WALKING
THROUGH
SHADOWS

A Novel by Bev Marshall

MacAdam/Cage Publishing
155 Sansome Street, Suite 620
San Francisco, CA 94104
www.macadamcage.com

Library of Congress Cataloging-in-Publication Data

Marshall, Bev, 1945-
    Walking through shadows / by Bev Marshall.
        p. cm.
    ISBN 1-931561-05-2
    1. Murder victims–Fiction. 2. Trials (Murder)–Fiction.
    3. Mississippi–Fiction. 4. Farm life–Fiction. 5. Girls–Fiction I. Title.

PS3613.A77 W35 2002
813'.6–dc21

                                                        2001058692

Manufactured in the United States of America.
10 9 8 7 6 5 4 3 2 1

Book design by Dorothy Carico Smith.

WALKING
THROUGH
SHADOWS

A Novel by Bev Marshall

MacAdam/Cage Publishing

San Francisco ◆ Denver

For Butch, Angela, Chess, and Dad
Your love carries me through the shadows

Between the idea
And the reality
Between the motion
And the act
Falls the Shadow

— T. S. Eliot, "The Hollow Men" 1925

My name is Leland Graves, and I'm a reporter here, in Jackson, Mississippi, for *The Clarion-Ledger.* I work on the crime desk now, but I wasn't always a hard-news reporter. In fact, I always fancied myself a novelist, and I would never have predicted that a murder that took place nearly five years ago, on August 31, 1941, would change my career — and my life forever.

Back then, I was working for *The Lexie Journal* in Zebulon, a small town about fifty miles south of here. I covered the society page, writing about local weddings and parties, and if Guy Peters had not quit the paper, I wouldn't even have been there on that day. But I was there, to capture and report the events of a story that would introduce me to a cast of characters I would never have known otherwise. They were, for the most part, good-hearted and simple people and no one, least of all me, suspected that on that hot, humid day, our innocence would be taken from us.

I remember, as though it were yesterday, them bringing the corpse up the small rise. As I stood watching them come, my anxiety grew until I felt light-headed. I had never seen a dead person except in a casket, rouged and neatly stitched. And though my recollection of the events of that day is muted by intense emotion, I will never forget the scene at Cottons' Dairy, where the first murder in Lexie County in nearly a decade occurred. Clyde Vairo, the sheriff, had everyone who had come out to join the search for the girl corralled like a herd of sheep. He vowed no one was going to leave until he had questioned them all.

These are the bare facts, written in my reporter's notebook, which I still keep here in my desk: "Sheila Carruth Barnes, found dead at 4:13 p.m., body found in Lloyd Cotton's cornfield. Nine-foot cornstalks. Muddy ground."

I recall asking one of the stretcher-bearers to cover her for decency and respect, but my notes do not reflect the true horror I believe we who saw the tiny body rolling to and fro on the canvas felt. My notes continued: "Green nightdress. Yellow trim. Purple bruises around the neck, several contusions, lacerations. A violent death. Victim may be 15 or 16 years old." Beneath these lines I wrote, "Bio: employed at Cottons' Dairy, married to Stoney Barnes. Address — Route 2, Zebulon, tenant house Carterdale Road."

I couldn't interview Mr. Lloyd Cotton, the owner of the dairy, that day, as he was given permission to go home to his wife. But I would get to know him as well as his wife, Rowena Cotton, their young daughter, Annette, and many others whose lives were affected by this tragedy when the awful truth of it all unraveled around us.

I tried to talk to the victim's husband, Stoney Barnes, on that gray day, too. But he was walking in a daze, his handsome face and six-three frame crumpled with grief. He was a boy really, no more than a teenager himself. He had asked me, "Who would want to kill her?" and had stared at my notebook as though I were going to write the name of her murderer upon it.

I wish it had been that simple. But we were all, then, living out a tragedy worthy of Shakespeare's attention, and I can only imagine the impact it had on those who knew and loved Sheila Barnes.

PART ONE

CHAPTER 1

ANNETTE

I never told Mama, but I saw the body. She had warned me to stay out of the way of the people swarming our land like fire ants escaping a poked mound. There were nearly one hundred pairs of feet stomping across our pasture, tromping down our tomato vines and butter bean bushes, kicking our milking buckets and stools across the slick cement floor of the dairy barn. But, despite the drama and confusion, I recall a sense of stillness that subdued the search. It seemed the mockingbirds sat like statues on the sticky resinous branches of the pine trees, and the bees, mosquitoes, yellow jackets, and dragonflies all seemed to slow the beat of their cellophane wings as they flew among the body seekers. From our raised back porch I could see fifty or more heads stretching out like sunflowers bobbing in the wind, swaying silently, seeming at times to float above the early morning mist that clung to the ground. The search had begun around six a.m. when Stoney had knocked on our back door to tell us that Sheila Barnes, his seventeen-year-old wife, was missing.

Her body looked older than seventeen. When the sheriff and three other men brought her out of the cornfield and laid her on the ground, she looked old and broken and defeated. Too short to see over the men's shoulders, I squatted down behind Mr. Wells to view the corpse between his bowed legs. Stretched out on the ground she looked like a pretend person, a puppet with legs and arms at odd angles to her short torso. She was tiny, not much larger than a blue tick hound, and her blonde shoulder length hair, turned reddish brown with dried blood and mud, was matted to her head in uneven clumps. Her eyes were open, staring up into the men's faces as if she had an urgent message for them; her mouth was an uneven oval, the bottom lip misshapen and swollen. Later I heard Bob Treacher retching in the weeds behind me. My stomach too rose up to meet my throat, but I kept the bile down even when I saw the beetle. It was stuck in her right nostril. Later when the facts were known, recorded in *The Lexie Journal*, I knew that, when her head was stomped into the ground between the nine-foot stalks of beautiful green and golden corn, the beetle must have tried to save himself by scurrying into her nose only to be squashed into death and entombed in her battered head.

Sheila was wearing a green nightgown that my mother had given her, with yellow piping around the armholes and neck. I remembered somehow knowing that she wanted to hug Mama when she held the gown against her flat chest, but I saw that she held herself back from that show of affection. When I read the words "love-starved" in a magazine left in Eatha's Beauty Shop, I thought of Sheila's yearning faraway look when she would watch Daddy crush my face in a hug against the bib of his overalls. Other words drifted in and out of my mind as I, with a giant-sized case of nerves, slipped in and out of the house the day she was found dead. I had heard neighbors and family members use the words "pathetic" and "feeble-minded" and "star-crossed" to describe her. But what I heard most was Sheila's own voice that sounded like tiny wren's wings flapping against window panes. One day beneath the fig tree she said, "Once I walked all the way to Brookhaven. Just took off and walked." Brookhaven was over twenty miles away. Why, why did you go? I wanted to know. She had giggled, covered her mouth with her hands. "Just felt the road pulling me pulling pulling." Had she been pulled to our cornfield? Or had she wandered there in a walking dream? Sheila believed all of her dreams held important messages that she didn't understand. "I dreamed of a snake, a giant garter snake with the head of a lion. It wanted to warn me of something, but I've thought and thought and can't tell what." Only two nights before this morning when her entire family of fourteen fearful souls had stumbled out of the yellow school bus that brought them to our place, she had told me she dreamed about a secret no one knew. "No one," she said. "And I ain't telling it neither. Not yet." We were sitting on the mossy ground beneath the water oak in her front yard, and she leaned into my body and bumped me with her elbow. "When I tell, you're going to be one of the first ones I tell." Then she grinned, a wide happy jack-o-lantern grin that scared me because it appeared unnatural on her thin, pinched face. I would never know the secret now, I thought. But I was wrong. By the time the trial began the whole state of Mississippi was privy to Sheila's secret.

It was afternoon milking time, before the searchers shouldered their rifles, shotguns, pistols, axes, shovels, and scythes to return to their homes. The cows had come up and stood patiently in the field beside the lot, lowing softly, swatting flies with their tails as if nothing had changed. The sheriff would have questioned them if only they could talk. Clyde Vairo hadn't expected to conduct a murder investigation during his term of office, and he went about this first one with a zeal that rivaled a puppy's frantic rooting for its mama's teat. After the body was loaded into the funeral home ambulance, the sheriff had looked around at the crowd of people standing in Sheila's and Stoney's yard. He held up his hands and yelled, "Nobody leave. This here is a crime scene now. It's murder." Somebody, Nellis Freeman I think, said in a high-pitched twitter, "Aw, sheriff, it was suicide. She beat herself to death," but no one laughed.

The sheriff finally left when the moon appeared and cast its light into my bedroom where Mama held me limp and crying against her soft stomach. My friend was dead. The battered puppet wasn't made of wood, but flesh and bone that I had touched and smelled and had once quickly and shyly kissed. I would miss our daily conversations, her hesitant walk, even the small hump that rose like a papoose from the center of her back. I would miss most of all having someone who would listen to me as if my words were important and not just sounds in the air to be brushed away like the gnats or mosquitoes that drove us all wild. I was not as a rule a crier, having learned by this my eleventh year that tears were generally wasted on my family who believed in "bucking up" when tragedy or disappointment visited, but that day I couldn't seem to stop the rivers of tears that parted across my cheekbones and filled the hollows of my ears and overflowed into my straight brown hair that Sheila had promised me would curl when I got my period. I got it that night an hour after supper and, holding my pink-stained panties, staring in the bathroom mirror at my lank, still-straight hair, I began to realize that she might have been wrong about many things.

Two years before, when she was fifteen, Sheila trekked barefoot up our graveled driveway looking for work and a new home. I remember the date, July 24th, 1939, because it was Mama's birthday, and Daddy had gone into town to pick up her surprise present, a new Singer treadle sewing machine. The storm that blew during the night, while I was dreaming of pulling taffy I could almost taste, had left puddles in the metal lawn chairs and I was mopping the seats with an old towel when I looked up and saw Sheila coming down Carterdale Road.

The first thing I noticed about her was the hump. Even though she hadn't reached our drive, I could see the small mound, the size and shape of a canteen, rising from the middle of her back like a camel's hump not yet fully grown. Her long blonde hair hung around the sides of her face obscuring all but her pointed nose which led her toward our house. She carried a cloth satchel like the one Grandma used for her yarn, and I guessed that it held only a few belongings as it swung so freely as she walked. Her feet were bare, muddy and wide. They looked much too big for her small frame and I remember thinking of butter paddles as they slapped along the road. She was wearing a yellow-on-white polka dot housedress that looked too elegant for bare feet, and I stopped my wiping and stood staring as she turned up our drive.

When she spotted me, she jerked her cloth bag to her chest and stood still as the lamppost sentinel beside our gate. Although she was standing near the sign that said "Cottons' Dairy" in large loopy black letters, she lifted her hand to her eyes to shade them and called across the lawn to me. "Is this here the Cotton Place?"

I dropped my towel and walked toward her. "Yeah. I'm Annette Cotton. Can I help you?" I asked in my most polite voice, the one I used for customers, teachers, and anyone related to us on Mama's side of the family.

She shifted her bag to her left hand, stuck out her right one. "Howdo. I am Sheila Carruth, first born of Thad and Effie Carruth out by the community of Mars Hill?"

I shook her hand heartily. Mainly because no one ever offered me a handshake before. Mars Hill was at least fifteen miles from our house and I wondered if she had walked all the way. Although there were no mountains around southwestern Mississippi, I pictured Heidi with her cloth-wrapped lunch gamboling over mountain paths to find our welcoming hut. I was a sucker for any tinge of foreignness, having lived with the dullest crowd of individuals I believed to have ever assembled in one spot. "You want to buy some milk or cheese? Orange drink?" My father had just begun bottling orange drink and it was fast becoming a best-seller and was the reason for my mother's extravagant birthday present.

She laughed. Her laugh was unlike any I had ever heard, a child's giggle reaching a shriek, but in a deeper adult tone. I hadn't thought my offer was particularly funny, but she continued laughing until she wiped tears from her eyes. "No, no," she said finally. "I'm not no customer. I'm here to work."

I lifted my eyebrows. No women had ever worked in the dairy. It was a man's place, a place of hidden whiskey bottles, drawings of half-naked women on tobacco-stained paper, and curse words, aimed at stubborn cows, that tickled my tongue when I repeated them to the chinaberry trees. "My daddy know about you?" I knew I sounded like a snotty kid and I immediately tried to take back my words by saying, "I mean he isn't here right now."

Sheila set her bag on the ground, brushed back her hair with the palms of her hands. "Oh, I ain't needing to see him right now. I reckon I can wait. Long as need be."

Her sleeveless dress exposed her freckled arms and I saw a purple bruise on the left one. The light brown freckles extended down her arms to her hands which, unlike her feet, were small and delicate-looking. A mismatch I thought to myself, like the one gray cat in the litter of black and whites, the battered straw hat my mother wore with her starched apron. I loved the unrightness of her, and I already knew somehow that she would become my Best Friend.

I invited her to wait in the house, but she pointed to her dirty feet and said she would just sit on the porch rocker. I brought lemonade and Mama out to her, thinking she looked in need of freshening and an adult who would most likely tell her my daddy didn't hire women. But Mama walked over to the rocker and said, "You must be Sheila. I'm Rowena Cotton."

Sheila jumped out of the rocker like there was a prickly bush under her butt. "I didn't know when to come. Daddy he just said to go, so I come down and now…" Her words had started out rapid fire and died off to nothing like a racing engine suddenly running out of gas.

Mama was smiling. "It's fine. Lloyd — Mr. Cotton — has gone into town, but he'll be back soon to show you around the dairy. It's my birthday, and he thinks I don't know what he's bringing home."

"You know?" I asked. I couldn't believe she had ferreted out our secret. I had congratulated myself for not giving a single hint and felt betrayed by her supernatural power to read my mind.

Mama patted the top of my head, taking the glass from me and holding it out toward Sheila. "It wasn't you. Your daddy slipped up this time. Told me not to sew up the rip in his armhole yet. Two and two. It was easy to guess."

"But what is it?" Sheila blurted out.

Mama and I laughed and said in unison, "A sewing machine."

Later I learned that Sheila didn't get presents on her birthday. "Birthdays ain't nothing to celebrate at our house," she told me. "Ten kids and no money. Just the little ones sometimes gets a candy or box of Cracker Jacks. I'm the oldest, so I stopped being young a long time ago." She told me this after I had taken a huge piece of birthday cake down to the little dark room that was the smoke house behind the dairy where she would live for over four months. I couldn't believe that anyone in their right mind would want to live in the place where Daddy used to hang hog carcasses, but Sheila acted like she had moved into the Taj Mahal. Mama told her she had some linoleum left over from the kitchen renovation that a hired hand would put down for her, and she gave her our old blue ruffled curtains for the one window, but looking around the cement walls, I doubted they would help much.

"When you been sleeping four to a bed, this seems like a triple-wide heavenly resting place," Sheila said, patting the thin single mattress Daddy had dragged out of our attic.

"You don't have anywhere to put your clothes and things," I said looking around the empty space. I couldn't believe I hadn't been told about something so important as a new person living in our backyard, but Mama said Sheila hadn't been expected for another week, and I suspected the handprint bruises on her arm were the reason she came when she did.

Sheila smiled. "I ain't got much, and I reckon I can keep them right here in this bag." She lifted the satchel onto the bed and opened it. She pulled out a wooden-handled hairbrush, a pair of panties with tired elastic, a toothbrush, a pair of badly worn and scuffed brown shoes, a beige man's work shirt, a calico skirt, and a small tin of saltine crackers. "In case I got hungry 'fore getting here," she said extending them in my direction. I shook my head, and remembering the cake, I pushed it toward her.

She fell on it. I stood beside the bed watching as she shoved large clumps into her mouth like a starving mongrel. I had brought a fork balanced on the blue-flowered saucer, but she ignored it, using her fingers to break off chunks of chocolate icing which rimmed her small mouth when she finally licked the last crumbs right off the plate.

"Delicious," she finally said. "I heared your mama was a good cook. A good woman too."

I nodded. Being Rowena Cotton's daughter had been a trial from my first step. People seemed to think I'd just naturally have all of her good traits, and no bad ones of my own. Suddenly, I felt envious of Sheila coming from a family that I had never heard of. The Cottons and the Bancrofts, who were my mother's people, were well-known in the Lexie County community, and I was constantly being reminded that "other" people did this or that, but "we" knew better. My mother expected more of herself, and unfortunately, of me.

Mama's goodness had reached its zenith when Lil' Bit had come to live with us. For nine years I had been an only child, pampered, petted, treasured because, by all accounts, Mama was barren after laboring for two days to shove my reluctant self out into Grandma's bedroom where Daddy had paced for all forty-eight hours of Mama's Terrible Ordeal. I still felt some guilt about my part in this horror story, which Mama still whispered to her friends at Baptist Circle Meeting. Mama said that, as soon as Grandma wiped me off and handed me to her, the late afternoon sun dipped in the sky to shine through the screen window so that my head was bathed in golden spots that looked like a connect-the-dots halo. I suspected much later that this story was embellished to curtail any devilish behavior unbecoming an angel.

Looking over at Sheila repacking her bag, humming a church hymn, I tried to imagine being one of ten children. As an only child, I had been reduced to begging cousins to come over for spend-the-nights, creating a cat and dog vocabulary, and summoning Janice, my pretend girlfriend who was so boring and predictable I had finally killed her off when I was six. But being a single child had advantages, too. I was assured of getting the pulley bone when Mama fried chicken, and I always got more toys for Christmas and birthdays than my cousins who had to share Santa's bounty. But I was lonely most of the time, especially during the long summer vacations, and so when Lil' Bit came, I was his most ardent fan.

As if reading my mind (Was she going to turn out to be supernatural like my mother?), Sheila said, "Your little brother sure is sweet. How old is he?"

"Nearly six months, but..." I was going to explain that Lil' Bit wasn't actually my brother by blood, but decided that would turn into a long story and I had lots of questions jumbled around in my head. "So what's gonna be your job at the dairy?" I pictured her in boots, shoveling oats into troughs.

"Cleaning mostly. Washing milk bottles, the floor, whatever needs a good scrub. Your daddy says the men ain't good at woman's work, and you got to be careful with the milk 'cause of bacteria. I think that's like a disease you can get."

"You're the first woman Daddy's ever hired," I said, hoping she realized the significance of this fact and would work hard to please him so I could keep my new Best Friend.

She stopped, belongings in mid-air. "That so? I didn't think about being the first one. Mrs. Bell, she's the lady at church who told your mama's friend about me, all's she said was she was maybe gonna find something for me to help out." Leaning over, she pushed her bag against the foot of the bed, then straightened the sheet and white chenille spread Mama had given her. She took a step back, an admiring smile on her face. "Oh, this is just wonderful. Don't it look nice?"

I disagreed, but I smiled back and shook my head yes. I was burning to know more about that family of hers but I knew it was impolite to ask personal questions of someone you'd only known a few hours. But it was nearly eight o'clock and the sun had turned the light in the room to cotton candy pink, and I decided at that moment that it was best to begin our friendship without rules. "Is the bruise on your arm why you came?" I was nearly whispering, frightened she would be mad at my audacity, which Mama said was unbecoming in a lady.

Sheila looked surprised, not by the question, but by the bruise itself as she raised her forearm and looked at the dark blue finger marks. "Oh that! Oh, no, that's just where my papa grabbed me. I broke the slop jar." She wrinkled her nose. "Whew, it were one big mess. I was taking it out and banged it on the wall and it spilled all out. Papa come in the room just then and law law you should of heared the hollering. He slapped me good too." A frightened, tight look came over her face as her jaws locked for a moment and her eyes opened wider. "I ain't too clumsy though. I ain't gonna break no milk bottles. I'm gonna be extra extra careful."

"Daddy wouldn't hit you for breaking something," I said, wondering if this were true. "Least he hasn't ever hit me, unless you count a regular whipping for big punishments. Even then, he doesn't hit you hard."

Sheila shook her head. "My papa says 'spare the rod, spoil the child' least once a day, and me being the leastest smart of his young'ns, I reckon there wasn't never a chance I'd be spoilt."

I ducked my head, supposing she was thinking I was one of those rotten kids who always gets their way. "Well, guess I'd better go." I didn't move, hoping for something from her although I had no idea what.

"Yeah, I better get to bed. Mr. Cotton said milking starts at two o'clock in the morning, and I'm supposed to be there at four o'clock sharp. Oh!" She reached beneath the pillow and brought out the wind-up alarm clock Mama had loaned her. "Better set this for quarter to."

Still I waited for more as I watched her struggle with the brass key. I breathed in the scent of the sooty walls, the residue of the bodies that had hung from the large rusting hooks above our heads. "Well…" I sighed. And then seeing that she had no idea of how to set the alarm, I took it from her and showed her how to work it. "Well…" I began again, taking up the empty saucer and unused fork. "Guess I'll say good night."

Sheila was already wiggling out of her dress, her back turned to me. "Night," she called. "See you tomorrow."

I grinned. "Tomorrow," I said, knowing now this was the word I was longing for. Her dress slid to the floor, and just before I turned to grab the door handle, I saw the horrible red welts that looked like hash marks across her hump, rising like a huge fiery boil between her shoulder blades. I bolted out the door into the fading light, panting and frightened, and somehow exhilarated by it all.

Mother's birthday sewing machine was already whirring when I awoke the day after Sheila came. Daddy and his brother Howard had carried it into Mama's bedroom and set it in front of the west window where Mama had been up half the night, feet pumping, palms on the wheel, her head cocked to guide the fabric beneath the steel needle. By the time I came into her room, she had already sewn up every torn piece of cloth in the house and was stitching around a bib for Lil' Bit, who was sitting on the floor playing with blue cloth scraps. I picked him up, kissed his fat little cheeks, and jostled him on my hip. He smiled showing his pink gums with two white bumps that we expected to erupt into teeth any day. Leaning over he chomped down on my hand and gnawed my index finger.

"This machine is a marvel," Mama said turning around on her stool. "It's even got attachments for buttonholes and fancy stitching. I'll make you some school dresses this year that will be the envy of all the girls."

I knew Mama was just saying that because she was always worrying about me feeling left out or jealous of all the attention she gave Lil' Bit. But I would have sewn things for Lil' Bit first, too. He was such fun to dress and so cute in the diaper shirts Mama had appliquéd with ducks and cows. "Great," I said, putting the baby back in the middle of his scraps. "Maybe I could help you cut out some overalls for Lil' Bit too. Corduroy ones for winter."

Mama turned back to her machine. "Yes, I'll teach you to use the machine. We'll have lots of fun together."

"I'm going to get dressed and go see how Sheila is making out."

"Eat something first." Mama ducked her head and pressed her foot back on the treadle.

I settled for a biscuit drowned in maple syrup and a glass of chocolate milk and headed for the barn where Sheila was just finishing up her first morning's work. When I opened the barn door, the scent of disinfectant overrode the usual smell of grains and cow shit. The concrete floor was wet, and I stepped over the puddles that had formed in the uneven surfaces. The big double barn doors were open, and the sunlight twinkled in multi-colors on the water all around me. Now that the cows had been let out to pasture, the barn was quiet except for the swishing of Sheila's broom. She was busily pushing the water toward the open door and hadn't heard me come in, and I stood for a moment watching her body sway with her strokes. She was wearing the light blue work shirt, the calico skirt, and the scuffed shoes I'd seen her pull out of her bag the night before. Her hair was knotted on her head, but escaped blonde strands fell all about her head, moving in rhythm with her long-handled broom. "Hi," I said.

She wheeled around, startled out of some reverie. She grinned, pushed her hair away from her face. "Morning. I'm just about done till they come back with the bottles to wash."

I wrinkled my nose. "Smells like a hospital instead of a dairy."

She nodded. "Yeah, your daddy said, since I come, he's gonna have the cleanest dairy in the state. There must've been eighty cows pissing and pooping in here this morning."

I laughed. "Daddy's got over a hundred head, and three, Wallie, Quinn, and Sal, are about due to drop calves."

Sheila leaned against her broom. "Why they named men's names if they're cows?"

"Oh, we name them after who we bought them from. Wallie Pearson, old man Ted Quinn, and Sal Delilo were the owners before us. Wallie is

Shorty's favorite and Digger likes Quinn best. My favorite is little June; Daddy let me name her 'cause she's mine. Lil' Bit's calf is named after him. Of course, he doesn't know he owns him yet."

Sheila hung the wet broom on the nail beside the door, and we walked out into the lot. I climbed on the wooden gate and sat straddled on the top rail. Sheila hesitated a minute and then wrapping her skirt around her thin legs, she pulled herself up beside me. "How come your brother is named Lil' Bit? He ain't none too little."

I had thought everyone in Lexie County knew all about Aunt Doris's cancer and Lil' Bit's birth, but Sheila, living out at Mars Hill, didn't know our story. "Well," I said, "When Lil' Bit was born, he wasn't anything like he is now. He weighed only three pounds and no one at the hospital thought he would survive. Mama's sister, my Aunt Doris, is his real mother, but she's dying of bone cancer, and so she gave him to us."

I explained to her that Uncle Walter, Lil' Bit's daddy, worked for the Illinois Central and couldn't take care of him and that Aunt Doris had come to our house one day and asked Mama if we would raise him as our own. Since Mama had wanted another baby, but hadn't been blessed with one, she was glad to get him.

When Lil' Bit was born Aunt Doris weighed seventy-four pounds, and no one thought either of them would survive. Mama went to the hospital every day, and after each visit, she would come home crying, doubtful that our baby would live. Weeks passed and finally Mama brought Lil' Bit home to us, but it was hard to believe he would survive. He was so frail, no bigger than a squirrel, and his cries were so weak we couldn't hear him unless we were sitting near his bassinet. Aunt Doris had named him Lloyd Jefferson Vitter after his real daddy and my daddy, but the nurses all called him Lil' Bit, and even though rolls of baby fat now encircled his arms and legs, that name had stuck. "Aunt Doris is a little better now. She comes nearly every week to visit him."

I didn't tell Sheila how much I hated those visits. Hated them for several reasons, some of them proving that the halo I had worn on my delivery day had tarnished to a deep black. I was scared Aunt Doris would change her mind and one day stride into Lil' Bit's room and take him away from us. On the nights after each one of her visits, I would kneel at the side of my bed and pray for her to die before she changed her mind. "Dear Jesus, she's sick and in pain. Don't you think it would be best for her to come live with you in heaven where all sickness ends?" I knew He wasn't fooled by my words, but I kept on. "You see all suffering. She probably wants to die, to live with You on streets of gold." Then my eyes filling with tears of shame, I said, "Take her. Take her." I did tell Sheila that, after each of Aunt Doris's visits, Mama would go into her room with the door shut for a while, and when she would come out, she was quiet for the rest of the day.

When I looked into Sheila's face, I saw that her eyes had filled with tears. "Your poor Mama." She shook her head. "I wish there was something I could do for her."

"There isn't anything to be done," I said. "Grandma says we just have to carry the burdens the Lord gives us."

Just as I was searching my mind for a happier subject, Sheila jumped down from the fence. She had read my mind again. "Hey, what's the name of the dark-haired boy that milks for your daddy?"

"Dark-haired boy? Oh, Stoney?"

A smile like I hadn't seen before on a girl except on the screen at the picture show spread across her face. "Stoney." She said the name with reverence.

I grinned. I had a crush on him too. "He's good-looking, isn't he?"

She was blushing, knowing that this time I had read her mind. She nodded. "I reckon he's about the best-looking boy I've ever seed in my whole life."

Stoney Barnes had come to work for my father only two months before. The Barnes lived three miles from us in a raised white house with green awnings. There were four sons, three living in the house and one married. Stoney was the youngest, but at sixteen, he was already a full-grown man. The first time I saw him he was leaning against the barn door, smoking a cigarette. I watched his lips as they drew on the white paper and then rounded and puffed out the gray smoke in perfect circles. Stoney was nearly a head taller than Daddy, and a lot more muscular. The sleeves of his work shirt were rolled to his elbow exposing the blue corded veins of his arms. His hair wasn't just dark; it was blue-black and shiny, cresting over his brow like a rooster's comb. But it was his eyes that made me fall desperately in love with him. They were the same blue as the purple-tinged irises that grew beside the barn.

I slid down to stand beside her. "Did you talk to him?"

Sheila shook her head so violently I knew she must have been as tongue-tied as I was in his presence. "All's I said was 'Howdo' when your daddy introduced me to everybody all at once." She pulled a piece of her hair into her mouth and sucked on it. "He done left, didn't go with them on the milk run."

"No, he doesn't know the route. Daddy and Robert make all the deliveries." I tried a taste of my own hair and spit it out. "He'll be back this evening though." I may have been mistaken, but I remember thinking Sheila's eyes got brighter at that information, and her little breasts rose up against her shirt. And I think I already knew with a black jealousy filling my gut that Stoney was going to fall in love with plain Sheila, hump and all.

CHAPTER 3

I don't know exactly when Stoney fell in love with Sheila, but he did. I never doubted his feelings for her although many people did. It was hard to understand how he could love a skinny girl with a hump on her back, breasts no bigger than green plums, and a seeming slowness in her head.

I had never thought of the dairy barn as being a romantic spot, but apparently it was. Maybe it was the feel of the cow teats, the warm frothing milk, the scent of the grains, the holy early morning darkness that held both fading stars and rising pink light.

Each morning, seven days a week, the cows ambled into the flood-lit lot outside the barn where the black and white Holsteins and tan Jerseys huddled together with their heads crowded over each other's flanks. The Holsteins were better milk producers than the Jerseys, but Jersey milk had a higher percentage of butterfat, so Daddy had bred both about equally. All of them waited patiently, swatting flies, lowing softly until their name was called. Digger, Stoney, Johnny, and Shorty were the milkers. One of them would lean out the door and yell, "Steve" or "Teddy" or "Bell," and like patients in a doctor's waiting room, when they heard their names, their heads would jerk up, and they would thread their way to the milking parlor. When a cow entered the barn, she would walk straight to the feed trough where the layers of grain were mixed with shovels, and when she stretched her thin neck toward her meal, the wooden latch on the trough would be lowered and locked into place. As the cow ate, she would relax like most of us do, and then her milk would come down, swelling her pink udder to sometimes an amazing size. After washing the bag with soapy water, strong rhythmic hands reached out to the teats to spray white gold into the bucket. Then after about ten minutes, when the cow was dry, she would be freed and ushered out of the barn.

The smaller buckets of milk were then poured into the big silver cans and taken into the next room where the liquid would be poured through cheesecloth into the cooler. Daddy or Robert would then take up the cooler and drain the milk into a can with a spout so that it could easily be funneled into clear glass bottles. The cardboard caps that said "Cottons' Dairy" were pressed on, the bottles loaded into crates and placed in ice in the truck. Finally, the cows, unaware of the business they'd created, were let out to graze in the pasture until evening when the entire process would be repeated. No one worried about pasteurization back then; people felt safe enough to drink milk right out of a teat, which I saw Digger do one afternoon.

Sheila's job began after the last cow left the barn. She would begin in the feed room, washing the floor with the hose, sweeping shit and pee and spilled grain out into the lot. But after a while, she came earlier to watch the Jerseys and Holsteins amble into and out of the barn. A lot of the Jerseys had nasty temperaments and they would kick at the milkers, scornful of the slaps and blows and curses that rained on them. One day soon after Sheila came to us, we saw Stoney get slapped back with a strong flick of Sid's tail.

When Stoney heard our laughter, a frown appeared on his face, but then he looked straight at Sheila and smiled. Mama called me inside just then to watch Lil' Bit while she went down to Grandma's for a visit, so I wasn't present when Stoney asked Sheila out the first time. They went for a ride in his battered Ford truck, which blew a tire on Enterprise Road. He didn't have a spare, so they walked nearly three miles back home on the dark gravel roads.

"On the walk home, I stumbled on some loose rocks, and Stoney caught my arm and nearly lifted me right off the ground," Sheila told me the next afternoon. "He is strong like a bull, but not bad-tempered like Franklin." Franklin was our 1,500-pound registered bull whom we fed with a pitchfork, his horn and nose roped in a half-hitch. Everyone was scared of him, even Daddy, who called his fear "respect."

We were sitting on the metal rockers in the front yard beneath the water oak. Lil' Bit sat on a pallet at our feet, laughing at the leaves that drifted down on the breeze. It would rain soon, and we were enjoying the unusual coolness of an August day. Sheila picked up a leaf and twirled it in her hand. "It were my first date, and I kissed him, let him rub up against my chest. Do you think that's wrong?"

I pretended to ponder her words, but I was actually thinking this was the first time anyone had asked me about right and wrong. Usually I was the one being told, not the one being asked. "I think it's romantic," I said. "I would've let him kiss me."

Sheila got up and flung herself down on the grass, and staring up at the aluminum sky, she whispered, "I love him. I do."

"Is he going to ask you for another date?" I asked, rising to pull the crab crawling Lil' Bit back onto the pallet.

She grinned. "Already has. Tonight." Her brow wrinkled and her eyes bore into me. "Do you think it's possible he might fall in love with me?" She shook her head fast. "No, not with this." She shrugged her hump.

I didn't know what to say. Here I was being consulted on problematic issues that were beyond my scope. I cuddled Lil' Bit, kissed his cheek. "Well..." I stalled. "Anything is possible, Grandma says," I told her.

Even Mama got caught up in the romance between Sheila and Stoney. After I told her they were "stepping out," she said, "but she doesn't have any clothes." And before an hour had passed, I was standing at the smoke house door with an armful of Mama's old dresses. They were all too big, hems hung unevenly over her hump to her ankles, shoulder seams to the center of her upper arms, but Sheila didn't care one bit. She twirled around the dark room in Mama's old green house dress like she was wearing an elegant evening gown. "How do I look?" she asked. "I wish I had a mirror."

"You can use the one over my dresser. Come on," I said, pulling her arm toward the door.

When Mama saw how pitiful she looked, she insisted on making emergency alterations, and she quickly stitched up the hem to accommodate the hump. We bunched in the waist with a belt, but we couldn't, on such short notice, do much about the drooping cloth that hung over her shoulders. When Sheila looked in the mirror, she slowly lifted her hands to her face; like a blind person her fingers traced her cheekbones and jaw line as though she were trying to discover her own identity. She did look different. I had never noticed the little green flecks in her blue eyes, but the watermelon green of her dress brought them out. The only words I remember her saying as she turned to Mama, who was standing behind her smiling at her reflection in my wavy mirror, were "God bless you."

God kept on showering blessings on Sheila, but He must have used them all up on her because before the month was out, Aunt Doris died. Sheila baby-sat for Lil' Bit when we went to the funeral. Daddy was a pallbearer, and he looked more unnatural than the corpse in his tightly buttoned white shirt, his red face protruding over his Adam's apple. Miraculously, Aunt Doris looked beautiful with her red hair curled softly around her face, her pale pink nails resting on a white lawn gown trimmed in blue ribbon. At the feast afterward, I sat with my head down and refused the fancy food the ladies from our church kept offering me. I had prayed for this; it was my fault Aunt Doris was dead. Ask and it shall be given. The Lord had given me just what I asked for. I hated myself. Was Aunt Doris looking down on me from heaven shaking her red curls at my blackest of hearts? Did she know I had been the cause of her being taken away from poor Uncle Walter who couldn't stop sobbing into his initialed handkerchief? I couldn't live with the guilt. I would go home and stab myself with the butcher knife Mama used for cutting up chicken parts. I would thrust the knife straight into my heart and blood would spurt out of my chest like it did from the hogs' necks when the blade sliced their throats on hog-killing day. I would drop the knife, sink to the floor, whisper, "I'm sorry," and then die.

When we finally got home that night after Mama had hugged Uncle Walter for the last time and invited him to come see Lil' Bit any day, I was too tired to kill myself. I had fallen asleep lying on the backseat of the Dodge on the way home, and I was barely conscious as Mama helped me undress and get into my nightgown. I remember Sheila saying Lil' Bit was "good as gold" and that he went to sleep with a smile on his face. He didn't know his true mother had been buried that day and that he would never see her face, hear her voice, or remember the kisses and hugs she had given him. But Mama said we would tell him about his true mama, and he would know her as part of himself. He would see her red hair when he looked in the mirror.

I kept worrying about needing to kill myself and face judgment. Mama asked me did I need a dose of castor oil, was I feeling poorly, did I want to talk about anything. No, no, and no I said. The last person on the face of the earth I would tell that I was a murderer would be my mama. I couldn't bear to see the look on her face if she knew me for the monster I was. Two days after the funeral I forced myself to open the kitchen drawer that held the knife, and I stared a long time at the wide silver blade that winked up at me, hissing "Pick me up. Do it. Do it." And when I slammed the drawer shut, I could hear a faint word rising out of the wood. "Coward."

The day when Uncle Walter came for his first visit with Lil' Bit was the day I knew for certain that Sheila was my true Best Friend. He knocked on the front door, causing a stir in our house because only the preacher and strangers ever lifted the big brass knocker, which sounded like a bass drum. As was our habit, Mama and I ran to my bedroom first to peer out the window before deciding to answer the knock. When Mama saw that it was Uncle Walter, she put her hand to her mouth. "My Lord!" she said. "It's Walter acting like company."

He looked like company too, dressed in navy slacks pressed with a crease, and a beige shirt that was scorched on the right sleeve. When Mama opened the door, he stepped back like he had changed his mind about coming to see us. "Walter, what a wonderful surprise," Mama said.

"I should've called, I reckon," he said inching toward us. "I just got up this morning and said today is the day I got to go see my son." He scratched his head like he was puzzling about something. "Got to go out on a run to Chicago tomorrow. I'll be gone quite a spell, so I thought, I'd…today… would be…"

Mama walked out onto the porch, and holding the door open, she pulled him inside. "Lil' Bit is in the kitchen. Come see."

I followed them into the room where Lil' Bit sat in his playpen chewing on a squeaky rubber toy. Every time he heard the funny screeching sounds the toy dog made, he chuckled, shaking his entire body with delight. Uncle Walter stopped dead still in the doorway. Finally, he spoke. "My God! He's got her hair. Just like her." And then he choked up and his shoulders caved in to his chest as he tried to walk toward his son.

I couldn't take it. I had had enough. It wasn't right for a murderer to be standing in the room watching the devastating results of her crime. Later it came to me that there would be a lot less crime if the people who committed them had to see the family grieve right in front of them. I doubted that there were many people mean enough in the world to stand it. I rushed out the backdoor and climbed the fig tree fighting the branches back like they were strong arms trying to stop me. I went as high as I could and lay out on a branch, rubbing my cheek into the bark. I wanted to wear away every bit of my skin, but I felt no pain.

"Annette." I looked down on Sheila's face tilted up toward me. "I seen you running out here. What's wrong?"

I sat up, shook my head. I couldn't tell her. She would hate me.

"I'm coming up," Sheila said. And I watched her as she climbed awkwardly, bracing her feet on forked limbs, testing a branch for strength, and then pulling herself up until she reached the stout limb across from me.

She looked down. "Whoa, this is great. I feel like a bird. I feel like I could just fly off here and not touch the ground."

I smiled in spite of the boulder-sized rock lying on my chest. She settled her humped back against the trunk and straddled the branch. She looked like an elf with her pixie bangs falling over her eyes. She was quiet for a minute, and then she reached across and tapped my arm. "You gonna tell me or not?"

"Not," I said. "Can't. It's too terrible."

"Ain't nothing as terrible when told as when kept locked up."

"You believe that?" I asked.

She nodded. "Shoot, I know it."

I looked into her blue eyes and saw the pond, the sky, blue jay feathers, sapphires, and Lil' Bit's blue diaper shirt. I saw the blue of unconditional love, true blue. She wouldn't judge me. "Oh Sheila, I prayed for her to die." Released from the bondage of silence, my words ran out and looped around the fig leaves, spun down the tree trunk, and cut through the heavy air toward my Best Friend. When I had called myself every name I could think, including coward for my inability to commit suicide, I ended up crying with great gulping heaves that felt like I had used the stabbing knife on myself after all.

Sheila waited until my wails dwindled to sobs. Then she touched my arm and pinched it hard. I was surprised I could still feel anything, but I winced in pain. "That's real," she said. "All this other is just shadow. You can walk through shadows if you watch the sun and do it just right."

I shook my head. I didn't understand.

Sheila licked her finger and wiped the spot on my arm with her spit. "Shadows is just imaginings. I thought on this one time after Papa beat me for eating the last piece of cornbread he were saving for hisself. I runned out in the yard and seen my shadow jumping up ahead of me. And I says to myself that ain't me; that's just dark lines shaped like me. But I knowed that I had to get rid of that black girl who was full up with fearing and worrying and sadness." She looked up and I followed her eyes through the green canopy of the leaves to the puzzle pieces of sky. "Now most folks think we can't get away from our shadows. You move, it moves, you stand still, it does too. But I learned how to walk right through my shadow." She smiled at me. "You wanna know how to do it?"

I nodded fast. I would practice every day if necessary. "What do you do?"

"Well, start like this. When the sun is positioned just right in the sky, that's when your shadow is near 'bout touching you, you just wait and watch, watch till the exact moment. And then, just as the sun bows to the west, you walk right into your shadow." She took a deep breath. "Then you ain't gonna have no more bad feelings." She frowned. "And what you got to do is remember that, when the sun goes down, when you turn off the lamp, the shadows disappear all by theirselves." She stopped and sighed as though worn out from all the talking. Then a slow smile spread across her face. "You ain't no coward. You can face what you done and see what you ain't done. Prayers is just words too. You couldn't change the time the Lord took your aunt no more than you can change the time the sun rises and sets."

"You don't hate me." It wasn't a question. That's when I leaned over, and nearly falling out of the tree, I grabbed her shoulders and kissed her right on the lips. "I love you, Sheila," I said.

CHAPTER 4

Late in November, Sheila and Stoney surprised us and ran off and got married. Sheila surprised us again by asking Mama if I could go with her to tell her folks. Mama thought Stoney should be the one to go, but Sheila said no, that it was best that she go without him. The third surprise was Mama saying we could take Daddy's truck out to Mars Hill. Sheila and I had both been practicing driving around the yard, but neither of us had ever been out on Carterdale Road. Why Mama would let her ten-year-old daughter be Sheila's first passenger is a wonder.

Sheila was nervous. I could tell by the way she kept fidgeting around my room while I got dressed. She fingered everything on my dresser, straightened my crooked bedspread, moved the curtains to look out the window three times. Finally, she sat on the bed while I put on a pair of pants. "Will I need a sweater?" I asked. Although I had just turned the calendar over to December, the temperature hadn't dipped below seventy.

"No, it ain't cold. Just wear a long-sleeve shirt." She leaned around me to stare at herself in my mirror. "You reckon they can tell right off? Do I look different?"

I took the question seriously and turned to look at her. She looked almost pretty in the red-and-white-striped dress Mama had made for her. Her hair was pulled back in a ponytail, and she had gained a little weight so that her thin face didn't look quite as sad as it had when she first came walking up our road. "You look like a candy cane," I said.

Sheila laughed. "Stoney said that! I wore this when we went to the justice of the peace's house last Friday, and he said I was candy, sweet sweet candy."

I pulled a yellow polo shirt over my head. "What did Stoney wear?" I asked through the fabric.

"Oh, a tie. He wore his Sunday pants, blue shirt, and a tie that had lines on it that looked kind of like railroad tracks." She leaned over and straightened my shirt over my jeans. "He was so handsome I thought I must be dreaming that it was me getting hitched to him."

I smiled. I had been disappointed when I found out they had eloped to Tylertown. I had planned a big church wedding with long dresses, lots of flowers, white veils, and me as the maid of honor in a pink net gown. Stoney had proposed after they had been courting for only two months, but Sheila said they couldn't get married until Stoney saved enough money for them to rent our tenant house. Stoney was still living with his parents, and she and Stoney certainly couldn't move into the smokehouse. Daddy had offered the vacant tenant house to them for ten dollars' monthly rent. There was no running water nor electricity, but when I expressed my doubts, Sheila said, "It's so big. Three rooms, and the well is close by. Stoney's Mama will loan us some furniture. It'll be perfect."

Actually, I was happy Sheila was willing to live in the house since that meant she'd be nearby and we would still be Best Friends. Daddy had given Stoney Saturday off and they had spent their first night in the house Friday. Today was Sunday, so Sheila had been Mrs. Barnes for two days, but I couldn't see any change.

"I wish I could have been at the wedding," I said.

"Me too," Sheila said. "But Stoney and me, we was scared my papa would try and stop us. It had to be a secret."

I nodded, remembering she was just fifteen, and the one time they had visited her parents, Mr. Carruth had told Stoney to stay away from his daughter. "Why doesn't your papa like Stoney?"

Sheila shrugged. "I reckon he thinks he's too good for me." She took the brush from my hand and smoothed my hair back into a ponytail like hers. "Papa said I was too dumb to get married and have children. He said I weren't like everybody else and couldn't expect to do things normal folks do."

I turned around, jerking my hair out of her hands. "That's stupid. He's the dumb one. You know about a lot of things."

Sheila nodded. "That's what Stoney said when I told him I couldn't read none. He said people can't eat books and writing good don't put food on the table."

The ride out to Mars Hill was like the pop-the-whip ride at the country fair. One minute we were veering left, then just as it seemed we were going to descend into a ditch, Sheila would whip us back to the right, fishtailing and skidding on loose gravel. It was exhilarating. We passed by the Parsons' Place, the Keppers', Johnny Moore's store, and by the time we got to the turnoff for Mars Hill, my maple syrup-drenched biscuit had risen up and gone down in my stomach four times. I was glad when Sheila slowed down on the rutted road so that I could enjoy the beauty of the season. The red holly berries against waxed green leaves added a festive air to our drive; an orchard of pecan trees, with gray limbs stretching and reaching out in the blue sky, looked like an artist had painted them there. I waved at a brown rabbit hunkered in a clump of yellowed field grass, and stretching my head out the window, I squinted up at a hawk circling a newly plowed field. When we turned into the Carruths' rutted drive, the smell of the turnips and collards planted in the front yard wafted toward us.

I don't like to remember all that happened next. I think Sheila tried to erase it from her memory too because, when we got home, we never spoke of that day again.

Mr. Carruth wasn't home when we got there, and I have asked God why didn't He keep him longer at his brother's house where he had gone to borrow an ax. Sheila's mama had seemed pleased when she lifted her daughter's hand and saw the band Stoney had given her. "It ain't real silver," Sheila said, "but it means the same." The children had assembled in the room and their thin arms and legs and pale hair filled all the spaces between the fireplace and the straight-backed chairs placed in a semicircle in front of it. Sheila stood with her back to the bricks, her mama's big stomach pushed into her side by one of the children.

"It's pretty," Sheila's mama said. I noticed she had no ring at all.

Just then his shadow fell across the rectangle of sunlight from the open door. The room fell silent. I looked from one child to the other and saw the fear mirrored on all their faces as they looked at the grim expression on their papa's face. He was holding the borrowed ax up in front of his chest. "What's all this?" he yelled as he walked through the parting children to his oldest daughter.

Mrs. Carruth twisted her apron, looked down. "Sheila's come home to tell us some news," she said in a voice so low I could barely hear her.

But he heard her. "What news?"

Sheila started toward him, backed up, and then held out her hand. "Me and Stoney got married, Papa. On Friday."

There was a peculiar smell in the room, and I remember thinking they must have cooked birds or something wild in the fireplace. The odor grew stronger and my already heaving stomach lurched and I tasted vomit. I watched Mr. Carruth frozen for a minute standing in front of his daughter and his wife. I couldn't see his face, but the faces of the women told me something was terribly wrong. He swung the flat side of the ax like lightning. The flash of blade moved so quickly I nearly didn't see it. He swung low and caught Sheila on the side of her left leg. She buckled, crumpled down like a piece of paper turning to ash in a fire. "Get up," he bellowed.

She didn't move and held her forearm over her face. "Papa, listen. Wait a minute."

Grabbing hold of her arm he lifted her up just as the clock chimed three times. I jerked my head up toward the mantel, startled at the sound and the idea that there was a beautiful clock in this ugly house.

Sheila was crying, squirming against her father's grip. "Stoney loves me; he's gonna take good care of me."

"He's gonna take your money you work so hard for at that dairy barn. That and your cherry." He spat in her face. "Reckon he's already got that. Next thing he'll plant a young'n in your belly." He dropped the ax, a relief to us all, but then he used his fists to smash into her nose, her eye, her jaw. And when she bent over, her hump rising up toward him, it became the target of the fire poker he snatched up from behind his wife. His wrist gave way and softened the blow, but Sheila's dress split open and red lines formed on her hump, matching the stripes of her dress.

I think we were all screaming, but no one tried to physically stop him until finally Mrs. Carruth grabbed the poker out of his hand and ran straight through her wailing children and out the door. When he turned to chase her, I ran to Sheila and lifted her up to lean on my shoulder. I don't remember how we got back to the truck, where the Carruths went, how I turned the key, and somehow slid forward on the seat so that I could push in the clutch. But I remember the clouds of dust that billowed after us and then drifted in our windows covering us with red silt as I shifted into first, second, and third toward home.

Stoney helped me get her inside the house and then told me to go home, said he would take care of her. I didn't want to leave her, but I didn't want to stay either. I wanted to close my eyes, open them again, and be safe in my bed. I wanted none of today to have happened. But what was before me was Stoney's frightening face looming like a monster's head over Sheila's broken body. "Go," he yelled at me. "Don't say nothing 'bout this either."

Tears stung my eyes, but I gulped them back and nodded. "See you later," I whispered to Sheila, but she didn't hear me. When I got back behind the wheel of the truck, I realized there was no way I could drive home, so I slammed the door and walked down to the barn where Daddy was worming cows. When I told him what had happened, he took off for Stoney and Sheila's house. I was worried what Stoney was going to say about me telling, but he never mentioned it. In fact, no one ever said anything about that day again. If it hadn't been for Sheila's wounds and bruises, I would have thought it was all a terrible dream.

CHAPTER 5

I had been secretly worried Sheila wouldn't remain my Best Friend after she was married, but my fears were unfounded. Although she didn't work as often at the dairy, she still came down to visit nearly every day. She would walk barefoot across the hard, coarse grass and sit on our porch picking stickers out of her feet. "One little sticker, two little sticker," she would say, laughing at Lil' Bit who was trying to master the art of walking. He went at it with a determination that surprised us all. Watching him, I wondered why most babies don't give up trying and settle for crawling through life. He would crawl over to the rocker and hoist himself up, sometimes mashing his fingers first. Then he would rise on his toes, actually on his very toenails, so that he looked like a ballerina. When he released his grip on the chair, he wavered for a second or two, and then his heavy bottom pulled him backwards, and he landed on the hard floor with a jarring thud that rocked his entire body. Several times Lil' Bit would roll on backwards and hit his head so hard you could hear it crack against the boards. But he wouldn't cry; he'd roll over, rise to his knees and crawl right back to the rocking-chair horse that had just thrown him.

Sheila and I were his cheerleaders. "Come on, Lil' Bit. You can do it," we would call to him as he stood, drooling and grinning his four-toothed smile, holding onto the rocker like a bull rider gripping a saddle horn.

"I can't wait till Stoney and me have a baby," Sheila said one morning when we were cross-legged on the porch, silking early corn together. She scraped her knife down a row of kernels and shook the red silk onto the newspaper laid out on the floor. "Course I don't want twins like Mama got this time. They're cute, but near 'bout ever time I seen them, one's awake and one's sleep. Then that one's up and the other down."

"I thought twins were brain-connected and do everything together."

Sheila tossed her ear of corn in the dishpan and picked up another one. "Well, them two ain't like that."

"Does Stoney want a baby?" I asked still working my knife on my first ear. I was most interested in how to get a baby and what that felt like, but I didn't know quite how to broach the subject.

Sheila wrinkled her nose, stilled her hands. "It's funny. Seems like he's sad when he sees I got the rag, but he don't talk about having none. When I'll say 'after we have our young'ns' or something like that, he just looks off and don't answer.

They had been married around six months then, and Lil' Bit had begun walking and had acquired an impressive vocabulary. He called me "Netty" and Sheila was "Sheshe." Ma-ma and Da-da were his first two words. Uncle Walter had visited him only a few times in the past year, but each time he came, Mama got nervous about Lil' Bit saying Daddy when he toddled over to my father. "He hears Annette call him that," she explained to Uncle Walter. And although I could see some pain in his eyes, he'd nod and say, "Of course, it's natural he would."

I looked over at Sheila dotted with bits of red silk. "Mama says men don't feel the same way about babies that women do. It's because we got wombs and they don't."

Sheila nodded. "I reckon, but your daddy sure does love Lil' Bit a whole lot."

"Yeah, well, Daddy's always loved babies, any kind. You've seen how he goes all moony over a new calf."

Sheila's eyes filled with tears. "But that's what I mean. Stoney don't have no feeling 'bout them calves. When Dusty had her kittens, he drowned them 'fore I had a chance to save a one."

I didn't know what to say to this. I had hated Stoney for that when I'd first heard about it. But lots of kittens got drowned on Carterdale Road. There were just too many of them to feed. I tried to turn the conversation back to where I wanted it to go. "But Stoney doesn't try not to have a baby, does he? I mean he still, you and him still..." I didn't know how to go on.

Sheila's eyes lost their sadness and she grinned. "Oh no. That ain't no problem. I ask him nearly every night for it, and he ain't never said no."

"You ask him?" I blurted out squeezing my ear of corn so hard that juice shot out onto my arm. From the conversations I had overheard between Mama and Aunt Leda and their friends, it was the men who did all the asking and the women who had to do their duty at night even if they had canned forty jars of pear preserves that day.

"Why not?" she said. "It feels good, and besides it proves how much he loves me. If he said no," she stopped, shook her head from side to side. "I can't think about that."

I wrapped a red silk around my forefinger. "I thought only men like to do it."

Sheila looked confused. She wrinkled her nose and worked her mouth from side to side like she did when Mama tried to explain to her how to whip stitch. "I don't think that's true. Seems like if it was, there wouldn't be so many children getting born around here." She started back on her ear with renewed energy and her knife flew up and down the cob flicking silks in all directions. "Maybe you ought to ask your Mama, but I'm telling you ain't nothing in this world any better as far as I'm concerned. Loving in bed is better than chocolate pie." She laughed. "And you know that's my favorite."

Of course, I was never ever going to ask Mama such a question. The one time we had discussed "becoming a woman" Mama had said that was God's way of giving us babies and calves, colts, and litters of kittens, puppies, and rabbits. Her face had turned as red as the apples in the fruit bowl on the table, and she had stared at them so hard for a minute I thought she was instructing them about wearing the rag instead of me.

No, I wasn't going to ask Mama about men. It was Sheila I told my secrets to. Nearly every afternoon, after the school bus dropped me off, Sheila and I would sit in the rockers and talk as we watched the cars and trucks speed down Carterdale Road. It seemed the whole world lay stretched before us as we gazed out across the green pasture where the cows looked like paper cutouts against the blue sky. The faraway pines and oaks seemed to be miniature trees set up on a play farm set, and I felt as tall and powerful as a giant. When the gardenias beside the porch bloomed, we would pick the creamy blossoms and pin them to our chests like corsages, and their scent would nearly make us dizzy. Sheila said she imagined the fragrance of heaven would be like swimming in an ocean of gardenias. These were my favorite times with Sheila, the times when we would sit on the porch and whisper our deepest thoughts to each other.

I told Sheila everything. She knew about the letter I had written to Jimmy Stewart in care of MGM Studios in Hollywood, California. And then the next letter I had written to Clark Gable offering him free milk, cheese, and orange drink if he would consider visiting our dairy. I never heard from either of them. I told her about my secret dream of becoming a writer. I would live in New York City and go to all the fancy nightclubs where I would dance the tango with Gene Kelly. I saw myself seated at a round table with a starched white cloth, sipping an old-fashioned, smoking a Lucky Strike in a long cigarette holder. I described my silver lamé dress, the open-toed high heels, dangling earrings that reached to my glitter-powdered shoulders. A stream of men in black tuxedos came to my table begging me to autograph my book about Hollywood stars.

Sheila said Stoney was ever' bit as good-looking as Clark Gable, and he had smaller ears. Except for craving the same fancy shoes, her fantasies were much less exotic. She wanted a Dodge like Mama's, two babies, a gas stove, and a matching set of dishes.

I confided my worries about my small breasts and large pimples. Sheila worried about her mother. Her life with twelve children, eleven still living at home, wasn't like the large family I had loved in the movie, *Cheaper by the Dozen.* The Carruths, Sheila told me, were the recipients of the church's donation box every Christmas, Thanksgiving, and Easter. "We used to dive into those boxes before the church lady left the drive. Mama was supposed to save the stuff for Christmas Day, but she knowed we couldn't no more wait that long than Papa could help drinking corn on Saturday."

Corn liquor was the bane of Lexie County. Most folks could count at least one drunk who had to be helped to bed on Saturday nights. In our family it was Grandma's sister, Aunt Molly. When she moved away to Louisiana, her new husband, a Cajun named Henri Fontenot, introduced her to beer. By the time I was old enough to remember Aunt Molly, she was well into her sixties, and when she came for visits, she preferred to stay in our guest room rather than with her sisters or brothers because Mama would buy for her. I remember walking by her room and looking in to see her passed out on the bed, her dress hiked above her knees, her orange-brown stockings rolled down to her ankles, and her thin blue-veined arm cradled around an amber-colored bottle.

But mostly it was men who swigged from bottles, jugs, and mason jars. I knew that Daddy kept his jug hidden in the dairy barn in the bottling room behind the milk cans. While Mama was willing to serve beer to her aunt, she wouldn't allow Daddy to bring a drop of liquor into the house. Daddy never took more than a few swallows at a time, and I never saw him drunk, but Mama said that the Lord doesn't use a measuring cup to gauge sin.

Sheila didn't mind Stoney's drinking. She said her papa vowed it was good for the digestion. I thought perhaps this could be true as Grandma gave me a tablespoon of whiskey with sugar for a sore throat, so alcohol, I reasoned, could have medicinal benefits. If liquor were in fact a life-sustaining drink, Stoney would live to a ripe old age. Sheila never worried about his binges, saying that most of the time he was funny, and not at all like her papa who was a mean and ugly drunk. "Stoney makes me laugh till my belly hurts," Sheila told me. "Don't tell nobody, but I had some brew too last night." Little crinkles formed around her eyes, and she grinned showing all her small crooked teeth. "I danced. Lord, you should've seed me, Annette. I whirled and did the Cotton-eyed Joe, and then Stoney come up to me and I hopped up on his hips and wrapped my legs around his back." She shook her head. "It were a sight, two of us dancing on one set of legs. Finally, his knees got wobbly and give out, and we fell down in a heap just laughing our heads off."

I knew my mouth was hanging open in wonder and I purposely closed it shut. I couldn't imagine Mama and Daddy doing something like that even when they were young. Mama said none of the Bancrofts had a bit of rhythm in them, and I reckoned the Cottons didn't either, judging from the times I stood next to Daddy in church and listened to him singing off-key two beats behind everybody else. But it was the playfulness of Sheila and Stoney's married life that amazed me. Nearly every couple I knew got solemn and dour right after the wedding. It seemed to me like marriage was about worrying and frowning till death do you part.

But I believed in the physical signs of love. I spied on Mama and Daddy, studied the love scenes on the screen at the picture show, and examined Sheila and Stoney's amorous behavior as if I were a scientist. I needed to understand why Mama's cheeks would flush and why Daddy's eyes took on a mysterious glow. Their touching was like feather tickling, quick and light, but with Stoney and Sheila, the caresses went deeper, right to their very bones. I found the word for their love in the big maroon-colored Webster's. "Passion, a strong feeling or emotion by which the mind is swayed." I could see that passion applied to Mama and Daddy's feelings for one another. Certainly, they swayed each other's minds; they joked about it. Daddy would say Mama's mind changed like the weather in December. But that word didn't fit the relationship between Sheila and Stoney at all. And then one Sunday morning when I was sitting in church leafing through our songbook, I found the word rapture. Webster said, "ecstatic, transporting, ravishing." Now I had a word for their love.

I wanted to be ecstatic, transported by love, ravished by a lover. I believed that Stoney was taken somewhere like paradise every time he stroked Sheila's arm, kissed the rim of her ear, smacked her pear-shaped butt. I studied his eyes as they traced the shape of her body like lines on a map, and when she would look back at him with a knowing smile, I knew that they were in total harmony, traveling toward the same destination.

One Saturday in June, during the first year of their marriage, they took me to the picture show with them. Sheila was so excited she could hardly sit still on the torn cloth seat beside me in Stoney's truck. Listening to her chatter, I thought how different the town suddenly seemed, and I was reminded of taking a walk around the yard with Lil' Bit. Every leaf, every flower, every rock was transformed into a wonder of nature. On those walks with Lil' Bit I felt like it was the seventh day of creation when God had just finished his project and was sitting up in heaven looking down on us, waiting for me and Lil' Bit to tell Him "it was good."

When we got to the lobby of the Palace Theater, the line was so long for popcorn, we decided to wait until intermission to get a box. It seemed like forever, but finally the lights dimmed and the show began. When Clark Gable appeared on the screen, I snuck a glance at Stoney. In profile the lines of his face were sharper, hinting of the Cherokee ancestors on his mother's side. His long, curly lashes were thick and dark, the lower set smudged in the dim light above his high cheekbones. Sheila was right; he was just as handsome as Clark. I sighed, turned back to watch Scarlett's white breasts heaving toward Rhett. Sheila was nothing like Scarlett; if anything, I thought, as the actors danced on toward the war, that she was more like Melanie. In fact, in a couple of scenes Olivia de Haviland looked nearly humpbacked in her mousy gray dress. Melanie's love for Ashley seemed more like the quiet love Mama had for Daddy. But I knew I'd rather be Scarlett and pursue rapture.

On the ride home, I learned about the power of fiction. I had expected Sheila to chatter like a chipmunk all the way back to the dairy, but she was quiet and thoughtful, sighing and still sobbing every now and then when she must have relived a particularly sad scene in her mind. I had heard my daddy say it was just silly women who got caught up in the stories they read and the shows they saw, but Stoney proved that day that men too can be greatly affected by fiction. From the moment we stepped out of the Palace Theater into the hour of dusk, Stoney was changed. I noticed it immediately when he grabbed Sheila around the waist and pulled her to him. Their hips bumped against each other as we walked down the sidewalk back to the truck, and by the time we started for home, he had kissed her neck twice. Stoney sat up straighter, drove faster, talked louder. I smiled inside thinking he was all heated up from the love scenes, imagining himself as a hero driving a buggy through the fiery streets of Atlanta. He was young and longing for an opportunity to prove his courage.

I had seen proof of this when he was courting Sheila. One day he had narrowly missed being gored by the Jersey bull, Franklin, when he jumped in the lot and waved his red handkerchief like a bullfighter. Another time on a Friday after the milk run, Stoney had dared Shorty to throw knives at him, and he had stood unblinking against the barn door as a reluctant Shorty tossed wobbling blades around him.

When we returned from the show that night, I had trouble falling asleep. I imagined Stoney's hand sliding up my thigh; I felt his eyes burning like hot suns through my chest. But the worst thought, the one secret I never told, was the monstrous idea that swallowed up reason in my brain. What if? I asked myself. What if Sheila got sick like Aunt Doris and died and Stoney fell in love with me?

CHAPTER 6

Grandma says you have to watch out for the worm in the apple, and perfect as my friendship with Sheila was, an occasional crawler wiggled into our relationship. One such time was the day we went on a picnic to Johnsons' Hole.

Johnsons' Hole was part of the Tickfaw River that ran along the eastern boundary of Lexie County and on into Louisiana where it widened and burst into Lake Maurepas. In some places the river was only four feet wide as it twisted and turned beneath the high red clay banks. On a narrow rutted lane jutting off from Johnsons' Road, you came to a horseshoe bend cut out in the tangle of cottonwoods and pine and ash. Here the water deepened and then turned azure against a small beach of white sand. This was Johnsons' Hole, our shady swimming spot that was always winter cold on the hottest of days. It was my idea to take a picnic lunch to this perfect place one hot July day.

Mama said the two of us could go if we promised to be back by afternoon milking. I loaded our picnic basket with leftover roast, biscuits, pears, and two pieces of chess pie. Sheila brought a quart jar of iced tea and a holey quilt which Stoney's mother had given them. Sheila had never been on a picnic except for the annual church one, and I told her that secular picnics were a lot more fun. For one thing you didn't have to wait for the preacher to bless the fried chicken for a half hour before you got some.

We rode out with the truck windows down, a hot wind blowing across our faces. I felt so happy I thought I should be singing or dancing or spinning around to show my feelings. I had dreamed of having a Best Friend on days like this, and now she was sitting beside me in the truck, laughing and teasing me about my scraggly ponytail. "You ought to brush your hair one hundred and one strokes every night, Annette," Sheila said. "Then it'll get thicker, and when you get your monthlies, it will be curly too."

I turned to look at her hunched over the steering wheel. "That so?"

She took a quick glance at me. She was a better driver now and she concentrated on staying straight on the right side of Carterdale Road. "Well, it happened to two of my Mama's sisters and some other folks we knowed, and I know my hair went wavy some the day I started wearing the rag."

I calculated that there were a lot more straight-haired people in the world than curly-locked ones, but I trusted that I would be one of the lucky ones that received the miracle. If Sheila said it would happen, then it surely would. She and Stoney had been married for eight months then, and she had become my personal encyclopedia from A to Z on all matters of the body and the heart.

When we arrived at Johnsons' Hole, Sheila spread out the quilt on the white sand and immediately sat down and kicked off her shoes. Pulling off her socks, she jumped up and ran to the water's edge where she dipped one foot in and quickly withdrew it. "It's cold," she said, hurrying back to where I stood on the quilt.

I shed the blouse and shorts I had worn over my bathing suit that Mama had made with a flounced skirt that nearly came down to my knees. It was long waisted, with yellow and green swirls on a white background, and I was glad there were no boys around because the suit plainly revealed that my left breast was the size of a hickory nut, and my right breast was missing altogether. I gathered up my skirt and ran into the water until it reached my waist. I shivered. Goose bumps rose up on my arms. "Come on," I called back to Sheila. "Put on your suit and come out here."

"Don't have one," she said. Then she shrugged out of her dress and tossed it backwards to the quilt. "I'm coming in the water in my birthday suit," she yelled and, laughing, she stepped out of her panties and pulled off her brassiere. I stood frozen in the waist-deep water. I had never seen a naked adult before. As she came toward me, a knot formed in my head and I shifted from one foot to the other trying to figure out how to act. I wondered should I look away until she was underwater, or should I act like her being naked wasn't any different than Lil' Bit running around with his little wee wee flopping. I looked down at the green water and thought that my flabby white toes seemed indecent to me now. The water rippled around me as she came nearer. I looked up and saw that Sheila was still grinning beneath her wrinkled nose and crinkled eyes. "Ooooh," she said. "It is cold as an icicle, ain't it?"

When I looked at the pale pink nipples marching stiffly toward me, I saw a purple crescent-shaped bruise on her left breast. "What happened?" I asked.

Sheila frowned. "What?"

I pointed to her chest.

"Oh," she smiled. "Just a loving mark."

I looked down at my white fish toes burrowing in the mud. "Did Stoney do that to you?"

"Yeah, but it don't hurt none now." When Sheila waded out to me, she held my hands, pulling me around in a circle. "Ring around the rosie," she sang. She kept pulling me in circles, around and around as the water swirled against our thighs. She threw her head back and looked up at the green canopy of leaves overhead. "Hey, there's a rope tied up there. We could swing off it and fall in the water."

I looked up. A frayed rope, looped over a high limb of the water oak, dangled down six feet or so above the dark water. Sheila's idea appealed to me about as much as a triple dose of castor oil. "It might break," I said. "Looks old."

But Sheila was already wading out of the water toward the beach. I watched her go. Water cascaded off her hump and fell onto her glistening white buttocks. My mouth went dry and I licked my lips trying to summon up some spit. "Sheila," I called. "Don't do it. It's too high in the tree. You'll get hurt." Then the piece of me that was Mama, and which I hated, caused me to scream. "You don't know how to swim. You'll be killed. Stop! Come back right now."

Sheila didn't answer me. She rounded the horseshoe beach and climbed the bank toward the tree. I squatted down and peed; the warm water against my leg comforting me. "Please God, don't let her die," I begged. "Don't take my Best Friend away from me." I kept on praying, bargaining with Him as I watched her awkwardly scaling the trunk of the tree. She hoisted herself to the thick branch just below where the rope was looped halfway down the overhead limb. When she crawled out hugging the rough bark, I could feel its scrape against the tender skin of her stomach and breasts. She sat up and straddled the limb, and grabbing the rope, she pulled on it, testing its strength. I held my breath, my toes digging deeper into the mud. She would be too far out for me to save her; I was a dog-paddler, not a strong swimmer. "Send someone to help me," I begged God. Sheila waved, then she stood up, teetering on those butter paddle feet, her toes curled over the limb. I closed my eyes. "Please. Please," I whispered. Then I started to cry.

Suddenly she was gone from the branch; where she had stood there was a patch of blue sky wavering against the bouncing limb. I looked out across the water and saw her hugging the rope like a lover, her knees wrapped around it, her hands crossed over her head. The thick braid nestled between her breasts and ran down the center of her body, and I felt the rough hemp chafing her skin. She swung far out and leaned back as the centrifugal force brought her around toward me. "Whoooooo," she screamed. "Whoaaaaaaa." Then scissoring her legs, pushing the rope away, she released it. She fell like an inverted arrow shot from God's bow toward the earth. When I saw the titanic splash where she went in, I began to dog-paddle out as fast as I could. She came up, laughing, treading water and slowly moving toward me; I wanted to slap her. I wanted to wipe that smile off her face and scream at her that she had ruined everything. Didn't she care that I loved her so much?

Later, after stuffing our bellies with roast and chess pie, we lay side by side on the warm quilt. I fanned my hair out to dry and looked up at the cotton ball clouds. "Weren't you scared?" I asked Sheila. "Didn't you think you might get killed?"

Sheila crooked her little finger over mine. "Nope. I weren't scared none." She sat up and looked down into my face. "I don't reckon I know what fear is really. I ain't never truly felt it."

I sat up too and knelt on the quilt facing her. "You mean you aren't scared of snakes, panthers, or getting gored by a bull? Of anything?" I couldn't imagine not being afraid. When I was little, I had been terrified of Aunt Bernice's wig, Grandma's outhouse, and even bunny rabbits, whose sharp teeth looked like white daggers in their pink mouths.

Sheila sat back on her hands, sticking her legs out in front of her. Although I was still wearing my bathing suit, she had thrown her dress on over her wet body and parts of it clung to her skin. She lifted the hem and pushed it back over her knees. "Well, there's bad things that can happen, but the way I see it is, if you go worrying about what might happen all the time, then you gonna miss out on what is. Take that snake over there. He ain't gonna hurt you if'n you leave him to his business." She rocked back on her hands. "Try this. Lay down with your cheek flat on the grass, close one eye, and look out between the blades. You'll see what that snake sees, get his point of view. Snakes is to be pitied. So why would you want to go worrying about him when you could be enjoying a walk or," she patted her stomach, "a piece of chess pie?"

I leaned back on my heels. "But Mama says you got to be prepared for danger. And Grandma says, 'Forewarned is forearmed.'"

Sheila shook her head. "I don't understand that. All's I know is I get up ever morning thinking something good's gonna happen, and most times it does. If'n it don't, I just walk through my shadow. Look here," she spread her arms wide. "We having a grand time right now, ain't we?"

I nodded. We were having a wonderful day, and as we packed our things and drove home, I pushed away my fears. I wasn't going to be like the Bancroft women, worrying themselves into a frenzy over nothing.

Stoney was waiting for her in the yard with a string of catfish. As I walked toward him, I thought of the bruise on Sheila's breast and felt my face heating up. I wished I hadn't seen it, wished she hadn't told me Stoney had put it there. Sheila let out a whoop and pointed to the fish. "Ain't this just the greatest day!" she squealed. "A picnic and catfish all in one day." Stoney was grinning, enjoying her happiness like it was his. I saw his violet eyes soften as she reached out to touch his hand. I saw the way she leaned into him going all soft and limp into his arms. I understood now. Sheila's breast was bruised with love.

CHAPTER 7

Every year, when the love bug season was over and the cool winds blew in from the north, my family began preparations for the fair. Mama entered nearly all of the contests. She won blue and red ribbons for cream-colored roses, red velvet cake, thick fig preserves, and her famous wedding ring quilt. I entered brownies annually and was usually awarded the tacky golden third-place ribbon. But it was Daddy who had the highest aspirations at the fair. It was his chance to show his best animals to his competitors, and after blue ribbons were tacked on the temporary stalls of his Holsteins and Jerseys, he couldn't be persuaded to leave the livestock barn for any reason. He positioned himself for most of the day beside his ribbons where he was available to answer any questions and accept all compliments from the people who strolled by. Mama and I took all his meals out there, and he would sit on a hay bale, enveloped in a cloud of smelly cow shit, and chew a fried chicken wing like he was eating steak on a snowy tablecloth in a fancy restaurant.

So it was Daddy who decided that we would go to the state fair in Jackson. He was especially thrilled because a man from Greenwood was bringing his Ayrshire cows for judging. Daddy had read just about everything ever written about the breed and he was crazy to own a few head. Maybe part of his interest stemmed from the fact that Ayrshires were from Scotland and Grandma Cotton was a Granstoun from the village of Heron in the southern part of that country. She claimed to be descended from Lord Granstoun, and over the piano in her living room she had placed a framed family Coat of Arms. It depicted a knight's head in armor with a white heron on top; beneath the knight three more birds walked across the orange shield, and horseshoed across the top of the images, the motto read "Thou shalt want ere I want." Daddy said the motto fit his growing-up years underneath Grandma's rule perfectly. Grandma and Grandpa Cotton lived on a farm twenty miles south of Jackson, so we would visit them on our way to the fair.

I had never been to the state fair, and I was wild with expectations. Daddy said I could take one friend and, of course, I chose Sheila, who easily cajoled my good-humored father into a day off for Stoney too. Since Lil' Bit had a cold, he and Mama would stay home with the extra hands that Daddy had hired to run the dairy for the day. So the four of us set out at five a.m. in Mama's Dodge, with its brand new Firestones. I hated the thought of stopping at my paternal grandparents'. I barely knew them, as about the only time we visited was on holidays. They were old old. Grandpa Cotton's back was bent into a u-shape, and he walked with his legs splayed so wide he resembled a crab inching down their front walk as he came out to hug us. Grandma had lost her dentures, and I couldn't understand about half of what she said. Most of her comments centered around Daddy's thinness and my nose turning up on the end like hers. It was hard for me to imagine Mama and Daddy as young people, but it was impossible to believe these two could ever have been capable of running or even managing a fast walk. As I sat in the hot kitchen, which smelled of rancid bacon grease, I chanted inside myself, "Stop talking. Let's go. Let's go."

Finally, after what seemed like hundreds of hours to me, we left my grandparents leaning crookedly on each other in the drive, withered arms lifted in a feeble wave. Sheila said, "Your granny and gramp sure are sweet folks, and I never seed a crochet toaster cover like that they got."

I rolled my eyes. Sheila and I didn't always think alike.

By the time we arrived at the fairgrounds, I was nearly worn out with anticipation, but when I saw the crowds and enormous rides that reached toward the perfect blue sky, I ran toward the midway. Daddy jerked me back with a strong hand. First things first, he told me. We would see the Ayrshires, eat lunch, and afterwards I would be allowed to spend the afternoon at the midway.

The livestock barns were easy to find because of the bleating, whinnying, and mooing homesick animals. Had the animals been silent, we would have found them by following our noses. Even though I was antsy and pouting about being in the barns, I instantly fell in love with a hinnie named Rhubarb. I preferred hinnies to mules because, since they are the result of breeding a stallion horse to a donkey jennet, they tend to be more horselike than the mule, and in my mind, much better looking. Rhubarb was small, as hinnies usually are, and he was wearing a flowered hat with holes cut for his ears. He brayed as I walked by and lifted his head, cocking the hat in a saucy greeting. Sheila loved him too, and when she reached out to stroke the taffy-colored point on his nose, he nudged closer, lifting his white socks like a show horse. Laughing, we moved on through the hog pens, the horse stalls, the goats and sheep pens, but after Sheila wasted so much time admiring every animal she passed, my mood turned black, and I began to hate every four-legged creature who was keeping me from the tilt-a-whirl.

The cows were in the last livestock barn. Here Daddy moved even more slowly, stopping at every stall to gaze at a Holstein, a Guernsey, or a Jersey. On his face was a look more reverent than Mama's in church, and his choice of a place of worship was suitable if you took into account the stable story of Jesus' birth. I figured Daddy would kneel when we got to the temple of the Ayrshires. He didn't, but when he got a glimpse of the red and white spotted purebreds, he yelled like a zealot. "Look. There they are. The Ayrshires!" I drew back from the foot-long polished horns which curved out toward our smooth foreheads. Mr. Patterson, the owner, showed up immediately. He ranted on and on about the Ayrshires and the Ayrshire Milk Program. He claimed the cow with the jagged red spot shaped like an accordion, was a descendant of Tomboy and Alice, who were famous for walking from Brandon, Vermont, to the National Dairy Show at St. Louis and still producing a record amount of milk on arrival. As I watched Mr. Patterson, rising on his toes, waving his arms, I was reminded of Brother Wells, our last revival preacher. When Mr. Patterson ranted about the ungodly dairymen who didn't officially recognize the impressive amounts of milk and butterfat his cows produced, his voice rose and fell exactly like Brother Wells' when he talked about the sinners who didn't know Jesus. And when Mr. Patterson forcefully grabbed Daddy by the shirt front to assure him the Ayrshires were hardier than any other breed, I could imagine Brother Wells jerking up one of those sinners and shaking him into belief. By the time we finally left the holy barn and headed for the oasis of the midway, Daddy was a convert and the owner of two registered Ayrshires and a brand new trailer for them to ride home in.

Ultimately the fair both enchanted and repulsed me. It was an island world set apart from normal civilization where children and adults of every description walk side by side anonymously, severed from their professions and neighborhoods and daily routines. The barkers and ticket takers took our money with ingratiating smiles, nodding at our eagerness to be whirled into the air, to throw balls at stuffed cats, and to stare at grotesque humans sitting behind gaudy curtains. But there was beauty, too, in the calliope music, the freshly painted black carousel horse I sat astride, rising and falling in the crisp air as I circled the crowd of waving hands. There was the sweet stickiness of pink cotton candy and the laughter of small children and teddy bears with blue ribbons around their necks, glass beads that glinted like diamonds in the bright sunlight, colored plastic fish with numbers taped on their bellies. And there were other exotic attractions that beckoned us to foreign lands.

From her raised wooden platform, Salome caught Stoney's eye as we walked by. "Hey," she called to him. "Come on over. See me do the hoochy koochy." She wriggled her hips, making the coins around her hips dance. The sheer green veil on her head was drawn across her nose and mouth, exposing only her eyes, dark with mascara. Her vest was brocaded with golden threads, and her harem pants clung to her hips. Above her bare feet wide bracelets jangled on her ankles as she moved across the makeshift stage. She clicked a pair of finger cymbals at Stoney, and rolled her hips in a wide circle. Stoney stopped walking so suddenly Sheila ran into his back. He turned and stood smiling at Salome until Sheila grabbed his right hand and sunk her teeth into it like a dog clamping on a steak bone. Stoney yelled and jerked away. When he lifted his hand and saw that he was bleeding, his other arm flew up. I heard the slap and the word "bitch" simultaneously as Sheila's head swiveled toward me.

I supposed this was the first time Stoney struck her because Sheila's face registered such surprise. And, watching Stoney's lavender eyes turn to deep purple, I think he was horrified too. I was righteous, thinking to myself that she shouldn't have bitten him for just looking, and I wished for Daddy to hurry back from the knife-throwing booth where he was trying to win me a bear.

By the time Daddy showed up holding a scruffy brown bear with a wrinkled yellow ribbon around its neck, Sheila and Stoney had walked away for a private talk. Accepting the bear with a frown, I wondered if I should tell Daddy what had happened or not, but before I could decide what to say, Salome came back on stage and set her hips to rotating like a big slow-moving fan. This time it was my father she called to. "Buy a ticket, and I'll show you my hoochy koochy." I was expecting Daddy to look away and hurry me on to the next attraction. But instead he lifted his eyes and ran them up the harem pants to the exposed navel, where they seemed to pause a minute, before traveling on up to the v-cut of the vest. When he finally lifted his gaze to her oversized red lips, he said, "How much?"

I gasped out loud. Was he actually going to mount those wooden steps, walk across the stage, and go behind the burlap curtain? He was, and he did after looking down at me and telling me to wait for him right where I stood. I turned my back to stare at the stupid kids who were riding a fake train around a track going nowhere. I made ugly faces at every one of them as they chugged by, waving their chubby hands and smiling at their good daddies who wouldn't be caught dead in Salome's den. But no matter how hard I tried to block it out, I could hear the provocative music wafting out from behind me. On the sides of the colorful train, I imagined Salome's hips grinding toward my father. I saw my mother's face; her eyes were swollen from crying, mouth open in pain. I hated Daddy and I hated those damned Ayrshires too.

I don't know what I might have said to Daddy when he finally came out from behind the curtain and tapped me on the shoulder, because when I turned to stare up into his red face, Stoney and Sheila came running up, holding hands and grinning. I saw that Stoney's hand was bandaged with a handkerchief and Sheila's eye had begun to swell. I tried to smile back at them.

"Well, here you are," Daddy said in this cheerful fake voice I had never heard before. "We've been looking all over for you." He gave me an even phonier smile. "Haven't we, Annette?"

I drew up my shoulders and moved toward Sheila. He was asking me to lie. I thought about Grandma saying something about how the mighty have fallen, from the Bible or some Greek play. And I remembered how she also told me that one small lie like a pebble can grow into a boulder and over time will become a towering mountain. Let Daddy pickax his way up the mountain alone, I thought to myself. But, as if reading my mind, he reached out and pulled me toward him. He bent forward until his face was even with mine. "No harm done, honey," he whispered. "It was all in fun. Don't be so hard on your poor old daddy."

A whiff of cheap perfume sailed off him and nearly hardened my softening heart back to granite, but when I saw his same old smile, his eyes clear and kind like the ones he'd come with, I forgave him. I nodded; a co-conspirator in his lie, I turned to Sheila and Stoney. "Yeah, we were looking everywhere," I said.

After the Ayrshires were put in their new stalls that night and Mama had admired them enough for Daddy's satisfaction, I lingered at the barn.

I walked up to the Ayrshire with the longest horns and looked her in the eye. "I hate you," I said. "Your real name is Salome, and someday I will butcher you and carry your head to my mother's table." The cow lifted her head and stared back at me. When she lowed mournfully out into the dark barn, I knew she understood.

CHAPTER 8

I learned about the awful pain that love can bring on the morning Sheila was supposed to come up to our house to make blackberry jelly. Year after year, every jar of Mama's jelly turned out so perfect it wiggled on your spoon and spread smooth on a biscuit. Mama had promised to share her cooking secrets with Sheila, who told us that her jelly always turned out too runny or too sugary. Our bushes were bursting that May, and I filled several gallon buckets with plump juicy berries. My purple-stained fingers were covered with briar nicks and my waist was ringed with red welts from red bugs who preferred my blood to berries. I was thinking that biscuits tasted just as good with syrup when Sheila came in laughing.

"Lordeee, lordece, y'all should've seen old Sid down to the barn. Stoney didn't get her mule collar on fast enough, and she started sucking her milk out 'fore he knowed it. When he tried to get her head back round, she butted him clear cross the barn." Sheila sat at the table and laughed hard. "Then Stoney, he got hisself up and went back over to her, and she's sucking fast as she can, one eye on him. 'Fore he got there she done backed up and turned her tail. I knowed she were ready to kick him like a mule, and he knowed it too." She looked over at Mama. "And you know what he done then? Stoney lit up a cigarette and walked right outta the barn. He said, 'Sid, you welcome to your breakfast. I ain't gonna get killed trying to keep you from it.' That cow got the best of him."

Mama and I laughed, but we were enjoying Sheila more than the story itself. Lil' Bit, who had been busy all morning stacking blocks on the floor and then knocking them down, heard our laughter and smiled up at us. He said in a most solemn voice, "You funny, Sheshe." That set us all off again.

Mama wiped her face on her apron. "Okay, now we'd better get to work if we're going to get these berries put up before dinner time." I had already washed all the mason jars, and when Mama went to hand the first one to Sheila, it slipped from her grip and crashed on the floor beside the tower of blocks. We all screamed, "Lil' Bit, no," as he reached out toward the glass. Mama grabbed him up into her arms at the same time that Sheila's arm shot out to move the broken pieces away from him. Her hand came down on a shard and blood began to drip from her palm.

"Oooh, you've cut yourself," I yelled.

Sheila held up her hand and licked the blood. The cut wasn't too deep, but it was nearly an inch long. "It ain't too bad," she said.

When Mama came over to get a closer look, Lil' Bit started to cry. "Shhhh, Sheshe is okay," she reassured him. Then she turned to me. "Annette, get some gauze and tape. Run."

After we got Sheila bandaged and Lil' Bit calmed with a cookie, we set about the serious work of jelly making. Mama stood at the stove with her wooden spoon, stirring the first batch that was nearly ready for cooling while Sheila carefully lined up the jars on the countertop. I dumped another bucket of berries in the sink to wash. I remember thinking that Sheila's accident was a bad luck sign, as I had dreamt about missing teeth only the night before, so when I heard the crunch of gravel, I looked out the window with a shiver.

I saw a bright red Chevrolet truck pull up beside our old rusted lawn mower that Daddy had set out for Digger to take home later that day. "Mama, company," I said.

"Who is it?"

"Dunno. Can't tell." But as those words came out of my mouth, I recognized the man getting out of the truck. It was Uncle Walter, Lil' Bit's real daddy, whom we hadn't seen since Lil' Bit's second birthday three months past. He had been spending a lot of time in Chicago working for the Illinois Central, and his visits had been sporadic and brief. Next I watched the passenger door open and saw a woman stepping out. He had never brought anyone with him to visit before. "It's Uncle Walter and a lady," I said, which sent Mama across the kitchen to the window. As we watched them walk toward the back porch, I noticed Uncle Walter had a new bounce in his step, and his hands fluttered around him as he talked to the woman and pointed to the dairy barn, the fig tree, our new tractor shed. The lady's head jerked around looking in whatever direction his finger led her. She was wearing a beautiful orange, pink, and yellow print chiffon dress, and I thought she looked like she was dressed for a party instead of a visit to our dairy. She wore yellow high heels with rounded toes, and I stared at her feet as they hopped like little canaries toward the house.

"Wellllll," Mama said, using a lot of air. "Wonder who she is?"

In the kitchen Uncle Walter introduced her as Gloria. Sheila picked up Lil' Bit and carried him into the living room where Mama turned on the lights and waved our company to the couch. After he sat down, Uncle Walter introduced her again. This time as Gloria Vitter. Mama and I looked at each other, both of us trying to figure out if she was a relative of Uncle Walter's that we didn't know about.

"We're married. Got hitched a week ago," Uncle Walter said, taking Gloria's left hand and displaying her gold band.

I waited for Mama to say something, but she was struck dumb. I think we both tried to smile, but we were so surprised I imagine our mouths looked like we had just swallowed iodine.

It was then, right at that moment, that Mama's supernatural powers came to her. She reached across and pulled Lil' Bit out of Sheila's arms and held him on her lap with her arms folded over his stomach. Uncle Walter kept right on talking about how he met Gloria in the hotel where he was staying and where she worked as the hostess in the restaurant. They hadn't known each other very long when they both realized they were "meant for each other." These last words they actually said together, and as I watched Gloria's hand squeeze Uncle Walter's knee, I thought about how he cried so pitifully at Aunt Doris's funeral. I remembered the hurt and dazed look on his face those times when we helped Aunt Doris into the truck after she visited Lil' Bit.

I suspected what was coming, but Mama knew before me, and when Uncle Walter stopped smiling and sat up squaring his shoulders, she kissed Lil' Bit's head three times. We had never cut his hair, and it hung down below his ears in soft red curls. He looked like a fat little angel, his blue eyes fixed on Gloria's colorful dress. "So Gloria's home is in Chicago. Her people all live there and naturally she wants to stay. I can get a transfer, no problem." I let out a long breath. Maybe Uncle Walter had come to say good-bye.

I began praying. "Please, God. Please please please."

Mama's eyes were closed and I knew she was praying as hard as me. The silence in the room was terrifying. I could hear the clock ticking all the way from the kitchen. A leaf blowing against the window sounded like a gunshot. I lifted my eyes to Gloria, and saw her pressed lips. She nudged Uncle Walter. He moved away from her on the couch.

Finally, when we were all about to break into a million pieces from the stillness, Mama's voice drifted out from above Lil' Bit's head. "So you're moving soon." The words were whispers, like the sounds of a weak person lying in a hospital bed.

"Yes, Rowena," Uncle Walter said. "I've got the house up for sale and the land, and I'll be packing up and going within the week."

"This week," Mama echoed.

Uncle Walter's face was chalky, and there were wet circles on his blue shirt beneath his armpits. I was glad of that. I wanted him to feel worse than he'd ever felt in his life. Just then Lil' Bit pointed to Gloria's yellow clutch purse which she held in her lap. "Candy," he yelled out. "I eat candy." Since Grandma had started bringing Lil' Bit a peppermint or a chocolate drop in her purse, he had gotten the idea that all purses held treats like these. "I want candy," he said smiling at Gloria.

Gloria didn't understand. "I don't have any sweets," she said. She turned to Uncle Walter. "Give him a penny or something, Hon."

I almost said, "No, he'll put it in his mouth and swallow it, stupid." But Uncle Walter wasn't listening to her. He stood up, walked over to where Mama sat on the edge of her chair and knelt in front of Lil' Bit. He held out his hands. "Come here, son," he said.

But Lil' Bit wasn't interested, and he craned his head around his father's back to stare at the yellow clutch. He pointed again. "Candy," he said, his face screwing up with fury.

Mama looked at me. "Annette, get him a piece of fruit slice."

I jumped up and ran to the candy dish, fishing out a sugared orange slice, and raced back to Lil' Bit, who grabbed it in his chubby hand and stuffed it into his mouth as he said, "Thank you" using the manners we had taught him.

Uncle Walter hadn't moved, nor had Mama or Gloria or Sheila. It seemed they were all frozen wax figures, the smell of the sweet candy wafting around their still heads. Mama's fingers moved when Lil' Bit's drool dripped down onto her hand, and without looking, she found his mouth and wiped it with her thumb. I stood right beside her chair, thinking about grabbing Lil' Bit and running out the front door. I saw the two of us flying down the road, Lil' Bit's overall straps falling down on his shoulders, my tennis shoes tearing up the grass as we sailed out of the yard. My right hand reached out, but Mama took it and laid it on her shoulder. As I stood there ramrod straight, I thought we must look like a tintype photograph in which I was the stern husband with my hand on the shoulder of the sitting wife, a serious-eyed baby seated on her starched skirt. Lil' Bit did look somber, now that his craving for sweets was satisfied. His round eyes bore into Uncle Walter as if he were memorizing him. Gloria was talking all this time, but I have no memory of what she said. I suppose she was telling us their plans because I heard Mama say, "The house sounds nice."

When Uncle Walter stood up, Mama and I knew that nothing could keep him from saying the awful words that would stab our hearts. "We plan to take Lil' Bit with us."

Pieces of the next hour come back to me, but mostly all I remember is the hollow sound of the voices, the sudden heat that made the air hard to breathe. I can still see the pink lipstick smear on Lil' Bit's cheek where Gloria kissed him. Phrases come to me. "Wonderful to him," "Appreciate all you've done," and finally the last hateful sentences as they walked out onto the porch. "We'll be back tomorrow afternoon. That will give you enough time to pack his things, won't it?"

I helped Mama pack his diaper pins, his sweet-smelling baby powder, the appliquéd sunsuits and bibs with ducks and cows on them. I folded the navy sweater and cap set Mama had knitted for him, and we boxed up the toys we had bought for Christmas although it was still months away. Now Santa would bring them to his new snow-covered home. Sheila cried for all of us. She sat on the floor in Lil' Bit's room, her tears wetting his undershirts, his sunsuits, his Sunday white shirt with the Peter Pan collar. She sobbed into the blanket we would throw over his head, asking, "Where's Lil' Bit?" until he would pull it off and laugh as we screamed, "Oh, there he is!" There he is, we said, but he wouldn't be there ever again.

Lil' Bit slept with Mama and Daddy that night. I tiptoed into his room to his crib to say a private good-bye, but the white sheet was stretched smoothly across the empty mattress. When I opened the door to Mama's room, I saw Lil' Bit's blue cotton rump sticking high in the air. His face was turned to Mama and his thumb was centered in the perfect O of his mouth. Mama and Daddy lay on their backs, their open eyes staring up at the ceiling that must have seemed like a giant coffin lid. I backed away from them and fled to my cold bed, where I lay in my own casket until the morning sun ruthlessly forced me to get up and become an only child again.

I didn't see Lil' Bit go. I didn't kiss him good-bye. I didn't help load the boxes and bags into the truck. As soon as I awoke, I pulled on my blue jeans and shirt and ran out the front door to Sheila's house. Stoney had gone on the milk run in Daddy's place since he needed to be with Mama and Lil' Bit, and Sheila was waiting for me on the porch. "I figured you'd come up," she said, as I pushed my two hundred pound legs up the steps. "Let's go for a walk."

May is an unpredictable month in Mississippi. Some years it is a summer month, hot and humid, so that all the town kids drive out our way to cool off in the river. Other times May is a spring month with a constant breeze that caresses our faces and cools our bodies. This day was perfect, a wind-kissing day, a day we Southerners brag about to our Yankee friends. Sheila and I set off slowly marching through the woods beside her house. We didn't talk for a long time, and when we came upon a doe with her white-spotted fawn, we stood motionless until the mother lifted her head and nudged her baby away from view. There were words and pictures in my head. I heard my voice saying, "They're giving him some crackers to take in the truck. He's crying and calling our names. He doesn't want to go."

We had been walking for hours, I think. I know we missed breakfast because I remember hearing Sheila's stomach growling like a hungry dog's. I didn't know where we were, but I didn't care. I would let my Best Friend take me wherever she wanted to go.

I later realized we were on the Whittingtons' property standing in a field of clover; we stood for a moment looking over the waves of vivid crimson stretched out before us. Above the field, the noontime sun sat like a golden orb in the sapphire blue sky. "Wow," Sheila said. "Ain't it pretty?" And then she pulled me farther out into the field. Taking my shoulders, she turned me around. "Now stand right there. Don't move," she said. I obliged her. Sheila pointed to the ground. "See your shadow?" I looked down and saw the outline of two legs, two hanging arms, a torso, a big round head. I nodded even though I wasn't at all sure the figure was me. Sheila looked back and forth from me to the sun. She danced from foot to foot, rocking left, then right. Shading her eyes with her hand, she stared up for a long time, and finally, she yelled out, "Okay, take a step. Now." I wavered for a moment, and then understanding and remembering, I lifted my foot and walked into my shadow.

On the way home, Sheila skipping along beside me, stopped and said, "This shadow will pass. The sun will come out again. It always does." When I left her standing on her porch, I walked home both full and empty. Nothing would ever replenish the empty cavern Lil' Bit had left in my heart, but I had been given something on this day. I walked on toward the sad quiet house, longing to feel Mama's arms wrapped around me, but knowing somehow that my scrawny limbs were the strong ones now.

CHAPTER 9

Mama took to her bed after Lil' Bit was taken from us. She had been grieving for over a week when I finally asked Sheila for help. Of course, she had
been lending a hand from the get-go by cooking and cleaning and picking
the early beans that second week in May. But Mama hadn't gotten out of
bed and there was a sour aroma in her room. Sheila said it was the smell
of sorrow, but I think Mama just needed a bath.

Sheila was bringing in a washtub of snap beans when I asked her if she
knew of anything we could do to get Mama up. She set the pan in the sink
and wiped her face with her forearm, then walked to the table where I sat
braiding the hair of an old doll I had rescued from the attic when Daddy
had carried Lil' Bit's empty high chair up there. Sitting on the chair beside
me, she pulled on her ear. "Hmmm. I got to think on it some. We know the
why of it; her heart is broken." I nodded. "So now we needing to figure out
the cure for heartbreak."

"If there is one," I said, giving the doll's brown hair a yank.

Sheila looked up at the white globe on the ceiling. "Well, if you got a
cold, honey in whiskey is good. If you got stomach gripe, baking sody helps
that." I frowned. She wasn't going to be much help if she was searching for
a physical remedy. But she ignored my glum puss and went on. "Now let's
see, wasp stings, tobacco and spit, blood root tea cures several maladies."

I was out of patience with her. My voice was too loud. "Sheila, she doesn't have a physical aliment. It's what's in her head that's the problem."

"No, Annette, it's not. It's her heart, and it may be the blood too. They're connected, you know."

I gave up. "Okay, so what's the medicine for broken heart and sad blood?"

"Dancing."

"Huh?"

"Dancing. It makes your heart beat real real fast and makes your blood swoosh like lightning all through your body. When you get up to racing speed, you start to feel better 'cause you're throwing out all the bad blood and the arrow in your heart comes loose and you can pull it out."

I saw the picture of a broken heart in her mind. It was a red valentine heart with cupid's arrow striking diagonally though it, rending it into two jagged pieces. "But, Sheila, even if that were true, Mama isn't going to get up and dance. She won't even come in here for meals; Daddy's been carrying a tray to her all week, which he brings back practically untouched."

My Best Friend looked me in the eye and said, "Wanna bet?"

I would have lost the bet, of course. When we went into Mama's dark room, the first thing Sheila did was pull up the shades, throwing light across the rumpled bed. I opened the window and breathed in the crepe myrtle and magnolia blossoms that grew beside the bedroom wall. No matter if Sheila was right or not about the smell of sadness, Mama just plain stunk. She struggled up to a sitting position and held her hands to her face. "No, it's too bright," she said.

"Now, Miss Rowena, you know the sun is good for putting roses in your complexion," Sheila said, beginning to pull the covers off the bed.

"What are you doing?" Mama said when the sheet got ripped off her thin legs that needed a shave worse than Daddy's three-day-old beard.

"I'm airing." Sheila grabbed Daddy's pillow and pulled off the case. She sniffed it. "Ummm, smells like hair tonic. Mr. Cotton must try to look good when he goes to bed."

Mama was flabbergasted and speechless. I looked over at her and my own heart ripped a little. Her brown hair was so greasy it was nearly as black as the deep dark crevices beneath her eyes. She was pale, and dry spittle made a little white trail from her mouth toward her chin. Mama was pathetic, and I nearly started crying right then, but Sheila wasn't having any tears in this room on this day.

She was laughing. "Lordy, Miss Rowena, you got purple violets embroidery on this case. There ain't nothing prettier than a field of them, is there?"

Mama wasn't going to answer, but Sheila waited and stared at her so hard, it was like Mama got hypnotized and had to answer. "No, no I guess not."

Sheila must have felt encouraged by this as she smiled and twirled around flapping the pillowcase like it was some beautiful scarf a dancer was showing off. "You ever seed the dance of seven veils?"

Mama was in a trance. "What?" Her voice was so weak I could barely hear her.

Sheila lifted the pillowcase and drew it over her nose and mouth. Her eyes met mine, and I knew she was remembering Salome, the hoochy koochy girl we had seen at the fair. She began to dance, humming a strange tune that captured the essence of the veil dance. She flipped the pillowcase over her hump and rubbed it like a towel between her shoulders. I stole a look at Mama's face and saw a hint of a smile.

When Sheila stopped dancing, she bowed, and after my enthusiastic clapping began, Mama did smile and clapped twice before she began to fall back into her bed. But Sheila was as good a miracle worker as Jesus, and before Mama's head hit the pillow, her hands were on her arms pulling her back up. "Wait, I got an idea," Sheila said, plucking at the ribbons on Mama's pink nightgown. "First we need to get you out of this old bed and into the tub." She turned to me. "Annette, you go get some magnolias, and camellias, all the flowers you can hold and bring 'em in here." I nearly saluted. Sheila was in complete control of me and Mama now.

When I returned with an armload of flowers, they were in the bathroom, Mama naked in the tub, and Sheila sitting on the side. This was the second time I had seen a full-grown woman naked, and I marveled at the difference between Mama's breasts and Sheila's. I wanted Mama's. They floated in the water like two pink sponges tipped with tiny brown rudders. They were buoyant and beautiful, and I nearly wished I were an infant again so that I could rest my head on one and pull the other to my lips. Before I had time to take in the rest of Mama's body, Sheila grabbed all the flowers from me and threw them in the tub. Mama squealed, but then smiled as she lifted a magnolia to her face and buried her nose in its yellow center. She cried, but this time no painful howl rose up to pierce my heart. These tears were soft and gentle, grateful tears, release tears, and I stored them in my mind for later in my life when I would need such healing tears myself.

When Mama, her body and hair clean and sweet-smelling at last, reached for another gown, Sheila's hand stayed hers, and she went to her closet and pulled out Mama's best blue chiffon. "No, this. Please?" She didn't need to beg. Both Mama and I would do her bidding, even if she asked us to burn our best Sunday dresses.

By the time Daddy came in for supper, which we hadn't cooked, Mama, Sheila, and I had formed a chorus line and were high-kicking like vaudeville show girls. "What's this?" Daddy said, but he knew and his relieved smile landed on his wife's face. Turning to Sheila, he lit up even more. "How'd you do it?"

Sheila ducked her head, suddenly shy and uncertain of what to say, I guess. "She gave Mama a flower bath and taught her the ball-and-chain shuffle," I said.

Mama smiled, and Daddy held out his arms to her. He looked over at me and Sheila, both of us grinning like fools. "Thank you, Sheila. Thank you for bringing our Rowena back."

I didn't know what Sheila meant when she said, "I'm the one owing you thanks."

CHAPTER 10

LLOYD

When they brought her body out of the cornfield, I was sitting on her porch beside Stoney. He was paring his nails with a pocket knife, and without raising his head, his eyes followed the men making their way across the yard with his dead wife laid out on the stretcher. "Well, I reckon she won't be coming back" was all he said. They should've covered her. Her nightgown was hiked up around her waist, and I could see the blonde hairs between her legs matted with mud and blood, and I wondered if she'd been raped before she closed her eyes on this world. Whoever killed her must've thought about it. She had an appeal. I won't say she was a beauty or anything close to it, but there was something about her that beckoned thoughts of putting your hands on her.

Clyde Vairo was strutting like a rooster around the ambulance, slapping his hand against the passenger door to signal Bob Underwood to take off for the funeral home where Casey Pottle would later perform an autopsy. Clyde looked up on the porch at me and Stoney before he hollered out for nobody to leave because he was commencing a murder investigation. I'd known Clyde since our school days and we were friends, but not the kind that invites each other over for dinner. Clyde was the same age as me, thirty-five, but he was single, and Rowena didn't like me hanging around with bachelor types. Still I knew Clyde was depending on me for help. The murder had occurred on my land, in my cornfield, and Sheila had worked for me for over two years.

So I got our sheriff a little table set up with a couple of folding chairs, and he began questioning folks in the shade of the oak tree in Sheila and Stoney's front yard. Stoney had gone inside the house and Clyde walked up on the porch and called him out. Figuring they'd be a spell, I walked back to the house to check on things while they sorted out the events of the morning. I was worrying about Rowena; she gets herself upset over nothing, and this day had certainly been something to get worked up about. I was thinking too that I was going to need somebody to help with the afternoon milking since Stoney wasn't gonna show up. I wanted to stop by the barn and take a big swig of whiskey from the bottle I kept in the overhead cabinet, but I decided that itch would have to wait to get scratched.

The weather was holding for now, but looking up at the charcoal clouds socking each other in an angry sky, I knew there'd be more rain before nightfall. I hurried on home, and when I reached the back porch, I heard Rowena's voice. She was on the telephone with her mama, and I stood at the door listening to her steady stream of words spewing out like cow piss over the few miles of wire between daughter and mama. I knew they'd be a while, so I settled onto the porch rocker and pulled off my mud-caked boots. The rain-soaked cornfield had sucked at our legs, and my calves ached with the effort of sloshing through the muddy furrows. I had been walking down a row near the fence line certain Sheila was gonna be found dead when I heard Cal Martin's shout. It was like when my best milk-producer Jersey, ole Gowan, had pitched head first into the gravel pit. I had gone lookin' for her knowing all along that she was destined for butchering. As I walked over to the men standing in a tight circle around her body, I already knew. I had known since early morning when I'd come back from the milk run that the girl was gonna turn up murdered. On my land.

I rocked back and listened to Rowena's voice. "Oh, Mama, I don't know where Annette is. The child has been running over the place like a wild Indian all day. You know she loves Sheila like a blood sister." She paused waiting on instruction from her mama. That was the way it was between them. Mama was the rudder on all three of her daughters' ships, and Rowena was the one most glad to hand the wheel over to her. Mostly, her meddling concerned raising Annette and taking care of the womb that held what she called our "miracle baby" so I didn't care if the old lady came around so often. What irritated me about her though was them constant little sayings she doled out for every crisis large or small. I could imagine her telling Rowena right now some proverb that would make Sheila's death seem like a blessing. I closed my eyes dreading the scene I knew was coming when Annette realized that Sheila wouldn't be running down to our house ever again.

I stood up and looked over to my right where thirty or more people were still milling around reluctant to go home, afraid they'd miss something if they did. Leland Graves, the reporter for *The Lexie Journal*, was talking to some of them, writing down their thoughts in the little notebook he carried everywhere. I doubted anyone had much to tell. I guessed only a few of them knew her to speak to. She was a good worker though. I'll say that for her. She could wash fifty bottles in less time than it took to milk three cows. When I started into the house, it dawned on me that I was gonna need to hire another hand down to the dairy for sure, and I damned to hell whoever killed Sheila. There would be plenty more trouble to come from this and some of it would be mine.

Looking back now, I wonder why I ever hired Sheila in the first place. No women had ever worked in the dairy; it wasn't a place for the fairer sex. Whenever Rowena came down to the barn for something or other, she looked like a bright flower sticking up in a pile of cow shit. It was a man's place.

No, I do know why I gave her the job. Rowena was the reason. She heard at church from one of her busybody friends that Sheila Carruth was getting the tar beat out of her at home, and if somebody didn't get her away from her old man, he was gonna kill her someday. So I agreed to give her a place to live and a job washing bottles, sweeping up, the chores the niggers usually did. And look what happened. Dead anyhow. A blind man couldn't miss seeing the irony of it all.

She came while I was in town buying a sewing machine for Rowena's birthday. Rowena tried to act surprised when I got home with it, but she knew all about it. Two weeks after we married I found out that it was useless to try and keep secrets from her. Her mama said all her daughters had powerful woman's intuition, but Rowena's knowing went beyond that. She met me at the door, grinning big, and behind her Annette was biting her lip. I shrugged and said, "Well, it's in the truck. Where you want it?"

Rowena laughed. Rose up on her toes and hugged me tight. "I've got a place cleared in Lil' Bit's room, in front of the windows. He's asleep now though, so let's wait to bring it in until he's up."

We walked out to the truck and she oooh'd and aaah'd over it. Annette was dancing around, impatient with her mama about something. She pulled her back from the machine. "Tell Daddy who's here. Tell him about Sheila."

Rowena's bright face clouded over. "Lloyd, the girl came early. She's down at the smokehouse. I sent Digger out there with some things to help her get set up." Her eyes filled with tears. "She's just pitiful. It breaks your heart to look on her." She pressed her lips together and then said, "Lloyd, she's got a hump on her back. Maybe some kind of growth or tumor. I don't know. She's so tiny I don't know if she'll be able to do much down there."

After my brother Howard came by and helped me get the sewing machine set up for Rowena, I went down to meet my new hired hand. When I knocked on the smokehouse door and Sheila opened it, I saw right off what Rowena meant about her looking like a deformed weakling. I tried not to stare at her back, but she pointed her finger over her shoulder and said, "This don't mean I won't be a good worker. It don't hinder me a'tall."

I didn't know what to say to that, so I just nodded. "Your name is Sheila, right? I'm Lloyd Cotton."

She smiled then and swept her arm out gesturing me into the room, which I saw Rowena had tried to make into a bedroom of sorts, but it wasn't a place I'd think a gal would want to live in. "You got all you need here?" I asked.

Sheila made a little dance around the floor skipping from the bed to the one window. "It's perfect. Thank you, Mr. Cotton. I ain't never had so much space all to myself." She came close up to me. "Mama and Papa got a pack of young'ns at home. We slept four to a bed no bigger than this'n."

I backed up a little, wondering why in the world I felt uneasy being alone in the dark room with her. She was just a child really. I needed to finish my business and get out of there. "I came to tell you about your duties," I said, and immediately she came to attention. "You need to come up to the barn at four a.m. sharp. I'll show you what-all I want you to do. I pay wages on Saturday. Fifty cents a day."

Her mouth flew open. "That much! Lordeee. My papa ain't never made so much." She laughed and covered her mouth with her tiny hand. "I feel like I done died and gone to heaven."

It didn't take but a day or two for me to see that hiring the girl wasn't a bad idea after all. She was ten times faster than the niggers, and she didn't mind wading through cow piss and shit like I thought she would. Her fingers was so tiny, she could get around inside the bottles better than anyone. I got to admit it; I liked having her around. She was always cheerful, never sick, never complained like the rest of the workers.

Sheila and Annette became fast friends, and soon she was up to the house, helping out with Lil' Bit and some of the housework. Rowena took pity on the girl and loaned her some dresses and such, and before long, between her and Annette, they had her looking right nice. Stoney must've thought so too as he and her began stepping out before too long. I didn't like it one bit, but I couldn't say why. Maybe I thought it might interfere with their work. But it turned out that their courting meant that Sheila came to the dairy earlier and started helping Digger shovel grain into the troughs, so it worked to my benefit, really.

After that, I didn't pay much attention to what-all was going on between them, because about two weeks after I hired Sheila, Doris started going down hill. Rowena was beside herself, knowing she was going to lose her baby sister. When she and Walter came round, I tried to be off somewhere. I hated trying to talk to Walter when the whole goddamned sky was falling in on him. Here we had his son, his wife looked like a corpse already, and he was wandering around with these dead eyes that it hurt to look at. It started me thinking on what if something happened to Rowena, or Annette, or me. You never know. You can't count on things staying the way you want them to. Hadn't I had a near epidemic of hoof and mouth? I could've lost the whole damn herd, but I got lucky on that, only lost four head of Holsteins.

Doris wasn't lucky though. She died before her thirty-first birthday. I was a pallbearer at the funeral, and it was a sad sad affair. After we buried Doris, Rowena, her older sister, Leda, and their mama were all looking to me for whatever they thought they needed. And their troubles and blues kept me running for a while. "Lloyd, my pipe is leaking. Lloyd, could you pick up some chops for dinner? Lloyd, change the facts and make me feel happy again." Walter was the one I felt sorriest for. His whole life was gone. He was on the road constantly, came by to see Lil' Bit only once before he left for Chicago. I think it hurt him more to visit the baby since the little fellow looked so much like Doris. Lil' Bit had a lot of me in him even though there wasn't any blood between us. He copied my motions and habits like a monkey, and his first word was Da-da, which he said looking straight at me. I was the only daddy he really knew.

After things around the place got back into a routine, Rowena was the one who told me Sheila was crazy for Stoney. I had already figured as much. I saw the way she looked at him down at the dairy. I caught them kissing once or twice, and then…well, hell, I admit it…I started looking for opportunities to watch them rubbing around on each other. I told myself it didn't mean nothing, that it was natural to want to see them happy together, and that's really all it was. Until one night they came down to the house and Sheila came out on the porch and flashed her titties at Stoney and me. I don't know if Stoney read my mind or if the heat of my sudden desire was flaring up on my face, but he got mad and carried her off to the smokehouse, and that's when I knew I'd best steer clear of the girl.

Rowena would be the first to know my feelings, and I took care not to be too affectionate with the girl; I tried not to look at her when she'd dance around the house. Rowena is the suspicious type, and I have to say, she has had cause for not trusting me. There was the one time back when she was pregnant with Annette, and I still feel bad whenever I think on it. I was younger then, filled up with hot blood, but that wasn't any reason for doing what I did.

The reason was Virgie Nell Jackson. She had been in my class at the Lexie County School, and there wasn't a boy over twelve who didn't notice her high tits bouncing by when she walked down the hall. Bad as I wanted to, I never asked her for a date; too scared she'd say no. After we got our diplomas, I heard she had moved off to New Orleans, and I didn't think about her again until one afternoon when I knocked on the door of 124 Front Street and she opened it. I had given Rowena my heart three years earlier, but not my eyes, and that day I had some view. Virgie Nell was wearing a low-cut blouse that opened two-thirds the way down her milk-white chest, and her skirt fit across her hips like a cap on a bottle. She invited me in, and before I knew it, I was tracking cow shit all over her expensive rug. Virgie Nell just laughed about it, said it was a good man's smell, and didn't she miss having that scent in her house. I removed my shoes, set them beside the door, and took her up on an offer of a cold beer.

She sat on the couch cushion right next to me, and I could smell her perfume when she leaned over and said, "So what brings you to my house, Lloyd? I heard you run a dairy out on Carterdale Road now."

"I do. That's why I came. Always looking for new customers. The Trasks who lived here took two quarts every morning. Lots of children."

She laughed, red lipstick flashing over white white teeth. She tossed her head, and blonde hair fell down her back. "Well, I don't have kids, but that doesn't mean I wouldn't be interested in your delivery." She batted her eyelashes and grinned. She heaved her tits up and down and let out a long breath. "I heard you married Rowena Bancroft." She slapped my arm. "Why didn't you wait for me, Lloyd?" This just floored me.

"I, well…" I didn't know what to say, wasn't sure if she was teasing or serious. "I reckon I didn't know you were coming back."

That was the wrong answer, and I knew it because my face got hot, and I could near 'bout hear Rowena saying "Oh Lloyd!"

We didn't do nothing sinful that day, nor the whole rest of that week, but it was getting harder and harder to leave. I didn't have Robert or Shorty helping on the milk run back then, so Rowena had no way of knowing what time to expect me home. I stayed a little longer each visit.

It happened on a Monday. I remember that because me and Rowena had a fight right after we got home from church on Sunday. I'm not saying it was the preacher's fault, but his sermon got me all worked up. The more he talked about David and Bathsheba, the clearer I could see her taking that bath and the wet, soapy body I was imagining belonged to Virgie Nell Jackson. So when we got home, thinking to erase sinful thoughts of her out of my mind, I said to Rowena, let's skip Sunday dinner at your mama's and have a little time alone. She knew what I meant, but she turned up that Bancroft nose and turned me down flat. Ever since Rowena had found out she was going to be a mother, when we made love she acted like her womb was an eggshell I was going to crack. Twice I hadn't even finished before she pushed me off and said she was going to be sick again. I didn't blame her about that, but that Sunday morning she was fit as a fiddle, and I suspected that her not wanting to stay home had more to do with worrying about missing the gossip at her mama's table than anything. Looking back now, I know better. I should have been more understanding about her fears and her delicate condition, but I didn't have an older man's wisdom in my young head back then.

I stayed mad the rest of that day and all of the next, feeling righteous and sorry for myself, until I knocked on Virgie Nell's door. It was like she was a snake who knew when and where to strike to get her man. As soon as I stepped inside her house, without one word, she pulled me up against her tits and started kissing me like I hadn't ever been kissed before. I never found out if she learnt all them things she said and done to me in New Orleans, but I know she didn't get them from anybody around Lexie County. She told me that I was the best lover she'd ever had, said I had a rare combination (that's how she put it — a rare combination) of brute strength and gentle touch. I still don't know what she meant by that, but I left her house that afternoon with my head swelled to the size of a pregnant sow.

By the time I parked the truck at the barn door, my head had shrunk back to normal size and I was sick with regret. All I could think about was Rowena. God knows I never meant to hurt her, and right off I saw that I was plain stupid letting myself get taken in by Virgie Nell's tricks. And tricks is what it was; it wasn't nothing like the love I had for Rowena. I deserved to live with the guilt and shame, without the comfort of Rowena's forgiveness, but Leda, the other snake in my life, had already struck. She told Rowena—and the whole town of Zebulon—that my truck was parked at Virgie Nell's house for over two hours. She said she just happened to drive past twice, but I know better. Leda was trying to pay me back for choosing her younger sister over her is what I think, but it doesn't matter why. The damage was done, and the feeling I had when I saw the hurt in my darling's eyes that night will never leave me.

But that was all in the past, and I hadn't done anything since to deserve her distrust. Oh, once and a while I'd sneak off to Howard's to play cards, and there was the whiskey I kept in the dairy barn, but I figured the little bit she didn't know wouldn't hurt her. To put it plain and honest, Rowena made me be a better man, and I was glad of it.

When Stoney and Sheila ran off to get married, I was some relieved, and I had hopes they'd go off somewhere far away and find a new life together. But then Rowena said I should offer them the vacant tenant house and told me to give them both a raise. I put my foot down then. All they got was a break on the rent on the house.

It wasn't much of a house, but it was a step up from the smokehouse, and Stoney was itching to get out from his daddy's rule, so they jumped on the offer and moved in before I'd had a chance to get Shorty to sweep it out. It wasn't long before Sheila and Annette had made a path running back and forth over the acre and a half between them. I'd see them hiking up their dresses jumping Rowena's flowers, always giggling, whispering in each other's ears about God knows what. I was glad for Annette; she didn't have many friends, and Rowena worried she was jealous of Lil' Bit. But she was wrong there. We all loved the little fellow to death. I got a soft spot for little ones. I reckon it started when my mama gave me my first puppy and it got sick and died. It was just a mongrel, but I treated it like a prize hunting dog, and when Daddy had to shoot it after it got the mange, I thought I'd never get over it. Of course, I did get over it, but to this day I can't stand to see no little creatures, human or otherwise, in pain.

That's maybe why, when I saw what Sheila's papa had done to her after she and Annette came from out there to tell them about the marriage, I threatened to call Clyde Vairo and have him lock the man up. Sheila wouldn't hear of it though, said she knew he was sorry for hurting her, and she didn't care anyhow because she was already married and he couldn't change that.

Then Stoney took up where Sheila's papa left off. I don't know when it started. He might've been whipping her since the beginning, but the first I knew of it was the day I bought the Ayrshires at the state fair in Jackson. I'd heard that a man named Patterson was bringing his prize Ayrshires to the fair, and that he was in trouble and aimed to sell them to settle his debts. I bought the cows all right, but I also borrowed a lot of trouble that day. Annette had asked if she could invite Sheila and Stoney to go to the fair with us, and so I gave them the day off. The kids deserved some fun, and I liked the idea of them seeing me buy the best damned cows in the state. We stopped by my folks' on the way up, but didn't stay long because Annette was about to have a hissy fit to get to the rides. I told her to hold her horses until I made the deal with Patterson. After a little half-hearted haggling, Patterson named a fair price, and when I pulled out my billfold, Sheila stepped up so close to me that I got a whiff of her toilet water. Her eyes got real big when she saw how much money I counted out for the Ayrshires and the trailer, and she said, "Mr. Cotton, you must be the richest man in Lexie County."

I laughed at that. "No, no. There's a lot of men got more than me." I winked at her then. "But I guess I do all right for a dairy farmer."

We spent the rest of the day tromping through the dust and trash that blew up around our legs. The noise bothered me most. When you live your days listening to birds calling, cows lowing, horses neighing, and such, the harsh screaming and loud music around a midway can near 'bout do you in. I won Annette a teddy bear throwing knives, which she accepted with a frown, and that told me it was time to go. We'd had our fill of the fair, and I said we should find Sheila and Stoney and head for home. Just then I heard this show gal calling out to me. "Buy a ticket, and I'll show you my hoochy koochy." I turned around and a woman, dressed up in some kind of Egyptian outfit that showed a lot of her skin, strutted across a make-shift stage toward me. I tried to ignore her at first, but she kept on swiveling her hips, and before I knew it, I heard myself ask, "How much?" When she said ten cents, I turned to Annette and told her to wait for me. Right away I saw Rowena's disapproval written on her face, but she didn't say a thing.

The show was a disappointment, not worth the dime it cost. The hoochy koochy girl didn't do much more inside the tent than she had on the little wooden stage outside. There was some strange Egyptian-type music playing from somewhere, and then she stepped out from behind a red curtain and began her dance. She switched around, jiggling the coins on her hips and shimmying her tits, leaned over so that I could see near 'bout all of them, but she didn't take off the veil or anything else. I had a front row seat on one of the metal folding chairs, and when the show was over, Salome (that was what she called herself) came over to me and took my hand and brought it right up to her left titty. My fingers were stretching out to touch her, and she laughed and dropped my hand. A real tease she was. I was ashamed of myself, and I felt my face heat up. I hurried out of the tent, wishing I hadn't wasted money on Salome and her lousy music.

Just before I got to where Annette stood with a big scowl, Sheila and Stoney came running up. I didn't take much notice of them as I was worrying more that Annette was gonna spill the beans about me going into that tent to her mama. I could already hear Rowena crying, asking me what was I thinking leaving Annette alone, disgracing the Bancroft family with my behavior. I'm not a man who acts on impulse ordinarily, but I reckon the excitement of buying the Ayrshires had affected me, causing me to forget myself that day. I stared hard at Annette and said to Stoney and Sheila that we had been looking for them, that it was time to go. Annette's face was frozen, and I knew she was mad as a setting hen. I pulled her close and whispered a plea for forgiveness and help. I saw the slow deliberation cross her face, and I smiled, hoping for understanding. Finally, Annette nodded and backed up my lie. She wouldn't tell, but I knew the reason was that she was looking out for her mama, not me.

I was in a hurry to get home, speed away from the loud noises, bad smells, and cheap women. I'd load my Ayrshires and by nightfall I'd hold Rowena in my arms. I turned to Stoney and Sheila and said, "Let's get started home," and that's when I noticed the handkerchief wrapped around Stoney's hand. I was about to ask him what had happened when Sheila raised her head and I saw that her eye was swollen some. It didn't take a genius to figure two and two. They'd had a fight, and Stoney had got the best of her. I wanted to punch his face, and I felt my hands balling up, but Sheila stepped in front of him. "I run into the edge of one of them booths," she said real low so that only I could hear her. "It were my fault." I shook my head, but then she reached out and touched my arm. "Please, Mr. Cotton. Let's go home." I gave Stoney a long warning look that said I knew what he'd done. Sheila's eyes filled with tears. "Please," she said again. I uncurled my hands and nodded then. I couldn't go against the husband if the wife had forgiven him. Stoney put his arm around Sheila's shoulders, and as he steered her toward the livestock barns, his face crumpled with misery. He was ashamed of himself, sorry for what he'd done, and I imagined that my own shame over my acts that day showed on my face, too. We'd been forgiven, but both Stoney and me were making the trip home with the heavy weight of guilt on our chests.

CHAPTER 11

It was a while before I took another trip out of town, but the rodeo down at Liberty coaxed me to take another day off. Rowena despised rodeos and wouldn't go to one if someone offered her a brand new cook stove to spend an hour there. Annette is a chip off the block though and wouldn't miss sitting in what her mama called the dirt pit of horrors, for anything. She begged for Sheila and Stoney to ride with us, and the four of us crammed into my truck and set out on a Saturday.

On the twelve-mile ride out, I found out that Stoney had entered the bull-riding contest, which was just the dumbest idea he'd ever had. I told him so, too. He wasn't even a good horseman. "A bull can gore you quicker than you could believe," I told him. "You fall off your bull, and if you're lucky, there'll be enough of you left to be carried off on a stretcher." Stoney's jaw was set though, and he didn't say anything to that. "You tell him, Sheila. You don't want to be a widow at the end of the day."

But she wasn't any smarter than Stoney. She laughed. "Stoney ain't gonna get kilt; he's gonna win." She was half-sitting in his lap, and she squeezed herself against him more. "Ain't you gonna win?"

Stoney grinned big. I could see his chest swelling up. "I reckon I might," he said, as I pulled the truck onto the grass and cut the engine. He took off to get signed up, and I ushered the girls over to the stands where we got good seats on the third row. I bought the girls some peanuts when the vendor came by, and Sheila dove into her little brown bag right off. She tossed the nuts into her mouth and threw the shells at the birds that circled overhead. No, she wasn't worried one bit. "The prize is twenty dollars," she told me. "If Stoney wins, think of all the things we could get with that much money."

"If," I said, "he doesn't get killed. Last year Bucky Moran was gored so bad in his thigh, he's gonna walk with a limp the rest of his life."

Sheila popped another peanut in her mouth. "Stoney's fast. If he falls off, he'll beat that bull to the fence. Hey! Lookit that."

I followed her pointing finger to the clown in the orange wig who was tossing a lasso around one of the barrels set up for the race. "I wouldn't want to be a rodeo clown," Annette said. "A couple of them get hurt bad every year, don't they, Daddy?"

Sheila wiped her fingers on the front of her overalls. "If they'd let women be one, I'd try it. They is so cute. It must be a real good feeling to make people laugh all the time."

Stoney came up to us about then, held up four fingers to Sheila, and walked off. She squealed and jumped up and down. "Number four! He's number four. That's my lucky number; he's gonna win."

I didn't have the heart to tell her that winning wasn't a possibility. Stoney would be competing against cowboys from the neighboring states of Louisiana and Texas who were well-known rodeo champions.

But Sheila kept on eating peanuts with a confident grin while we watched the other events. Darnell Glascock won the calf-roping by expertly throwing his lariat over a running brown calf and tying its thrashing legs in eleven seconds. I was pulling for my second cousin Eric who entered the contest and embarrassed our family by taking twenty-eight seconds to truss his calf. My friend, Homer Knight, was in the bull-dogging event and he wrestled his steer to the ground in eight seconds, which earned him second place. The saddle bronc and bareback riding were next, but my seat was getting hard. So I stood up and stretched. "Let's go see how Stoney's making out and wish him good luck," I said to Sheila and Annette.

We found him squatting beside a muddy truck talking to some other men I didn't know. When Sheila called out to him, he stood and smiled at us. "Come to wish me luck?"

"Uh huh," Sheila said, pulling him away from the men. "I'm gonna give you a magic kiss that'll keep you safe, too." She stuck out her tongue and ran it in a circle around Stoney's lips and then thrust it into his mouth. She drew back and laughed. "You never had a magic kiss before?"

I heard Annette's breath sucking in, but I couldn't look away from them. Stoney laughed. "My mouth ain't what needs magic. Kiss what parts you don't want that bull to puncture."

Sheila bent her knees and ducked her head. "Okay."

I thought of those times I'd watched them in the barn then, and I knew she'd do it. But Stoney caught her by the arms and pulled her up. He whispered something in her ear which made them both laugh. I felt my face turning red; I didn't like standing there watching Sheila make a fool out of herself, but she didn't give a hoot. She giggled and kissed him again.

She wasn't laughing an hour later when we saw Stoney's brown hat sailing off his head as he and a monstrous Brahma bull shot out of the gate. To win, a cowboy has to stick for eight seconds, and Stoney lasted for only three. The only thing we saw was the white hump of the furious bull who turned to charge at the puny rider he had just thrown. Sheila was right about Stoney's speed; he fell on his back and somehow managed to flip over, jump up, and scramble to the fence rail before the dust covered him from our view. All the while Sheila was screaming at the top of her lungs, "Stoney, Stoney, Stoney." When we saw that he was safe, I turned to Sheila figuring she was going to be filled up with disappointment, but she was laughing. "Did you see that? Ain't he something? He done so good, y'all. I can't believe it. Do you think he won?"

Not one other person at that rodeo would have asked such a question, and for a moment I wondered if my eyes had played a trick on me and I hadn't seen what she had. I knew better, of course, but that's when I understood what that saying about rose-colored glasses really means. When

Stoney strutted over and proudly accepted her compliments, I thought maybe that kiss she planted on him sure did have some magic power — over Stoney anyway.

Sheila didn't have much power over herself though. I don't think it ever occurred to her to stand up and fight when she needed to. There was a time when I tried to make her see things straight.

I remember that it was on the morning Rowena and me had had a little fuss over me going to Howard's to play cards. I don't know to this day how she found out, but she did and she was slamming pots around the kitchen when I came back from the milk run. Didn't fix me any breakfast, said she was too busy to be feeding sinners who gambled in dens of iniquity. I turned and walked out of her kitchen and stayed away from the house all day. When Rowena gets like that, there's no use trying to reason with her. She gets over it fast though, and so I figured she'd come around by nightfall if I stayed out of her way. About mid-morning Annette came sailing by the barn door loaded down with pine cones for making Christmas decorations. I figured that would lift Rowena's spirits and she'd forget she was mad at me. I ate some brisket out of Shorty's dinner pail and then Stoney and I took off for town.

I had returned from the late run and was in the bottling room when I heard Sheila come in, her boots scraping slowly on the floor, like she was reluctant to get to work. I turned around just as she came through the door. I had switched on the overhead bulb, but it doesn't cast out much light, and Sheila was in the shadows. When she didn't come on in and start gathering up the bottles, I walked over to her. Before I got there I said something like, "How'd the Christmas doodads turn out?" She didn't answer, and then I saw the bruise on her face. I've seen enough injuries to have a fair idea of how to judge what caused them, and looking at the circle of red slits inside the puffy purple rise below her eye, I would say the fist that made it was wearing a ring. I lifted my hand to her face, and she shrunk back from me. When she limped over to the bottling table, she winced. I followed and knelt in front of her. "Let me have a look," I said.

She lifted her dress. The large mass of blackish skin on her leg made the face wound look like nothing. I kept my knees on the damp floor waiting for words to come to me. "Stoney?" I asked, trying to keep my voice low.

She grabbed my shoulder. "No. No, he didn't." She was crying now. I hadn't ever seen her cry, and I rose up and took her in my arms. I was surprised at how soft she was against me. The hump wasn't the heavy rock I thought she carried all this time. She buried her face against my chest, and I took a breath and then I smelled it. She had been taken along with the beating. I let her cry awhile, and finally she pushed back from me and hung her head. "I'm sorry, Mr. Lloyd. I done wet your nice shirt." She ran her hand across Rowena's embroidery that spelled out Cottons' Dairy.

"Sheila, you can't allow this. Stoney is gonna hurt you bad one day."

Her hair whipped back and forth against her face as she shook her head. "No, no. I told you. It weren't him that done it."

I cupped her chin and lifted her face to look into her eyes, and I saw that she was telling the truth. Stoney had been with me most of the day, hadn't he? I read fear in her eyes. Sheila was scared of my finding out, but I knew. It had to be her papa who'd done this. I felt sick. "Goddamn him," I said. "May he burn in hell." I thought then that I should have called the law on him when she came back from Mars Hill all bruised up after she announced her marriage to her folks.

Sheila put her hand over my mouth. I know it was crazy; I don't know what came over me, but when her palm touched my lips, I grabbed her wrist and kissed the spot where the blue vein ran up her arm. She allowed it, stood quiet while I lifted her bangs and touched my lips to her forehead. I just wanted to comfort her like I would Annette; that's probably all I was feeling.

She drew back from me. "Mr. Lloyd," she whispered. "Please. You don't know. You can't tell. If Stoney finds out, he'll kill him." She clutched my shirt in her fist. "Please. Please."

She was right; Stoney would kill him. I wanted to do the job myself and she wasn't even my wife. "He's gonna see what's been done to you. How're you going to explain this?" I touched her face.

Sheila chewed on her lip. "I'll think up something. Stoney believes near 'bout anything I tell him."

I had to smile at that. She was simple, but she was most likely right about Stoney. "Next time," I said. "Get a gun, and you use it on that bastard you call Papa."

Sheila shook her head. "It weren't him," she said. "That's all over and done with now."

I wondered how she could protect such a devil, but I guessed that Rowena's mama was right about blood being thicker than water, so I didn't push her to say the truth. After she left, I decided to keep a closer watch on who visited up there at my tenant house.

CHAPTER 12

It was around five months later, after that day in the barn, when Walter and his bride showed up at our house. God knows I'd have done anything in this world to be fair to Walter; he had lost his wife and suffered plenty. Lil' Bit was his son; he had every right to ask for him back, but it went down hard and bitter for all of us.

Rowena, of course, took it hardest. It was like she was ghost-walking that morning they came for him. She wandered around the house, in and out of rooms, standing in front of the stove when there wasn't anything to stir. I did what I could. Held her and rocked her in my arms all that night, but she wouldn't cry, wouldn't say Lil' Bit's name. Annette was sad, but she was young and kids bounce back from worse things than this is what I told myself.

The day after Walter left with Lil' Bit sitting on the new wife's lap, I was set to take down the crib in the middle room, but Rowena wouldn't have it. She hung onto that baby bed like it was a life raft in a room full of raging water. I reckoned she thought as long as we kept it there that maybe Lil' Bit would come home. Then the next day, Rowena took to her bed and just flat gave up. I told her we would go to Chicago to visit them; I said I'd get her a new set of china; I read the Bible to her; then I called her mama. But even Mama Bancroft couldn't get her out of that bed. She left the house shaking her head and wiping her eyes with that fancy little lace-edged handkerchief she keeps in her sleeve.

It was Sheila who brought Rowena back. I never did understand exactly how she did what she did, but one night I walked into the front room to find her dancing to some old ragtime music on the Victrola. Annette and Sheila were high-kicking along with her, and I thought it beat all I'd seen since Darby had delivered twin Jersey calves in the back pasture. I didn't know how we could ever pay Sheila back for helping out like she did, but she didn't want any thanks.

The opportunity to return a favor came when I began looking for a bull to breed with the two Ayrshires I had bought back in the fall. Roger Moak over in Tylertown said he had a registered Ayrshire, but I took one look at the old bull and knew the papers were doctored. He wasn't fit for old Patch, our sorriest cow. Then I read in the *Farmer's Journal* that there was a breeder over in Louisiana who had the finest Ayrshire bulls in the country. That man turned out to be Doug Patterson, the fellow who had sold me my cows at the Jackson State Fair. When I telephoned him, he remembered me, and I arranged to take both of my heifers over there for a visit. Stoney was hot to go on the trip. He hadn't been out of Mississippi but once for a ball game in Alabama one of his brothers was playing in, and he hadn't ever stayed in a roadside cabin neither. I needed a hand all right, but I had figured on taking Shorty or Digger. I told Stoney no and I thought that was the end of it.

The next afternoon after I got back to the dairy from the milk run, Sheila was waiting for me in the barn. She was all lit up about something, smiling, moving fast around the barn like a little hummingbird going from one chore to another. "What's got you humming?" I asked her.

She giggled. "Might be you."

"What's this about?" I stood watching her swish the broom around like a dance partner.

"It's a secret," she said. "Can't tell yet."

More foolish nonsense is what I thought. "Well, let's get going on these bottles," I said lifting a crate to the table beside the sink.

"No. Not yet, Mr. Lloyd. Uh, you is needed up to the house. That's right. Miss Rowena, she said you best come up there quick."

I straightened up from the load and wiped my forehead. "Oh Lord," I said. "I'll bet her mama's hit another tree with her old Buick."

Rowena told me earlier in the day that her mother was picking her up and they were going shopping in Zebulon. "Why can't you pick her up?" was my reaction. Rowena's mama was a terrible driver. The worst I've ever seen. She hadn't learned to drive until she was in her fifties, and, like a lot of the older folks in the community, she couldn't break the habit of pulling close up to trees and posts like she had done when she drove a buggy and needed a hitching post. Her eyesight wasn't the best, and her spectacles didn't help with her distance judging. "I don't like you to ride with her," I said.

But Rowena was determined. "I can't go hurting her feelings telling her you think she's a danger to her own family." She set her flowered Sunday hat square on her head, and I knew there was no talking her out of it. "Anyway, she hasn't had a mishap in over a month," she said over her shoulder as she sailed out of the house.

Before I went in the house I looked for Mama Bancroft's banged-up Buick in the driveway, but there wasn't a vehicle in sight. I was worried the damage might be so bad she couldn't drive home. I went in the house and called out for Rowena, who answered me from the front room. "In here, hurry, Lloyd." I dreaded the sight. She must've been hurt bad this time; she might be lying on the couch in a leg cast maybe, maybe worse. The old lady didn't make it, or she made it and was gonna be moving in with us for round-the-clock care. I squeezed my eyes shut once and then quickly opened them. I was prepared for whatever this afternoon would bring.

"Hi," Rowena said, unbandaged, alone, pretty in her clover-colored dress spread out on the couch.

"Where's your mama?"

Rowena patted the cushion beside her. "Gone home. Come sit."

I eased down beside her. "She have a wreck?"

Rowena smiled. "No. She had a little trouble parking, but we got that worked out." She kissed my cheek. "Ask me where we parked."

I was relieved, but aggravation was setting in now. She was acting more like Sheila or Annette than herself. "Rowena, I got more chores to do. I don't have time to play a guessing game."

Rowena kept her smile. "Okay, you can go in a minute, but you've got to hear what I have to say first."

I stood up. "Say it then. Time's a-wasting."

She took both of my hands in hers and looked up at me. "Lloyd, I went to Dr. Brock's office. I thought I might be and I am! Lloyd, we're going to have a baby."

I was stunned, struck dumb as a fence post. The thought ran through my head that she might be crazy, having some kind of hallucination, and I wished for the first time that her mama hadn't gone home early. "A real baby?"

"Uh huh. Middle of February. Or thereabouts. Doctor said I'm fit as a fiddle, too."

I looked at her stomach, couldn't see any sign of it. "You're sure?"

Rowena stood up and put her hands around the back of my neck. She jiggled my head back and forth. "Get it through to your brain, Lloyd. You're going to be a daddy to another child."

I believed her then. "It's a miracle," I said.

She kissed me all over my face, cheeks, chin, nose, eyelids. "Exactly," she said breathless with her efforts. "We're having a miracle baby."

I hated to leave her, but there was still work to be done, so I left her and went back to the barn. Sheila was nearly finished with the scrubbing when I walked in. She turned and grinned as wide as her lips would stretch. "Congratulations, Mr. Lloyd."

I was a little disappointed that she had been told before me, but I didn't let that show. "Thank you, Sheila. We're both real real happy. It's a true miracle."

Sheila disagreed. "No, it were just everyday magic. Ever since Lil' Bit left, I've been telling Miss Rowena y'all need another young'n to put in that crib, and that I knowed how to get one."

Here comes more foolishness, I thought, but I leaned back against the table to listen. "And how's that?"

"Well, the best way is to tie a magic cord around the, uh, the daddy-to-be's, uh, private."

I laughed at that in spite of myself. "Oh, Sheila!"

She looked down at the floor. "It's true, but Miss Rowena said she knowed you'd never let her do that. Stoney won't let me neither, so then I come to the next plan, which was already part set up with the crib still in the room."

I thought how Rowena had hung on to that baby bed, insisting she couldn't allow me to take it up to the attic with the high chair and playpen I'd stored. Surely, she hadn't believed Sheila's silliness.

As if reading my mind, she said, "I didn't tell Miss Rowena, but four times when I come to the house, I snuck in the room and tied the magic cord around the legs of the bed, one on each leg. And, of course, I didn't know for certain that would do the trick, like I said, it's better if'n the string goes on the man, but it works on cribs too. We know that for sure now."

Oh, ignorance, Sheila is thy name, is what I said to myself. "If you're right, I guess we owe you a big favor" is what I said instead.

Sheila twisted her hair around and sucked on a strand before she spoke. "Well, there is a favor I would like; it ain't for me so much as for Stoney."

"And what would it be?"

"Stoney, he's a-wantin' to go on that trip over to Louisiana bad. Said you was taking Digger instead of him. So what I'd like is for him to get to go with you. He's wild to travel the world, Mr. Lloyd, and he ain't got started on none of it yet."

I gave in right off. I knew she'd had nothing to do with Rowena's pregnancy, but she had been her savior after Walter had taken our son. And in a way, she had helped us conceive the baby because, after Sheila left on that night of the girls' dancing, we got into bed and Rowena showed me just how recovered she was.

So a couple of weeks later, Stoney and me lit out in the truck pulling the trailer and headed for Louisiana. It turned out to be a good trip in that both Ayrshires were impregnated, and the fees weren't as high as I had thought. Stoney did pretty near what I told him to most of the time, and I have to admit I enjoyed having the boy along. As we drove northwest along the pine-scented highways, we talked about the war in Europe, speculating on whether we'd get into it. I said I thought we would; Stoney was hoping I was right. He wanted to kill himself some krauts, he said. I told him that my daddy was in the Great War and he didn't think much of it. Bad food, sleeping on the cold ground, your buddies getting blown to bits right beside you. Daddy said he prayed every night to come home with just one limb missing; that would be something to be grateful for. And his prayers were answered; he came home after he lost an ear when a sailing bullet shaved it clean off.

Mostly, we talked about the dairy business, hunting, and fishing. We were heading west into the setting sun, and I was squinting against the glare when Stoney brought up the subject of women. "Mr. Cotton, you remember your first time with a gal?"

I laughed. "I reckon any man who hasn't lost his mind remembers that."

"No. What I meant to ask was when you first done it with your wife, or someone else who hadn't done it before, a virgin, well, how did you know for sure that you was her first?"

I saw where he was headed, and I thought about Sheila in the barn that day, her smelling of sex after her papa's visit. I considered before I spoke. "It's hard to know for sure. Some women bleed a lot, some hardly at all. I reckon it's a good thing we don't hold shivarees anymore because the old maids used to check the bride's sheets after the party, and I've heard tell of young girls getting accused of not being pure just because they didn't bleed."

Stoney's arm was propped on the open window with his elbow sticking out into the warm wind. He leaned out and let the air flow over his head as if to cool it down. He turned back to me. "Sheila didn't bleed none."

"That doesn't necessarily mean anything, Stoney. Rowena told me Leda broke her cherry horseback riding." I had known better when she told that whopper, but I passed it on now to where it might do some good.

"Yeah, I've heard that old tale." He mimicked a high-pitched woman's voice, "Oh, I fell on a monkey bar when I was just a little girl, I was riding a boy's bike and hit myself on it."

Stoney wasn't quite as dumb as I thought. I grinned. "Well, thing is, we can't prove whether they're lying or not. Just no way to tell for sure."

"I think Sheila's papa got hers." His voice was quiet, filled with hurt, and I was taken aback.

"She tell you that?"

"No. She don't like to talk about her papa. That's one reason I think it's true."

I saw a sign for Sinclair gas ahead and decided it was a good time to stop and end this conversation. I stuck my arm out my window to signal a turn. "He's a mean man. Hard as nails. He beat her. We all know that. As to the other, well, best to bury that thought. She loves you; she's happy now."

"Yeah. She loves me more'n anybody could believe. As to being happy, I don't think Sheila knows how not to be. She can take the smallest thing and make a real big deal outa it, make you think something real ordinary is special. Magic, she calls it."

I smiled over the wheel and cut the engine. "She does that," I said. "She thinks her magic cord is why Rowena is pregnant."

Stoney frowned. "Yeah, she tried to tie that cord on me on our wedding night. I don't want no kids, and no magic cord, witchcraft, voodoo, praying or nothing else gonna change my mind on that."

I figured he would change his mind; Sheila would find a way to turn him around, but I got out of the truck and said, "They got a restroom if you're needing to use it."

CHAPTER 13

On the way home from Louisiana, we stopped at a roadhouse next to some cabins called The Cottonfield. We'd got a late start that morning, and I decided we would spend the night on the road. I checked the Ayrshires, shoveled them some grain in the trailer and then joined Stoney inside the bar. The place was a dump, sawhorse tables, a few rickety chairs; the floor was so filthy I couldn't tell whether it was pine or oak. The bartender was a woman, and I hadn't ever ordered a drink from a woman. I reckon Stoney hadn't either because when she came over to our table and said, "What'll you have?" he answered, "Can you pour us a drink?" She laughed and said she guessed she could since she owned the place.

We joked awhile about my name being Cotton and us planning on staying at "my" cabins next door. Peggy, that was the gal's name, sat down with us and said she owned that too, but I was welcome to a discount on a room since my name was Cotton. She was nice to me, but all the while she talked, she kept her eyes on Stoney. She was old enough to be his mama, and when he kept on calling her "Ma'am," she finally started looking interested in me.

Two fellows came in, locals I guessed, since Peggy called them by name. The one she called Wallace was over six feet and skinny. His jeans, slung low on his hips, looked like they might slide plumb off. The other one, Eugene, was about the same height, but a lot heavier. They were brothers, I knew, because they both had noses and chins that stuck far out on square faces. Neither of them took off their hats, so I couldn't read their eyes as they passed by us to a far table and ordered their beers.

Stoney and me had consumed a considerable amount by then, and when I looked over at Stoney, I saw that he wasn't seeing too clear by the way he held his head back trying to focus on my face. I let him order another drink on me though. If he passed out, I could sling him on my shoulder and throw him in the truck to sleep it off, and then I'd have the motel room to myself. Peggy raised her eyebrows when she brought the drink, but smiled at me and pressed her tit into my arm as she set the glass on the table. I touched her arm with my fingers and slid them up to the sleeve of her dress. She didn't pull away. Just then the brothers yelled for her to get her butt over to their table; didn't she care nothing about saving thirsty men from dying, they shouted, and she whirled around and was gone.

When Peggy delivered the drinks to the other table, Stoney started singing a cowboy song. On the morning when we had left the dairy, he had come down toting his guitar along with his gear, and I told him there wasn't room for it. Sheila had taken it from him and said she was gonna put it beside her in bed to keep his spot warm. So now Stoney's fingers strummed the air, and he moved them so precise like, I could nearly see a real guitar in his hands.

The brother named Wallace talked real loud, saying to his brother, "Eugene, that boy can't carry a tune in a bucket."

Stoney raised his voice and sang out more.

"That goddamned racket has got to stop," Wallace said and stood up. Before I knew it, the two of them were standing at our table. The brother leaned up close to Stoney. "I said shut up the noise."

Stoney stopped singing then. He smiled at the two men. "What you got against a Tex Ritter song?" he asked.

The big one, Eugene, answered. "What you got against us?"

Peggy came over then, shaking her head at them. She grabbed Wallace's forearm. "Wallace. Eugene. I told you last time you was in here there'd be no more fighting. You broke two chairs, and," she swept her arm out, "I ain't got but eight left."

Wallace shook her off so hard, she fell up against Stoney's chair. I saw the danger in Stoney's eyes; just like my bull Franklin gets before he charges. I said shit shit shit to myself. Last thing I wanted was to get into a fight with these fellows.

Stoney was up so fast, his chair went over. "Apologize for pushing this lady," he said in a low voice.

Eugene laughed. "Peggy ain't no lady. She's a whore. You can have her all night for a dollar."

I heard myself saying, "You told us you owned this place. And the cabins."

She grinned, but still her face took on a deeper color. I think she said something like, "Well, I am the manager," but I'm not sure as right then Stoney's fist shot past her ear and landed on Eugene's jaw.

God knows I've seen a lot of fighting in my time from schoolyard fracases to serious fisticuffs over poker pots and family disputes, but I'd never witnessed such as I did that night. I never threw a punch, didn't need to. Stoney had them both on the floor before I could get up from my chair and around the table. He would have killed them; I'm sure of it. After Peggy and I finally got him off them, he staggered around the room like he didn't know where he was. I turned around and saw Eugene getting up, holding his eye that had nearly been gouged out of its socket. Walter was bleeding from a chunk of chin that was hanging off his face caused by Stoney's teeth, and he was already on his knees, ready to come after his assailant. I grabbed Stoney's arm and dragged him toward the door. We made it to the truck before they came running out to the parking lot, and I scratched out, leaving them in a cloud of dust.

We didn't say anything for about ten miles. Stoney had a few bruises and one deep cut on his cheek. Finally, I slowed and pulled off on the shoulder. "You okay? You hurt bad anywhere?"

Stoney raised his arms and looked at his torn shirt sleeve. "This were my best work shirt," he said. "Sheila's gonna be mad as a wet hen." He squawked like a chicken and giggled. I say giggle, like a girl would, because that's how he sounded. I guessed he was still drunk and so I pulled back on the road and headed on south toward home. In less than five minutes, he was out cold.

I drove on through the night, suddenly more alert and sharp-minded than I'd been in a long time. First my mind turned onto that Peggy. She was a liar, getting me worked up with her tits pushing on me, and all the while planning on charging me for it. I've never paid for it, and I sure wouldn't have started shelling out for it on this night. She wasn't much anyhow. Couldn't hold a candle to Rowena. Then Rowena's face came looking up at me in the windshield. I saw her with her eyes a-shining like stars, honest to god, they were that bright on the glass. Right then and there I got an ache for her. I was so damn lucky that Stoney had started that fight. I was going home to my little love pure as a white lamb, and I was glad of it. It was the being away from home that had made me think crazy. Rowena was all I'd ever want for the rest of my life, and I'd treat myself like a lame horse and shoot myself in the head if I ever hurt her again.

There wasn't any traffic this time of night, and I looked off into the dark woods as I drove on. Every so often a house light winked out of the dark, but most of the light came from the moon that slid in and out of view as I crested hills and coasted toward bottomlands. It seemed like I was the only man left on the earth after some great catastrophe. I shivered in my aloneness and looked over at Stoney slumped against the window. He looked like a child sleeping there, like innocence itself. It was hard to believe he was the man who had whipped two people so bad less than an hour before. I was reminded of one of our yard dogs. Stew was the name Annette gave him. He was a mutt, came to us in a rainstorm, barking from underneath the house, till I threatened to shoot him. Annette had dragged him out next morning, cleaned him up and fed him some leftover stew, the reason for his name. He had turned out to be a good cattle dog, helping herd like he'd been trained for it. He hung out at the barn and made us all laugh because he acted like one of the cats when we milked. Stew would line up with them beside a milk stool and wait for Digger or Shorty to turn a teat out and squirt milk into his mouth. Then he got rabies. I don't know where or how, but one morning I noticed he wasn't around, and as the day went on and he didn't show up, I figured he'd got himself killed by a car or some animal in the woods. Then the next day, just as I was coming up to the house for supper, there he was in the drive, foam dripping from his mouth, a wild look in his eyes. He growled and staggered toward me. I knew he'd attack me any minute, and slowly I backed up to the barn and lifted my shotgun off the wall. Then I heard the guineas screaming. He was in their pen and had killed two already and was now lunging toward the fence where one was trying to fly up to safety. I was calm though, took a quick bead and shot him behind his left ear. I remember standing over Stew's bloody fur, thinking how quick things can turn from good to bad. That was the way it was now with Stoney. Looking back over at his hands crossed on his chest, I remembered how those fingers picking the pretend guitar one moment had curled so quickly into fists smashing flesh and bone the next.

I figured then that those hands could also have caused the bruises Sheila told us came from run-ins with doors and tools and such. She hadn't blamed her papa and she wouldn't tell on her husband, but I was sure she needed protecting from both of them. I told myself it wasn't my worry, not my duty to see after her. I knew Rowena would say it was. She'd quote the parable about the Good Samaritan or some other verse in the Bible that instructs us to become busybodies in the name of Christianity. Well, she could read the whole Sermon on the Mount to me, but I made up my mind that night, I wasn't getting involved. It was between the two of them; it's not right for a man to speak up for another's wife. I had nearly slipped up already, been taken in by her bruises. I felt my face heat up thinking about that day in the barn. I remembered the softness of her hump when I held her against me, the scent of her hair when I lifted her bangs to kiss her forehead. No, I wasn't going to allow such as that to happen again. Sheila

Barnes might be persuasive, she could try to cast spells and use magic charms, but like Stoney said about them having a baby, none of her fool-ishness was gonna work on me.

The boy slept all the way home. It was dawn when I turned onto Carterdale Road, and as the sun's early pink light washed over Stoney's face, his lids fluttered and opened. He stretched like a cat and looked out of the window. "We nearly home already?"

"Yep, you had a good sleep," I said.

He wrinkled his forehead, remembering how things had been before he'd passed out. He grinned. "I bested 'em both back there, huh?"

"You did that," I said. "You were drunk as a skunk, too; you went at them like a mad dog."

"Yeah, hooch can make you faster, not slow like folks say."

We were passing the turnoff for Flowerdale Road, and I lifted my hand to Mr. Brister, who sat high in his black truck waiting to pull out toward Zebulon. "Drink slowed the other two though, and if they'd been sober, you might be dead now. They were big men."

Stoney jabbed his fist in the air. "Boom, bang, I got one. I got to tell Hugh how surprised that biggest one was when I bit his chin."

My place came into view, and I slowed to enjoy the quarter-mile ride up to our drive. The cattle were coming through the gate to the back pas-ture, milked and fed, ready to saunter across the green field. I filled up inside at the sight. If the dairy kept on prospering, I'd buy more Ayrshires, more land. My son, if that was to be the outcome of Rowena's pregnancy, would have a legacy that would be the envy of the county. Rowena would fix me a hot breakfast, sausage, eggs, grits, biscuits with syrup. Before I took my seat at the head of the table, I would take her in my arms, hold her sweet-smelling hair against my face. I wouldn't think of last night again. That woman, the whiskey, the fighting, all of that was behind me, a bad memory that I rubbed out of my head like clotted cream from the bot-tom of a bottle. I smiled then, thinking of the little verse Annette memo-rized for Sunday school. "God's in his heaven, all's right with the world."

That night lying beside me in our soft bed, Rowena turned to me and said, "Lloyd, don't tell this, but Sheila thinks she might be expecting a baby too."

"Does Stoney know yet?"

"No. She says she wants to wait until she's sure, but she's so happy, I don't think she'll be able to keep it a secret long."

I thought about Stoney's vow, remembered his eyes darkening when he said he wasn't having any children. I remembered the defiant tone of his voice when he said Sheila's magic would never change his mind. Then I looked over at Rowena's face glowing in the moonlight that slanted across our bed and decided to keep counsel with myself. I pulled her into my arms. "There's a lot to be happy about around here these days," I said. She snuggled against me, and when I reached for the ribbon on her night dress, she moved in even closer.

CHAPTER 14

ROWENA

Digger is the one who told me that Sheila had been found. He stood in the backyard, yelling up to the porch where I stood waiting for news. "Miss Cotton! Miss Cotton! They found her. She dead. Murdered in the cornfield." I remember opening the screen door to go inside. I'd have to tell her mother, but my knees felt like jelly and I stood hanging onto the door, wondering if I could walk at all. Effie Carruth had heard the shouting, and she came running toward me from the living room where she'd been nursing her new baby.

"I'm afraid it's bad news." My voice was a whisper. "She's been found. She's dead."

Effie was already crying, she crossed her arms over her chest, and began rocking back and forth. "No, no, noooo." The room began spinning around her face, and I knew if I didn't sit down quickly, I would collapse in front of the poor woman. I made it to the kitchen table and fell into Lloyd's seat. Effie was moaning between her words. "I knew it. I knew she were dead. I said it. I said it." Her dress was open, and I could see the blue-veined breast, the nipple wet and dripping onto the floor. I wondered what she'd done with the baby, but I felt bound into the chair and couldn't manage more than a hand stretching out to her grief.

I watched her stagger toward the door and realized she was going to her girl. I summoned strength then and stood. I held her shoulders from behind her. I didn't want to look into her face. "Wait. You don't want to see her now. Stay here until your husband comes."

"But she needs me. My baby needs me."

I pulled her back to the chair where I'd been sitting and she crumpled like a rag doll over the table. We both heard the half-nursed baby crying then, and Effie lifted her head. She looked confused as if maybe she thought it was Sheila, her firstborn, who was crying instead of her last-born child. There were so many Carruth children I had wondered how she kept their names and ages straight in her head. Did she remember each birth separately or did they all blend into one painful memory? I could recall every detail of Annette's birth. They say you forget the agony when you look on your baby's face, but that's a bald-faced lie. I cupped my stomach, thinking I would have it all to remember again in just a few months. Effie's baby stopped crying and I heard one of the children's voices saying, "Here, boy, suck my finger." Yes, there were other children in the house; most of them were sprawled out on the floor in exhausted sleep. Where was my own child? I hadn't seen Annette for hours. Annette! She would be devastated. Sheila was her closest friend. It seemed that Effie's crying was coming from high above me, and I saw Annette's grief-stricken face in a green haze. "The Lord is my shepherd. I shall not want," I said aloud. "He maketh me." I couldn't think straight. What? He maketh me to lie down beside still waters. Or was it He leadeth me beside still waters? Make or lead? Which one? It seemed so important to know. I was actually headed to the front room to get my Bible when I came to my senses and turned back to the kitchen. I turned on the light and saw that Effie sat staring at her hands like they belonged to someone else. I walked over to her and buttoned her dress. I longed to lay my head on the table and grieve for Sheila, for myself. I would miss her so terribly. But I couldn't, mustn't. Her mother was in my keep, and I didn't know how long it would be before somebody came for her. It was nearly supper time. I had the catfish Lloyd had caught yesterday, the crowder peas in a dishpan in the sink, corn already silked. Would that be enough though?

I felt his presence before he knocked, and I looked up at Mr. Carruth, who had altered into another man since I had met him that morning. His face was a terrible mask of grief, rage, disbelief, the Lord only knows what he was feeling for sure, but I was frightened out of my mind when he opened the door and grabbed his wife's shoulder. He lifted her up and shoved her toward the door, where she stood with her head bent into the crook of her raised arm as if it would shut out the sight of him. He hadn't spoken, and I cleared my throat, trying to summon up some civility, but I didn't need to think of that because he was out of the room already, headed toward the children. In seconds, it seemed, they filed through my kitchen, a parade of tow-heads bent like broken flowers of varying heights. Mr. Carruth followed them all with the baby slung over his shoulder, the baby's head bouncing upside down against his father's back.

I headed straight for the telephone chair and asked for Mama's number. I wouldn't allow myself one thought, one feeling, one aching sob. I stroked my stomach with one hand while I held the receiver close to my ear. Mama would know what to say, she would help me take care of my little unborn baby. But as I listened to the static on the line, I wondered if I would be able to speak. When I heard Mama's hello, I couldn't open my mouth, and then she said, "Rowena, is it you? They found her, huh?"

It was her saying my name that let the floodgates open, and I burst into tears. "Mama, she's dead. Our little Sheila is dead."

Sheila came to us on my birthday. Lloyd had gone to town to purchase a sewing machine that was meant to be a surprise for me. I wanted something more personal like jewelry, but except for buying my wedding ring set, I doubt Lloyd has ever been inside Dauber's Jewelry Store even though it's right next to Vest's, where he buys his work boots.

Annette met Sheila out by the road and brought her up to the house but she wouldn't come inside. When I went out to the porch to welcome her, I needed a moment or so to collect myself before speaking. I never saw anything more pitiful. Besides the hump that rose up like a small hatbox on her back, there were the bare feet, the wispy blonde hair, the white eyebrows over blue eyes too large for her pinched face, all of which put me in mind of one of Mr. Charles Dickens' characters.

Lloyd had been against hiring the girl, but I had persuaded him that it was his Christian duty to help her get away from that tyrannical father of hers. I said, "Now, Lloyd, how will you feel if the girl's father kills her one day and you didn't do a thing to help?" He blew out his breath in a big "Psssss" like he always does when he's resigned to something or other, and I started thinking about curtains for the smokehouse right away.

I wanted to do more for her, but you have to be cautious with charity. Mama warned me that plenty of people do bite the hand that feeds them and it's because they resent your taking away their dignity. So I was careful not to overdo it with the child. I say child; she was fifteen, but she was so tiny and playful, she seemed as young as Annette, who was nine that July Sheila came.

At first I thought she was simple-minded, and I wondered if maybe her father had hit her in the head too often and caused damage there. But naiveté doesn't always mean ignorance, and while Sheila was never going to be a scholar or even understand the punch line to Lloyd's silly jokes, she had a sort of wisdom about life that, at times, astonished me. After she'd been with us for a couple of weeks, I saw the proof myself.

Doris had visited that day, and I was so blue I didn't feel I had the strength to cook the noon meal. I was standing in front of the pantry shelves staring at the rows of mason jars filled with figs and peaches, thinking nothing sweet was going to take away the bitter taste of Doris's suffering when Sheila called my name. I turned to see her standing in the kitchen door holding a tiny biddy. "A newborn," she said. "Lookie, Miss Rowena, it's already trying to peck my hand."

"I see," I said. I guess I've seen thirty or more biddies break open their shells and I wasn't in a mood to humor Sheila's fascination with a chick that was going to turn into a squawking hen destined for our Sunday dinner.

Sheila ignored my sour tone. "Ain't it just the cutest little thing?"

I glanced at the bit of yellow fluff in her palm and said, "It looks like a normal biddy to me. I guess some people think they're cute."

"But ain't it the miracle that starts you considering?" She was standing so close to me I could smell the residue of birth on the chick, and I wrinkled my nose. "I mean, I was thinking about your poor sister, Miss Doris, and how she must feel so thankful for her own place in the Lord's plan."

I stepped away from her. "Thankful? How can you say such, Sheila? You know she's dying of cancer."

Sheila stroked the back of the chick with her forefinger. "Yesum. I do, but Lil' Bit is here, healthy and happy, and that's a miracle, ain't it?"

"Well, yes, of course, but he nearly died before we got him."

Sheila bobbed her head exactly like the chickens did when looking for bugs in the ground. "That's what I mean. The good Lord needs your sister up there in heaven, but He knowed her leaving was gonna put a hole in your heart, so He showed you how to patch it by mending her baby. He knowed you was longing for a baby you couldn't have, and He let Miss Doris be the one to give a son to you. I know when your sister takes her trip to heaven, she's gonna lift up with a happy heart, knowing what she's leaving here on earth. I know I feel thankful just to be here with folks like y'all." She ducked her head and whispered. "I feel like I'm part of the miracle too."

I stared at her for a long while. Sheila didn't mind the silence between us; she stared back at me with eyes filled with a knowledge alien to me. I considered her words. Hadn't Doris just today said she felt such peace in her heart when she saw her little son in our house? When my sister bowed her head and said the Lord's Prayer, was it possible that she sincerely meant the line, "Thy will be done on Earth?" Had God's will been to give us a miracle? Even so, I couldn't be happy or grateful or even peaceful that Doris was being taken from us, but I thought that perhaps I could learn to accept what couldn't be changed and I did take some comfort in Sheila's words. "Thank you," I said. Before she turned and left my house, I touched my finger to the soft down of the sleeping biddy. "It is a cute chick," I said. "And to think it came out of an eggshell. It is a wonder."

That was the way of it so often. Sheila opening up my mind to what was seemingly complex and then in her halting, limited vocabulary guiding me to see a simplicity that felt, well, more natural to me. I suppose it is the Bancroft blood that causes me, in Lloyd's words, to make mountains out of molehills. Lloyd's people are so matter of fact, and if you can't see it, smell it, or taste it, well, it doesn't exist as far as they're concerned. But the Cottons are a good family; Lloyd's mother was a Graunston of Scottish descent. On our first visit after Lloyd proposed, his mother showed me their coat of arms, and when I told Mama about that, she gave up on try-ing to marry me off to Harry Gatlin, who was studying law at Ole Miss and laughed like a girl. I admit though I had to feign regret when Lloyd's par-ents moved up toward Jackson. Every time Mrs. Cotton visited our home, I felt like a schoolgirl who didn't know a thing about running a household.

Of course, my own mama could make me feel much the same, and not just about housework. But when Mama points out my mistakes, it's not to show off what-all she knows, it's for my own good, and those are the same words she used back when she had to punish one of her girls. "This is for your own good," she would say in a real sad voice. Poor Leda is the one of us who heard that sentence the most.

Mama also believes acquiring culture and refinement is good for you. She raised all three of us girls to revere Shakespeare and Wordsworth, and we took both piano and elocution lessons until tenth grade. Leda was on the debate team and went to the state contest, which she lost to a boy from Greenville whose daddy was the former mayor. That was two years before Leda began dating Howard, Lloyd's brother, and that's how I met Lloyd. Leda and Howard set us up on a blind date, and well, we just took off from there. Then Howard jilted my sister, and she turned her eyes on Lloyd, causing a big rift between us for quite a few years. When I said to Sheila that in his play, *Othello*, William Shakespeare wrote that jealousy is a green-eyed monster, she shook her head and said she didn't believe in monsters, just fairies and trolls. I had wanted to follow Mama's example and help Sheila learn the things she needed to know for her own good, but I gave up on trying to educate her through book learning and tried to teach her more basic skills like how to can vegetables and how to crochet and quilt.

Sheila's first lesson involved courting. She didn't know the first thing about the etiquette for a young lady, and I had assumed that her ignorance would most likely never become apparent since I doubted anyone would ever ask her to step out. Boy, was I wrong! In just a few weeks, Stoney fell for her. At first I didn't believe Annette when she told me about them. I even admonished her for telling a cruel joke. "The Bancroft women do not participate in that kind of humor," I said.

"But, I'm telling the truth, Mama; they've already gone out last night," Annette told me with her hands on her hips. "And she doesn't have any nice dresses to wear."

I went straight to my closet then. There's something so satisfying about giving hand-me-downs to someone who really appreciates them. When Annette brought Sheila up to the house, I got right to work on the dress she'd chosen for her date, and by the time she went out to wait for Stoney to pick her up, she looked nearly lovely — at least from the front where her hump couldn't be seen.

Over the next weeks I thought about Sheila and Stoney as a couple quite a bit. It just didn't make a lot of sense to me that a handsome boy like that would fall for a girl like Sheila, but as Mama says, if the man's private gets hard, his brain gets soft, and I could tell that was the way with the two of them. I don't like to think about it, but something in me just knew that Sheila wasn't being a lady on those dates, and I worried Stoney was taking advantage of the poor girl, and she'd come up with a seed planted in her belly and no husband. Mama and I discussed this possibility, and she said, if I were correct, he'd never marry her. "Why buy the cow when the milk is free?" was her mantra when Doris, Leda, and I were dating. Doris and I believed her and were both virgins on our wedding days, but I suspect Leda gave a few gallons to some thirsty men in her younger days. Of course, this proves Mama right as Leda lives with a woman now and has never worn a wedding ring. I tell her she shouldn't give up on finding a husband, that it's never too late, but Leda doesn't seem to mind being an old maid. She says she and Sylvia are happy as clams, and although I'll never understand her choice, I have to admit they do have fun together.

I needn't have worried about the courting though. Stoney and Sheila were married, if not properly in the church, at least legally. I talked Lloyd into renting out our tenant house to them, and they seemed truly happy over there.

Before the wedding, Doris died, and we had to get through the funeral and help Walter sort through her things. It was a terrible time for all of us, especially Annette, who was of an age that magnifies the sorrows of this world. She spiraled into a deep depression, against which I felt helpless. Then suddenly, she recovered and was her old self, running around the dairy like always. I'm certain that it was Sheila who somehow lifted her spirits. She had a power over Annette that was near magic, and more than once I caught myself wondering if those fairies of hers might not exist. Then I'd laugh at myself, wishing something so frivolous and silly to be true, and me a grown-up woman with a family to see to. But Sheila could do that to you; she was so earnest and convincing. I noticed even Lloyd would lean closer to her when she'd tell some made-up story about magic coins or some such. He'd say it was nonsense after Sheila went home, but his eyes and ears were all hers when she was around.

"Admit it, Lloyd," I said to him in bed one night. "You're glad I made you give Sheila a job. You like her, don't you?"

Lloyd turned over and laid his head on his arm and grinned. "I like you best," he said. "She doesn't have those." He was pointing to my breasts, and I blushed. I take after Mama; we both wear D-cup brassieres.

I won't say what happened next, but Lloyd excelled beyond his usual that night. I had to put my hand over his mouth so Annette wouldn't hear him. She might have heard something though, because the next morning when Lloyd came in from the milk run for breakfast, she wouldn't look at her daddy, and when he asked her did she sleep well, she turned a deep pink and barely nodded yes to him. I knew I should talk to her about the birds and bees, but I couldn't make myself do it just yet. Right after Lloyd left, Annette said she and Sheila were going to play jacks on the porch, and I laughed at myself for making a private joke about what kind of balls interested her the most. I thought about sharing it with Mama, and then came to my senses and scrubbed down Lil' Bit's high chair until it looked brand new. If I didn't understand Stoney's attraction to Sheila, I certainly couldn't fathom what other men saw in her. I would never have believed any man would find her appealing except I overheard a conversation about her between Lloyd and his brother Howard. Howard, like my sister Leda, hasn't been fortunate in love, but therein the similarity ends. Lloyd's brother is a cad with women. I suspect he knows ladies of the evening and there was talk that Howard runs a poker game on Friday night. More than one of my friends has told me that they've seen him out with Fred Prather, who succumbed to the sin of gambling before he was out of high school. With all that, I forbade Lloyd to visit his brother's house without me, but still Howard is welcome in my home. He is, after all, Lloyd's blood and his only brother. When Mama questioned my wisdom on inviting him for Sunday dinners, I told her that, if Jesus could allow Mary Magdalen to wash his feet, I guessed I could fry a chicken leg or two for Howard.

It was after one of our Sunday dinners when I inadvertently heard the brothers talking about Sheila. They were sitting in the living room listening to the radio and Annette and I had just finished cleaning up the dishes. I folded the dish towel and walked quietly down through the dining room intending to join them, but I stopped when I heard Lloyd laughing. "Really, Howard. You can't be serious. Sheila Carruth has a hump on her back, no tits, and a strong wind would blow her off those little stick legs of hers."

"You just told me she's stepping out with the Barnes boy."

"But he's not you. He's sixteen and probably hasn't ever had any of a woman's candy. First time a boy will settle for anything." There was a pause then, and he said in a louder voice, "Besides you're way too old for her."

I could imagine Howard's leer when he spoke. "Old enough to have experience. That little filly needs an expert."

What surprised me the most were the next sentences out of my husband's mouth. He used the same tone of voice that he spoke in when Annette came home from the Tucker girl's house with her face painted and handkerchiefs balled up for breasts beneath her dress. "Howard," he said. "You stay away from the girl. She's not for you. I mean it. You go messing with her and you'll have me to answer to."

After Howard left, I waited for Lloyd to tell me about their conversation, but he didn't have a word to say, and I decided to take Mama's advice for times like this and keep the wisdom in my head from falling out my mouth.

So when Stoney proposed, I was greatly relieved. Sheila's being married would change everything, erase any thoughts men had about her. That's what I thought back then.

Sheila certainly seemed happy being married to Stoney. During the months that followed, each time she came to the house, she brought her happiness with her, spreading the sweetness of her new life over our house like a blanket of chocolate. Sheila couldn't stop talking about Stoney, their silly games, their plans for the future. "Stoney said his papa might loan us some money for a new truck. Stoney is wanting one bad," she told me. I knew better; all the Barnes were tight-fisted. Everyone knew that, everyone except Sheila. However, she was right about Hugh, the oldest son, being good-looking. I saw proof of that for myself one day when he came to our house looking for Stoney.

I remember that it was in early December because Sheila and Stoney had just celebrated their first wedding anniversary and it was the day that we had set to make our Christmas decorations. Sheila and Annette had gathered pinecones in big bushel baskets, and we were daubing gold paint on them with small sable brushes. The three of us were sitting around the newspaper-covered kitchen table littered with cones, ribbons, paint, and glue. Lil' Bit, dressed in his favorite overalls with a train appliquéd across his chest, was toddling around the room dragging a wooden cow on a string that clacked clacked as he went round and round the table. I remember Sheila's quick fingers cutting lengths of red ribbons which she handed to Annette to tie on the tops of the cones. We would make wreaths and a table arrangement by adding greenery, nuts, and candy canes. After a while Lil' Bit got tired and dizzy from running around and he stood by my chair yelling for "duice" which meant orange drink.

"Annette, get him some juice. Maybe we can finish a few more decorations before his naptime," I said.

Sheila was spinning a small cone on the table, and as we watched the gold and red top, she giggled. "I ain't never thought of taking an old pinecone and turning it into something so pretty. I'm gonna make some for me and Stoney." She looked over at me. "We didn't have no tree last year, but I want to make some paper cutouts and string popcorn and we'll have us a little tree in the front room."

Annette got up from the table to search for Lil' Bit's cup right then, and Sheila craned her neck around to her. "Annette, you'll help, won't you?"

"Sure," she said. "It'll be fun." She rose on her toes and looked out the window. "Mama, company."

I went to the window and watched a man get out of a brand new Ford truck. Sheila came to stand beside me. "It's Hugh," she said. "I reckon he's lookin' for Stoney." Although they lived nearby, I hadn't met any of the Barnes' boys except Stoney. Oh, I had seen them all go by in various vehicles from time by time, but I wouldn't know any of them to recognize on the street. I did know that Hugh was the oldest and married to Earlene Farmer, who was a real snob for no reason at all that Mama and I could see. Her people were from some wild state out west like Utah or Montana. They had two sons; Sheila had told me that they were "corkers," which meant little heathens most likely. The two other Barnes boys were more like their mama, according to Sheila. "Kinda plain and quieter than Hugh and Stoney. Stoney's the best lookin' one," she had said to me, tossing her chin up with pride.

As I watched him coming across the yard, I disagreed. Hugh was far more handsome than his brother; he was heart-stopping. I walked out on the porch to greet him. As he climbed the steps, I watched the pale yellow shirt and string tie with silver ends coming up toward me. He smiled. Big white teeth, tanned face, a square jaw that would make a young girl's knees wobble. "You must be Mrs. Cotton," he said in a baritone that rivaled our best singer at church. I nodded. He reached the porch and bowed at the waist. "I am Hugh Barnes. Stoney's big brother."

"I'm Rowena," I said. "Can I help you?"

Before he could answer, Sheila walked out barefoot with Lil' Bit wrapped on her hip. Orange juice dribbled down his chin onto the front of her blue house dress, and Sheila wiped at it with her free hand. "Hey, Hugh," she said. "You lookin' for your little brother?"

His eyes, black as a raven, left me and traveled over his sister-in-law. He tucked his thumbs into his belt behind the big silver buckle, and I quickly looked away from his privates. "I need my plow point back, honey. You know where he left it?"

"I reckon I do." She shifted the baby on her hip. Behind her I saw Annette's admiring eyes and frowned at her.

Hugh saw her too and winked at her. "This your little brother? He's a fine-looking fellow."

Annette was struck dumb. "Yes," I said. "His name is Lil' Bit."

Lil' Bit was shy with strangers, and upon hearing his name, he hid his face in Sheila's neck.

Hugh reached out to pat the baby's back, and his hand moved from Lil' Bit to Sheila's bare arm. "You look real natural with a baby," he said. He dropped his hand and returned his thumbs to his buckle. "Want to come up to the house with me and show me where that plow point is?"

Sheila looked down at her bare feet. "I can tell you where it's at."

He smiled at her. "But I might not see it. You come with me."

She hesitated, then turned to me and held Lil' Bit out. "I'll get my shoes," she said and went inside.

Hugh looked around the porch at the ferns and rockers and clay pots of begonias I had started last fall. "Nice place you got here, Mrs. Cotton. I reckon Stoney's pretty happy working for your husband."

I knew I should say something, but a chill came over me and was making its way down my back. I shivered slightly and hugged Lil' Bit tighter. "Thank you. I'm glad Stoney likes it."

Sheila came out then, leaned over and kissed Lil' Bit's cheek. "Bye bye. I'll be back in just a little while."

Lil' Bit held up his hand. "Bye bye bye bye bye bye."

We all laughed, and then Hugh swept his arm out for Sheila to lead them down the steps. She stopped midway. "Miss Rowena? We'll finish them decorations soon as I get back. Okay?"

"Sure," I said, and then I detected something in her face I couldn't identify. Misgiving perhaps. Guilt. An apology of sorts. It was as if she had felt my uneasiness about Hugh's eyes on her and wanted to tell me that it wasn't her fault. I called out to her. "Sheila?" She turned on the bottom step and gazed up at me; the look that bothered me so was still in her eyes. "Nothing," I said. "We'll see you later."

But we didn't see her later. Sheila didn't come back all that day.

That night I lay in bed thinking about Stoney's brother. Hugh Barnes was arrogant; he knew all three of the females on the Cottons' porch admired him. He did look like a moving picture star; no doubt about that. I told myself I was just shoveling dirt to make a mountain again. He was her brother-in-law after all. But when I closed my eyes, I saw his thumbs, thick and bulbous, pointing down inside his jeans. I saw his fingers pressing into Sheila's flesh, and the chill I felt earlier came back over me. I turned to Lloyd and laid my head against his warm body. The rise and fall of his chest against my ear and the soft snores that rose in the dark soothed me like I was Lil' Bit drifting off to sleep to the rhythm of a lullaby. I opened my eyes and sat up in bed. "A baby," I whispered to her across the night sky. "Sheila, you need a baby to keep you safe."

CHAPTER 16

When I thought that about Sheila having a baby, I never dreamed that five months later I would be losing mine. I found that out on a perfect day in early May, the kind of day that makes you grateful to live in Mississippi, where spring begins sometimes as early as February and occasionally continues through June. Annette was in a snit, griping about a few scratches and red bug bites she'd gotten picking blackberries. Sheila's mood was opposite, buoyant, telling us a story about something or other Stoney had done. A bit later that morning she cut her hand on a broken jar, and Lil' Bit got hysterical over the commotion, and I remember we had to give him a cookie to calm him.

Walter drove up in the midst of our work, and when I saw the woman with him, I wondered out loud who she was. I was speechless when he told me they were married. I tried to congratulate them, but just as I opened my mouth, I noticed that Walter's hands were shaking and a line of sweat had appeared around his hairline. He hadn't come to my house for a marriage blessing. I think I knew then how this day was going to turn out, but I wouldn't allow the thought to form in my head.

We went into the living room and made small talk, just nervous chatter on my part. Lil' Bit sat in my lap, shrinking back against me, maybe sensing my discomfort. Discomfort? Rising terror, really. I could feel something hard and cold weighing inside me, hammering against my chest, and

I wondered if I might be coming down with a flu. When Walter's new wife said they would live in Chicago from now on, I knew for certain what was coming. I asked when they would be going, but it really didn't matter, one week or two, I knew what the verdict would be. I tried to go on. I was mistress of this house, the hostess, a lady taught to use good manners. I inquired politely about the house they would live in. They. All of them.

Lil' Bit was eating an orange slice, dripping juice all over the both of us when Walter stood up and said the words. "We plan to take Lil' Bit with us." There. It was finally said. That wasn't so bad I told myself. You can survive this, Rowena. Stand up and accompany them to the door. You knew this was a possibility from the first day you agreed to raise Lil' Bit. Silly woman, thinking he was yours forever. I chided myself thus, like a schoolgirl, as I said things that must have made sense to them because they left my house without calling for Lloyd, or a doctor to commit me to an asylum, which is where, I think, I was longing to go.

But I stayed. Stayed and did what a mother does for her son. I tried to think of it as a trip Lil' Bit would take, like I was packing for him to go off to camp. I folded his shirts, wrote his name with a laundry pen inside the sunsuits, the sweaters, the little corduroy pants that were so small they seemed like trousers for a doll. I remember Sheila's tears, Annette's set face, pale and frightened, Lloyd's stoic silence. Mama came over to say good-bye, but I wouldn't talk to her. I stayed in my room listening to her sobs as she kissed her grandson farewell.

Annette left the house before they came. I hadn't slept all night, and I heard her slipping through the silent house, but I didn't get up from where I lay with my hand on Lil' Bit's soft back. Let her go, I thought. I would run too if only I could. My mind may have already fled from the house that morning. I can barely remember the loading of Lil' Bit's toys and clothes, the rocking horse. I suppose Lloyd attended to most of that. What I do remember is the scent of my son snuggled against me, his special smell that isn't just baby powder or lotion. I would know him in the darkest room from that special scent that is his alone, and if I met him on the street, unrecognizable as a grown man, I would sniff the wreath of scented air that would surround him, and say, "Lil' Bit, it's you."

The days that followed could be few or many for all I know. Lloyd told me that we would go to Chicago someday. He would get someone to mind the dairy, and we would take the Illinois Central up there. We could go in a month, or maybe wait until the fall. Don't the leaves change to gorgeous colors in the fall? Yes, yes, I said. We'll go in the fall, and we looked into each other's collapsed faces, knowing we'd never go.

Everything seemed to wither and rot around me. Trays of food made me gag. Sounds entered my body like roaring cannons. When Lloyd put his hands on me, I slapped them away in pain from the pressure of his light touch. I would hear my baby's plaintive calls, and I would sit up in my bed, thinking to go to him, until I would look around the dark room and know all over again. I would remember that part of me had died, and the rest of me couldn't remember how to live.

It was Sheila who saved my life. No, I don't think it's an exaggeration. Had it not been for her, I might never have recovered from my partial death. There had been a parade of people through my bedroom hailing me with false cheer, phony promises that life would get better. They told me I would forget. Chicago, they said, isn't so far away. I closed my ears to all of them. I tried to lock them out, but Lloyd took the knob off the door and sent Annette in with another plate filled with food from the church ladies. I would throw their fancy dishes against the wall until anger left me. Then I fell into another kind of existence where light hurt my eyes, where I couldn't distinguish between sleep and wakefulness. I drifted through the nights and days, too tired to care that I was lying in my own stink. Then Sheila came.

Annette brought her into my room, and I pretended to be asleep. I couldn't bear another "You'll see. The dark cloud will pass." All lies, lies, lies. I was sick of platitudes and Biblical quotations and voices with false promises. Sheila let the shade fly up, and the noise made me open my eyes, which I quickly closed. "It's too bright," I told her in a stern voice, but it was as if I hadn't spoken. She strode to my bed and pulled the covers off me so violently, I shrank back from her. She started talking about my pillowcases, Lloyd's hair tonic, nonsense. She was laughing, and I began to take interest in her as I imagine one crazy person attracts another in an insane asylum. She began to dance, and I watched her carry on as though she was not in my bedroom where grief hung in every corner. I think I clapped for her; I know I was scared of making her angry. She was crazy and there was no telling what she might do next. Then I was in the tub, naked as a newborn baby, surrounded by white blossoms and purple and red ones, and there was a lovely scent rising up to awaken my senses, and I felt the warm warm water, and I was an unborn baby floating in a safe, sweet-smelling womb. I caught a magnolia drifting toward me and lifted it to my face. It was as soft as Lil' Bit's silky hair, and I remembered the feel of his rust-red curls on my fingers. He was gone, but my mind had returned with the memories of him. I cried then; I wouldn't die, and I gave myself up to the sorrow of living.

Sheila dressed me and pushed me and Annette into the living room where we danced like show girls on a stage. I was weak and my legs wobbled badly, and when I nearly fell, Sheila grabbed me and lifted me up. I hung on to her strength; I could feel it like a current running into me, giving me the energy to move toward the coming days.

That night I lay in Lloyd's arms. I was open to his love again because Sheila had given me a great gift that day. The gift of hope. I would feel strong again with the love of my husband, my daughter, my family and friends, and maybe someday I would hold Lil' Bit in my arms again. I never dreamed that my long-ago hope of holding another child of my own was about to be realized.

I couldn't believe it. It was a true miracle. Lloyd and I had tried and tried to conceive after Annette was born, and as the years went by, I had accepted that my womb would bear no more fruit. I was surprised, but Sheila wasn't. "I knowed it," she said. "When something bad happens, two good things always follow." This idea was in opposition to Mama's opinion that troubles come in threes. "Wonder what the other good thing will be," she said. "Maybe Stoney and me will have a baby too." When I looked into her yearning eyes that were set on my stomach as she spoke, I said a silent quick prayer that the Lord would bless them too.

After I told Sheila about the coming baby, our relationship changed. Although she was a married woman, often I would catch myself thinking of her as one of Annette's young friends. I suppose it was her naïveté, or perhaps it was her unwillingness to succumb to the drudgery of running a household. She certainly wasn't interested in beautifying her home. The first time I went up to the tenant house, I was appalled at the living conditions. Sheila was no housekeeper; there was an inch of dust on every stick of furniture, which was in deplorable shape to begin with. I found a chicken feather on her dinette set and a spider web in nearly every corner. Of course, it is more difficult to keep house with no running water, but the well was only twenty paces from the back door. As I sat on the tattered couch in her front room, I thought about how many hours I spent mopping the kitchen floor, scrubbing woodwork, dusting whatnots, and I wondered what I might do with all those hours if I were more like Sheila.

On one of my last visits to the tenant house, Sheila offered me coffee; Stoney had bought her a really nice coffee grinder, but I declined, thinking of how slapdash she most likely washed her cups. Annette was off somewhere that day, and I now can't remember the purpose of my visit. I was probably needing something Sheila had borrowed as she frequently left my house with her arms filled with our belongings.

Since Sheila's mother had borne so many children, I naturally thought that Sheila was knowledgeable about babies, but really she knew no more than Annette. "Miss Rowena," she began, leaning toward me with an eagerness I could nearly feel myself. "When do you think you'll feel your baby movin' round inside?"

"Well, I…I…can't be sure," I replied. "Don't you remember when your mother felt life?"

Sheila shook her head. "No, ma'am. Mama weren't never one to speak on such. She never telled us she was gonna have another one till the day come to birth it."

"Really?" I didn't know what else to say. Sheila's life before she came to us was so different from ours that it was like she had lived in a foreign country with a different language and customs.

"So when will you feel it movin' round?"

I smoothed my dress over my stomach. "I think around the fourth or fifth month was when I felt Annette. It was so long ago now; I'm not certain."

Sheila reached across the couch and patted my stomach. "And when do you have to close your legs?"

I pulled back, unsure of what she meant by that. "What?"

She grinned. "Uh, leave off with the lovin' beneath the sheets."

I nearly stood up to leave then. I hadn't discussed such with anyone, not even my own mama. I felt my knees pressing against each other, and I suddenly saw myself as a schoolgirl swapping secrets with a friend during recess. I couldn't help smiling now. "It depends on how you feel. During the last few months before I delivered Annette, I was just too uncomfortable to want to…uh…and…I was worried it might hurt the baby."

Sheila looked puzzled. "But before that, when you ain't feelin' bad, or uncomfortable, can you do it up till that?"

My school days vanished and I was a mature woman again entitled to refuse to answer a question that was too personal. "I'd rather not talk about this topic anymore, Sheila."

She wasn't the least offended though, or even put off by my tone. "Okie dokie, I understand how you feel, but, Miss Rowena, I'm needin to know 'cause I might be, might be…" She crossed her hands over her chest and then her fingers too. "I might be gonna have a baby too." Before I could congratulate her, she dropped her hands and grabbed both of mine. "Don't say nothin' though. To nobody. I ain't sure yet, and I don't want to disappoint Stoney if it ain't so."

"Oh, of course not, sweetheart," I said and then hugged her. "I won't tell a soul. You have my word."

Sheila was bouncing up and down on the couch so that I was getting thrown backwards and forwards. "Won't it be something? You and me and our two little ones to play together?"

"Yes, yes," I said. "That truly would be wonderful."

CHAPTER 17

Not long after Sheila had told me that she might be expecting, Lloyd and Stoney went off to Louisiana to breed the Ayrshires. I was still at the early stage of my time where I needed a soda cracker before I could get up in the mornings without vomiting. I dreaded their going, but I knew Lloyd had been planning the trip for over a month, and Sheila was thrilled that Stoney was going too. Mama offered to come over and stay with me for the one or two nights they'd be away, but I told her I had Annette if I needed anything. The truth was that Mama was getting on my last nerve, and I really can't say why. She always gave sound advice, which I generally followed, but she was getting to the stage in life where she couldn't stop giving it. I found myself being short-tempered with Annette too though, and Lloyd, as well. I was sure it was my being in the family way that caused me to get upset so easily. Dr. Brock told me not to worry, that lots of women got "out of balance" when expecting a child. He said that it's something doctors call hormones that were changing inside me, and he advised a cup of chamomile tea before bedtime, and of course, the soda crackers for the morning.

So after my nausea passed that morning, I rose and helped Lloyd pack his travel bag and made biscuits for the trip. You would have thought Sheila was the one going as she danced around the truck blowing kisses, hanging onto Stoney's guitar which she was going to sleep with. She kept waving good-bye long after the truck was out of sight, and I finally said,

"You want to come in and have a cup of coffee before you go to the barn?"

Sheila jumped back into reality then, literally lifted off the ground. "Oh no, I got to get to the barn right now. I'm helping with the milking since they short-handed till Stoney gets back. Ain't that something? Me, doing the milking!" Her smile could have stretched a mile.

I watched her running down the hill and wondered what it would be like to live just one day in her head. My own mind was always filled with so many thoughts of obligations and responsibilities and yes, regrets and some guilt. But my destiny was to be born smart and that blessing can also be a burden. I turned back to the house, actually jealous of Sheila's simple ways. Why couldn't I feel excited about milking a cow? Why wasn't I happy for Lloyd to go on a trip with his beloved Ayrshires? Hormones, I decided. I hoped I wasn't going to be in a bad mood for the entire confinement.

I didn't see Sheila for the rest of the day, and I supposed that she was out shoveling manure singing a happy song over every pile she scooped. I wandered around the house feeling sour. I just couldn't make myself sit and crochet even though I had a cap and bonnet set nearly finished. I sat at the player piano for a while and pumped out a few songs. "Danny Boy" brought tears to my eyes, and I started worrying Lloyd was going to be killed in an automobile accident. I imagined Clyde Vairo coming to the door, hat in hand, twirling it around the brim. "Rowena," he'd say. "I'm afraid it's bad news. It's Lloyd." I laid my head on the piano keys and cried then. What would I do if Lloyd never returned? I couldn't run the dairy, could I? Well, I thought, maybe I could. Didn't I keep the accounts, order supplies, figure weekly wages? All I would need would be workers to do the milking. I'd paint the barn, too, a nice brick red like I'd seen in magazines. I'd increase production of the orange drink, as Lloyd always ran out before his last customer. I'd redesign the bottle caps. I'd be alone though. Lloyd wouldn't lie next to me each night. There'd be no one to enjoy going over the profit and loss statement I prepared each month. Who would care about new bottle caps? I bowed my head. "Oh, please, dear Lord, bring Lloyd home safe to me. Don't let anything bad happen to him."

"Mama?" I turned and saw Annette standing in the door leading into the dining room.

"What?" I had snapped at her again. I softened my voice. "What is it?"

She wrinkled her forehead the way I've told her not to. She thinks she's never going to get old and have wrinkles. "Something's wrong with Sheila I think."

I sat up straight and wiped my face with the hem of my apron. I wasn't alarmed right then. Annette has a liberal imagination. One time she was convinced that she'd seen a rhinoceros in the woods behind Mama's pecan orchard. Then for weeks she had hoarded a bit of coke bottle glass shaped like Leda's marquise-cut diamond ring thinking it was a valuable precious stone. And nothing could persuade her that her hair wasn't going to spontaneously curl when she got her period. "Why do you think something is wrong?" I asked.

Annette stood like a stork with her right foot resting on her left knee. "I went up to her house and knocked after the truck left, and she wouldn't come to the door."

"Whose truck?"

"I don't know. I knocked and knocked and finally Sheila came up to the screen on the window in the front room. I hollered that it was me, and she said, 'I can't talk to you now. Please go on home.'"

"Hmmm, well, maybe she just doesn't feel like having company right now," I said, knowing this was unlikely. Sheila was always happy to have Annette up there.

Annette dropped her foot and walked to the piano. "But, Mama, something might be wrong. She didn't sound like herself. Her voice was all, all, all scary sounding."

If Stoney hadn't been off with Lloyd, I wonder if I would have gone up there. But he was and I felt responsible for her. It crossed my mind that she could be sick, maybe miscarrying. I had to go help if needed. I told Annette to stay home and practice her piano, that I'd go up to Sheila's house and set things right.

The sun was an orange slice bobbing low in the late afternoon sky, and I shaded my eyes with my hand as I walked on the path up the slanting ground to Sheila's house. I stood on the porch a minute, collecting myself, before I knocked and called her name. "Are you okay?"

The dark outline of her appeared in the door, but she didn't open it to welcome me in. "Miss Rowena, is it milking time? I ain't late, am I?"

I remembered then she was replacing Stoney today. "I imagine they're getting started," I told her. "But that's not why I came." I hesitated unsure of how to say what I wanted. "Annette said you might be sick, and I was worried that if you were, you know, p.g., well that maybe something had happened?"

I heard her breath coming out in a big whoosh. "Oh, no. That ain't it. I'm pretty sure I am now, but…" I could see her hands moving to her stomach. "It's fine. Ain't nothing gonna hurt this little one."

Why wouldn't she open the door? My irritation with her rose up. If she wasn't sick, then what was the matter with her? Annette had mentioned a truck; maybe something had happened to someone in her family and they'd come over to tell her about it. "Is everyone all right at your mama's?"

"I reckon so."

"Well, is there anything you need? I mean if you have trouble maybe I could help?"

Sheila didn't say anything for a long time like she was considering telling me, but then she said, "No, I ain't needin' no help."

Frustrated isn't the word for what I was feeling then. I took a firm tone with her. "Sheila, Annette said you had company and then she came up here and you wouldn't let her in. She said you didn't sound like yourself." There, no more of this avoiding the obvious.

"I'm sorry. Oh, I hate to think I made Annette feel bad." She lifted her hand to the screen door, and I thought she was going to open it at last, but she rested her hand against the thin wire. "Miss Rowena, don't be worrying about me none." Her hand moved to her head and she stepped farther back into the house. "Please don't tell Stoney nothing. There ain't nothing to tell."

She was right about that; I didn't know any more now than I did when I left my own house. "Okay, Sheila. I'm going now. If you say everything's all right."

Finally, she sounded like her old self, her voice was light and happy again. "Yes, yes. It is. I'm gonna get my boots on right now and get to work."

It wasn't until after Lloyd got home from his Louisiana trip that I found out that Sheila didn't go down to the dairy that afternoon. Digger told Lloyd that he had to do the cleaning-up and bottle-washing, but that the next morning she showed up early and milked more cows than Shorty ever did and in less time.

When I told Lloyd about the truck parked up there and Annette's worrying, and my going to see about her, he said it was most likely that her papa had gone there and hurt her again. Lloyd said, "Sheila's scared Stoney will kill him if he finds out he's still beating her. She wouldn't want you or Annette to know, especially Annette, as her tongue slips pretty often."

So that all made sense to me. Lloyd was right about Annette spilling the beans. I wasn't about to tell her about Sheila's baby until she told Stoney, and for whatever reason, she was still keeping her baby a secret.

That night I turned the puzzle of it over and over in my head until I got myself too upset to sleep. I thought about Doris dying, Lil' Bit far away in Chicago, Mama getting old, Sheila's papa beating her, Lloyd getting kicked in the head by one of those mean-tempered Jerseys. I woke up Lloyd and told him I was in a state. He rolled over and patted me like a child, but he never opened an eye. I got out of bed and went to the window. The moon and stars were hidden by dense clouds and before me there was only the endless darkness of the night. I thought of Genesis, the world as the void, a black abyss. Nothingness. I shivered, frightened beyond reason, and my fear turned into panic. I ran across the room, back to the comfort of my bed. Once safely beneath the soft sheets, I told myself that my awful hormones were making me think wrong things, and I must calm down. I began breathing slowly and deeply, and that was when I felt my baby move. It was the tiniest flutter, but I knew my child was okay, and I snuggled against Lloyd's warm back with a mound of hope for my pillow.

The next morning Sheila came down to the house wanting to borrow the wish book. I sent Annette for the catalog, and when she left the kitchen, Sheila leaned over and whispered, "I'm gonna tell Stoney about the baby tonight. I'm gonna wear that pretty nightdress you gived me."

"You're sure then?" I knew she hadn't been to the doctor.

"Yep, I know I am. I'll tell Annette tomorrow; she's gonna be so excited."

I smiled. "She will. Come up as soon as you're done at the barn. I'll make a cake and we'll celebrate."

Annette came back then with the Sears & Roebuck catalog and held it out to Sheila. I saw that when she reached for it, Sheila's hands were shaking, and I had to look away so she wouldn't see the tears in my eyes. I remember thinking that God had finally blessed her by giving her this baby to love. I thought of Mama's adage about it being darkest before dawn, and I recalled the previous night's torment that lay behind the joy I felt at this moment.

After Sheila left, I walked out on the porch and watched her trot up the path to her house. She held the wish book against her chest, the hump on her back, which I hardly noticed anymore, bobbing up and down as she ran. She stopped midway, and I followed her gaze across the yard to Stoney. He stood on their porch waving his arm overhead, urging her to hurry on home.

CHAPTER 18

STONEY

It was like some kind of amazing dream I couldn't wake up from, like I was caught in a net somebody had throwed over me, like I was watching myself — not Stoney Barnes — not that self, but some other fellow sitting on my porch paring his nails with a pocketknife. I seen their heads first, bobbing up and down as their boots traveled on the uneven ground coming up the rise toward the house. Mr. Cotton was sitting beside me in Sheila's chair, and when they started across the yard with her, I heard him suck in his breath like he'd been hit with a board in the gut. I kept to my nail cutting, saw the oval white peelings falling on the porch twixt my boots. I didn't want to look on her face. When I glanced at the mound of her, I pretended she was a cloth dummy or a sack of chicken scratch being loaded into the ambulance. I said something or other to Mr. Cotton 'bout her not coming home no more, and I went in the house and sat on the couch, listening to the engine crank, the tires on the gravel, the sheriff yelling couldn't nobody leave now. I wanted them all to go on home. I wanted every goddamned one of them out of my yard, but I didn't have no say even if it were my own property. Rented, but mine by payment just the same.

I headed for the kitchen, half expecting to see Sheila slicing up a tomato for my dinner, wiping her hair off her face with the back of her hand like she was in the habit of. I was expecting to hear her singing some little ditty, stopping when she'd look up and see me. Some days I'd take her right there on the kitchen floor, tomato juice dripping off her fingers onto my chest, her giggling and kissing me all over my face and down the side of my neck, squirming like a wriggle worm till I'd hold her so hard a bruise would come up on her arm. When I seen the empty room, I squeezed my eyeballs shut, and I felt tears pushing against them. I got the heaves choking on my loss. That's when the sheriff come to the door hollering my name.

He said to come on outside, and I went and sat on the folding chair that didn't belong in my yard. I looked up when a wild turkey flew overhead, its shadow darkening the sheriff's face. Then my eyes fell down to the gun snapped in the holster on his side. I had a twelve-gauge in the closet. Hadn't ever shot anything much with it though. I wasn't a good shot like my brothers.

Sheriff told me I was in shock, said to answer best as I could in my condition. I said I reckon I would try my best, but he was right about me; I couldn't stop crying and all them people standing around staring at me. I hadn't cried none since I was thirteen and Daddy took the strop to me for the last time. That time I had grabbed that long strip of leather he used for whetting his razor and curling it around my fist, I jerked him to me till I could see the dark hairs inside his nose and I banged my head against his face till I seen blood spurting out and that's when I stopped crying.

I didn't tell the sheriff much of nothin' about Sheila and me. It was private; none of his goddamned business. I told him that when I left for the early milking, she were lying on her side on her bed, all curled up, sweet dreaming, and when I said that, I could see her there. Some mornings she would turn over to me, lift her arms and hike her nightgown up. "You got time," she'd say grinning as big as her little mouth would stretch.

"What time was that, when you left the house?" Sheriff Vairo wanted to know.

"Must've been around two-thirty. Milking commences about then," I said. "We started late though 'cause Mr. Cotton weren't there until maybe another hour."

I let out a hoot when the sheriff asked me if'n I locked the door to the house behind me. We hadn't never used the big skeleton key to the front door; most times Sheila left it wide open. We didn't have nothing worth the trouble of stealing. He frowned at me, and I said, "I ain't checked to see if anything is missing. Sheila might've had a little money put away. She sometimes held back a little for presents and such."

I started thinking about the tie bar she bought me for my birthday. I needed to go get it, hold it in my hand, feel the heft of metal, the heat from her that might be left there. She gave it to me a month ahead of my day. Couldn't wait to give it to me once she'd bought it. Sheila was like a child in that. I swear she believed in fairies and ghosts and trolls that she said lived underneath the Flowerdale Road bridge. She could make you believe crazy stuff. She could make you go crazy, turn you into a real loony once she got a hold on your mind through them eyes of hers.

Sheriff asked me a few more questions about Sheila's daily doings, where she went to, who she knowed, and he wrote fast in his notebook, and then left off with me. Said he wanted to question the niggers next and they better not be run off somewhere. Right away then, Digger come shuffling out from behind the tree with his head down. "I ain't gone nowheres," he said, "but I don't know nothin', Mister Sheriff, sir."

I walked back toward the porch. My fingers was scratching on my legs, and I couldn't stop them. A fire was inside my head. I seen her staring eyes, her opened mouth, and I leaned over and spewed white vomit on the goddamned holly bush Sheila had planted beside the steps.

The first day I ever set eyes on Sheila Carruth was on a Wednesday. I know that because it was four days after I had my last date with Kathleen, which was on Saturday night. Sheila weren't nothin' like Kathleen, and I sure didn't plan on dating a girl with a hump on her back. I could do better. Had done better. Kathleen was some dish. Big jugs like cantaloupes, long blonde hair, a switch in her walk that took your eyes to her warm hips. She was smart too. Worked in a bank as a teller, and I seen her count money out faster than a professional gambler dealed out cards. Money was the cause of our breakup. There wasn't no other reason it could've been. Kathleen said I was the best-looking boy in Lexie County, said she got chills just thinking about my hands running over her. I satisfied her all right. No question there. That Saturday night she wanted to go to the show, and I told her I didn't have no money to waste on Jimmy Stewart, and that was the end of it. She were always figuring on how to get me to spend more money on her, expecting presents when it wasn't her birthday, saying she was dying for a pearl necklace. I had told her straight out from the git-go that I wasn't makin' nothin' down at the dairy. Mr. Cotton didn't pay fair wages in my mind, and I had to lay out a lot of cash on my durn truck which kept breaking down on me. Piece of shit was what it was, but my old man wouldn't loan me enough for something better.

Sheila thought that truck was a queen's chariot. She'd sit up high, flapping her hand out the window like she was waving at her subjects. She was like that, always living some fairy tale kind of day. I reckon that was part of how she got me. I hadn't never knowed a girl who could make believe so good that I felt like I was some goddamned hero in a picture show.

First time I saw Sheila though all's I thought was, man, she's got a hump, and she don't know shit about cows. She didn't look at me when Mr. Cotton said who I was. She didn't look at nobody, put her hand over her mouth and nodded at the concrete floor smeared up with cow piss and grain. That were her job, to clean out the barn after milking.

After a week or so, Sheila started coming down to the dairy during milking, before she had to be there. I suspected it were me, and not them cows, that was drawing her there, but I didn't pay no mind to her. I flirted with little ole Annette, who had a giant crush on me. The girl couldn't pass by without her face turning the color of a ripe tomato. But Sheila, she didn't interest me, not at first. Then one afternoon she was there when I was milking old Sid. Usually, I watched Digger's pace on the teats and tried to time my finishing with a cow, so's that he would have to milk Sid, but on this day, Digger was still pulling on Bell's teats, and Sid was the only Jersey with a full bag left. All Jerseys got nasty tempers and will kick and butt us milkers, but Sid was the meanest one of the bunch. Sid wore a mule collar backwards around her neck because the crazy cow liked her own milk. Without the collar she would turn her head, bending her body like it were rubber, and suck her own teats dry. I reckon she thought I was stealing the drink she wanted for herself, and when I sat on the stool, she side-stepped and used her long tail to swat my face so hard I fell backwards off'n the stool. I heard them two girls, Annette and Sheila, laughing their heads off, and I was about to cuss Sid and them, when I felt Sheila's hand on my arm pulling me up. I came up close on her, and she looked right into me for the first time, and I swear to this day, I don't know what it was that made me want to kiss her right then and there. It might have been them eyes of hers. I felt like they were magnets and I was a tenpenny nail sliding toward them. Them blue centers were clear and perfectly round. They reminded me of my hound watching me eat, begging with eyes that made you toss your cornbread at him. Annette's mama called her in just then, and Sheila and I were left standing there in the dark barn. She said something about Sid being a "caution" or some such, and I grinned down at her to watch her eyes light up like fireflies winking in the night. She were about to leave, and I caught her arm. "You wanna go for a drive tonight?"

Sheila didn't look surprised like I had expected. She nodded and smiled. "I reckon I could," she said. "What time?"

I told her seven and she run off then and I hit Sid's head with my fist and told her she were gonna give up her milk whether she liked it or not. After we finished, I hurried home to eat and clean up for the date. Daddy near ruined it all. He threw the wire cutters down on the table beside my plate and said he wanted me to fix the back pasture fence before dark. When I told him I had a date and would do it next day, he snatched up the cutters and threw them in my lap. Gave me a bruise, but didn't hit my jewels, and I was grateful for that. "I said I'll do it. Tomorrow," I told him, and he saw my jaws locking up and walked over to his seat. Pete and Daniel kept their heads down like they wasn't my brothers who could help with the fence if they weren't the lazy asses they were.

Ma tried to ease up the air like she always done. "Hugh and Earlene might stop by with the boys later," she said. "Seems like we don't see enough of our grandsons even if they don't live but two miles from us."

Daddy was a fool for Hugh's two boys, Arthur and Billy, who were two and four. He never played with any of us that I could remember, but when them two showed up, he'd get down on all fours and let 'em ride him like a horse. So he brightened up right then and said he reckoned the fence wasn't going nowhere before tomorrow.

When I knocked on the door of the Cottons' smokehouse where Sheila was staying, I heard her singing "Beautiful Dreamer" and she hit the high notes like a little songbird. I saw right off she'd spent time fancying herself up for our drive. She had on a dress nice enough for church and she'd tied her hair up with a green ribbon trailing down the back of her. I thought to myself then that if it weren't for the hump she was almost pretty.

She slid right in the driver's side of the truck and didn't move all the way to the window so that I could feel her thigh against mine. I turned out onto Carterdale Road, and she started humming the melody to a song I didn't know. "You got a nice voice," I said to her. "I heared you singing 'fore I knocked."

Sheila giggled like I'd told a joke. "Ain't nothing to singing. You just open your mouth and let the songs out."

"I play the guitar," I said. "It's my fingers that makes my songs." I turned off on Flowerdale and thought about the woods a mile down where I had taken Kathleen the first time. I wasn't sure about what to expect with Sheila yet, but I figured to keep all my options open at this point.

"Ooooh, you got a guitar? Maybe you and me could sing together sometime."

"Maybe," I said. "I'll bring it next date." I didn't say what I was thinking which was if we have another one, depending on how this one turns out.

Before we'd gone another quarter of a mile, the goddamned tire blew. Bang! It were done for just like that. The tires were bald, but I hadn't expected one of them to blow. Sheila fell up against me and started laughing crazy like. Ha ha ha ha. What was funny about us having to walk home because I didn't have no spare?

I got out and started kicking the shit outta the busted tire. I reached down and picked up some rocks and threw them at the truck bed. "Junk! Heap! Piece of crap!" If I could find a board I'd smash the windows too, and I was looking around for something else to throw when Sheila came over to me and held my arm. I snatched it away from her. I wasn't gonna listen to no "You're scaring me. Don't be upset." whining like I'd heard so many times from Kathleen. But Sheila opened my fist and put a big rock in it.

"Throw this'n. See if you can hit the rim. It'll make more noise." She was grinning so big I could see near 'bout all her teeth.

I took the rock and did like she said. "Bull's eye," she yelled. "Can you do it some more times?"

I couldn't help grinning even though I was still plenty pissed off at my truck. This little gal had taken the edge off me though. She was holding another rock out to me, and I grabbed her wrist and pulled her up close to me. I could feel the rock against my chest, and then she let it loose and I could feel her little jugs a-rubbin' up against me. "You're something, girl," I whispered. I leaned my head toward her and she rose up on her toes and kissed me. I say it were a kiss, but I hadn't never had one like it. Her mouth went sideways and up and down, and I felt like she must have had four sets of lips a-workin' on that one kiss. My peter started getting into it then, and I ran my hands over her back, pulling her into me. It weren't till I got home and was laying on my bed still aching from her that I realized I were rubbing that ugly hump like it was a golden egg.

After that night I was done for as far as the single life goes. In just a week's time I couldn't do nothin' without thinking about them eyes of hers, her little jugs that was so sweet to taste, her pretty voice that could follow any note I strummed out on my guitar. She'd let me do just about anything to her that I could think up, and I didn't think near as good as her. One night when we was stretched out on a blanket in the bed of my truck, I asked her where she learned all them things about what pleases a man and she told me she didn't know how she knew. Said she just done what felt natural to her. I had my suspicions though. I didn't think I was her first, but she swore I was and I didn't figure her for a liar. She was like a kid in a woman's body and that combination is hard to resist for somebody like me.

I asked her to marry me right after our first fight. We had been down to the Cottons' that night. Mrs. Cotton had turned in with the baby, and Mr. Cotton and me were sittin' on the back porch smoking. Mrs. Cotton didn't allow no tobacco in the house, nor any kind of spirits either, so Mr. Cotton kept his hooch down to the barn and smoked his cigarettes outdoors. I wouldn't live with a woman like that. I'd tell her a thing or two about who was boss of the home, but it didn't seem to bother Mr. Cotton none to live with what he called a "delicate lady." We wasn't talking much. I remember blowing out a smoke ring, watching it rise like a blue halo in the dim light, and here come Sheila out of the house all painted up like a whore. She was wearing a low-cut dress without no brassiere and when she bent over my rocker, I could see her pink nipples plain as day. Mr. Cotton seen 'em too, and he didn't look away neither. I grabbed her arm. "What you trying to look like in that paint?" I asked her.

Sheila just smiled like I wasn't hurting her though I was sure I was. "Annette and I were just playing. She's coming in a minute. I done her hair up and we'se pretending to be moving picture stars on our way to some fancy place Annette heard about in New York City. The Ritzy something or other."

I didn't let go of her, but pushed her back as I got outta my chair. "You get that paint off'n you right now. Come on," I yelled at her. We left then, went down to her room, and when she got inside, I slammed the door and threw her face down on the bed. "You showed your titties to Mr. Cotton," I said, looking down at her with her legs splayed out like she was ready for taking from behind. "You're mine, and I don't share what's mine with nobody."

Sheila's eyes watered up, and she scrambled down to the floor and grabbed hold of my ankles. "You whup me," she said. "I'm bad. I shouldn't done what I done."

"I'll whup you." I jerked her up by her forearm and slung her back on the bed. I raised my leg and my boot came down on her hump. She didn't say nothing, didn't cry out for me to stop, so I gave her another good hard stomp. I thought I'd make her good and sorry she ever put on that paint and whore's dress. I'd make her cry and beg forgiveness. What happened next is what happened from that time on. She flipped over on her back and held her arms up to me.

"Do it now. Hurry," she whispered. I saw the look in her eyes then and my breath starting coming out in short pants. She was askin' me for something I never figured on. A feeling come over me that was just like how I felt when I skinned my first squirrel. I had run my hands over them slick intestines, and dug my fingers into the bloody fur. I licked the brains when I cracked open the head, and now the taste of them was in my mouth. I grabbed her hair and flipped her over. I ripped her dress and my shirt and came away with bits of skin beneath my nail. Then her hump was in my stomach, my head between her legs, and I bit into the soft flesh of her thigh and tasted her blood.

I asked her to marry me that night. I didn't figure I had no choice really. Somebody had to give her what she needed, and her eyes were set on me, Stoney Barnes, who didn't have no power against a blonde witch who screamed my name at night and laughed when the sun come up every blast day.

Sheila and me moved into the Cottons' tenant house the weekend we got married. On a Friday we drove over to Tylertown and got hitched by this old geezer who read out the vows so loud Sheila started giggling and covered her ears with her little hands. I didn't have no money to buy her a proper ring, but she was tickled to death with the tin band I gave her. It didn't take much to please her, and that's one of the reasons I felt I'd picked good for a wife. By the time we got back to our new house, we was so hot for each other, we done it on the floor in the front room. I had a bottle of hooch my brothers had give me, and I was planning on a few celebration drinks, but Sheila didn't allow me no time to think of it. She was like a wildcat that night, a-screeching and hollering out. She kept shouting "I love you" and such every time we done it. What nobody would believe she done was she tied a string on my peter. We was both used up and ready to get some sleep and I had rolled on my back and shut my eyes when I felt her fingers on me. "What you up to?" I asked her, lifting my head up from the pillow.

She smiled without opening her mouth and kept on with her fingers. When she'd made a little bow on top, she looked up at me. "It's loose, won't hurt you none."

"Okay," I said. "But what the hell is it for?"

Sheila leaned down and bit the end off the string, held up the piece.

"This here is a magic cord. It gives you powers."

I sat up then to get a better look. The string was tickling my leg and I moved my thigh out to the side. "What kind of powers?"

"To have perfect babies," she said. "Babies without no humps, smart ones."

I yanked the string off me. "Tying a hundred strings on me ain't gonna make no difference 'bout us having kids. Put your lips around it instead," I said. Sheila looked kinda hurt for a second, and then she smiled, made a big "o" with her mouth and bowed her head to it.

Next morning was more of the same, and we had another whole day and night of loving before Sheila went out to tell her folks about us getting hitched. That visit ruint our first week. Sheila's papa beat her so bad she couldn't do nothin' in the bedroom 'ceptin' sleep. When Annette pulled up in the drive and helped her in the house, I didn't have to ask who done it. I got rid of Annette soon as I could. She was crying all over Sheila, shaking, her teeth a-chattering, like it were her who was bloodied up. Sheila didn't cry; she just laid still on the bed, looked up at me and said, "Papa were mad about us gettin' wedded." She whimpered when I tore what was left of her dress off her, but she said she didn't need no doctor when I offered to go down to the Cottons' and call for one. "I been a lot wors'n this," she said. "It'll be all right. I should've said it different. I knowed he was gonna be mad at me."

I went out to the well and saw Mr. Cotton a-hurrying up to our house, and I figured Annette had spilled the beans about what happened. I waved him away, shouted to him that I would take care of my wife, I'd do what had to be done. He looked like he wanted to come on anyhow, but he waved his hat, turned around and went back toward the barn. I drew some water and went back to the house and bathed the blood off'n Sheila. Then I went to the closet and took out my gun. Sheila cried out when she seen it. "No."

"You ain't got no say," I told her. The hard metal felt good in my hands, and I breathed in the scent of the oil from the barrel. I would smash his head in with the gun before I put a bullet through his heart.

Sheila half fell off the bed and crawled over to me. "Please, please, please. Don't do it. He didn't mean it. He just lost his temper is all. He didn't mean to."

I understood about losing your temper. I knew all about red eye rages that come over you and cover your head with ruby fog so that you feel like your head is in a vise getting screwed tighter and tighter and you got to do something before your head comes off. I knowed what her papa knew all right, but I couldn't be a man and let this go without taking action. "He's got to pay for it," I said.

Sheila was hanging on my knees, squeezing me hard. "Stoney, he will. I promise. He will, but don't go over there now."

I kicked her off. "I'm going."

She laid her head on the floor. "He ain't there. Run off. Mama went after him, but she won't find him. He'll be gone for days. Done it before when he beat me this bad and the first time after he..."

I gripped the gun tighter. "After he what?"

"Nothing."

I looked down on her and seen them eyes, big and scared. There was blood on the floor. She had broken open again. I laid the gun down, carried her back to bed. I knowed nothing was something, and I suspected what something was, but I didn't ask her no more that day. I had my secrets and she had hers. Maybe it was best to leave it that way.

Ma invited us over for dinner the next Sunday. It was supposed to be a celebration dinner to welcome Sheila into the Barnes' big happy family. I knowed Ma weren't gonna fool Sheila though; she would see the truth of us right off. It went better than I expected. It were plain as day that Ma had told everybody not to look at my wife's hump because ever' time Sheila turned her back to any of them, they ran around to the front of her. Earlene, Hugh's wife, acted kinda uppity like she always does, but Sheila just smiled and told her how cute her boys were. Hugh and me got into an argument about whether Fords or Dodges was the best automobile on the road. Hugh drove a Ford, and I like the looks of the Dodge, but Hugh let it go this time, and they left without us gettin' into it. Daddy surprised me too. He acted real nice to Sheila, conversed with her in the polite voice he used when he talked to the preacher's wife, and that made Ma light up like a bright star. I asked him for a little loan when we were alone in the hall; it seemed like a good time, him being nearly jolly all day. I told him it were for Sheila to set up housekeeping. "She come to me poor as a church mouse," I said.

He reached in his pocket and pulled out a few bills and handed them right over. "See that you pay it back." He looked hard at me then with them dark eyes of his that put the fear in me when I was a little boy. "You treat her good. She ain't strong like Earlene and your ma."

I wadded the bills up, thought about throwing 'em in his face. But I needed the cash. I stuffed the money in my pocket and said, "You don't know nothin' about Sheila, Daddy. You don't know her a'tall."

I reckon nobody exceptin' me really knew her. She had two faces and I was the only one she showed 'em both to. When we was out with folks, she was one way, and then when we'd get back home, she'd turn around and there was the other Sheila who drank whiskey with me and liked the taste of it. Next to me Annette knowed her the best. Them two was always going off somewhere with their heads together. I asked Sheila what was they talking about, and she giggled and said it were girl talk, not for men's ears. I kept on, thinking they might be talking about me, and finally she says real sweet like that she tells Annette how happy she is being married to a man like me. "She got a crush on you too," Sheila told me.

"Ain't you jealous?" I asked her.

We was in the kitchen sitting at the little rickety table Ma had gived us and Sheila reached across and took my hand. "No, I ain't jealous. She's my friend."

I squeezed her fingers real hard. "Well, no friend of mine better be thinking about you. I'll kill anybody ever touches you."

Sheila didn't blink. She nodded real slow and then said, "I know it,

Stoney. I know you would." Then she jumped up and pulled me outside. She said to look up at the moon, it was shaped like a boat full of water, and wasn't we glad it would rain on our garden come daylight.

We skipped church the first two Sundays after our wedding day, but Sheila was about healed up the third week and we lit out for the service at Mars Hill, where she got saved. Her mama was there and a bunch of the kids, but her papa hadn't come with them, and I could tell Sheila were glad of it. Mrs. Carruth was a nice lady. I had met her before when Sheila and me visited out to their house before we got hitched. She hugged me and said she hoped we'd be real happy, and then she looked down at the Bible she was carrying, and said she knowed Mr. Carruth would come around to the idea of us. I knowed that were a lie she was telling, but I acted like I believed her. After the service I offered to give them a lift home. Mrs. Carruth didn't drive, and she and them young'ns had walked the two miles from their house to the church. She looked real scared then, and said, "No, no. You two go on your way. We'll catch a ride with Mrs. Tucker." I knew then how it stood between Sheila's papa and me.

CHAPTER 20

Sheila was right about Annette having a crush on me. I came to see that clear on the day the three of us went to the picture show in Zebulon. Sheila knowed who all the big stars was but she hadn't never seen one of them on the big screen at the Palace Theater. I'd been to the show lots of times with Kathleen, and before her with Pete and Daniel when Ma would give us a dime each to go. We took Ma once to see Shirley Temple in *Bright Eyes*, which us boys thought was the dumbest show we'd ever seen, but she loved every minute of it and thought Shirley Temple was "just the smartest and cutest little girl that ever lived."

We'd been waitin' a whole year for *Gone with the Wind* to finally get to the Palace, and when Annette heard it was playing, she come running up to the house, screaming we had to go. There'd been so much talk about it that I didn't figure it could be as good as what folks were saying. Over in Atlanta there was a near riot over Clark Gable, and I wasn't too keen on Sheila mooning over him. But she were set on it, told me I looked like Clark, but was more handsome since my ears laid flat on the sides of my head. What cinched us going though was Mrs. Cotton offering to pay our way. I said I'd take the girls on Wednesday night, but Annette's mama said that Wednesday is Klondike Night, and the jackpot was up to $50, so it would be too crowded. Annette told me and Sheila that her mama's sister, Miss Leda Bancroft, had been present to win one time and had embarrassed Annette's mama by jumping up and screaming and showing her garters when she grabbed her jackpot of $32. Annette thought it was a funny story, but her mama didn't like to talk about it. As it turned out Mr. Cotton wouldn't let me off early on Wednesday anyway, so we had to go on a Saturday.

Sheila was near beside herself. Her and Annette acted so silly on the way to town, that I told them they better behave or I'd put them out on Carterdale Road. They laughed their heads off at that. Everything was funny: the old men lined up in rockers in front of Johnny Moore's store, a stray dog with swinging teats, an old lady with her hose turned down around her ankles. When we finally got to Main Street, Annette calmed down some, but Sheila kept on squealing over ever' thing she seen. She carried on over a dress hanging in Feldman's window, apples on a stand, a man wearing garters on his sleeve. Ordinary stuff really.

The Palace is on State Street and I found a parking spot just around the corner on Third. We was an hour early for the matinee, but there was already a line of people waiting to buy tickets. I crooked both elbows out from my side, and said, "Ladies, may I take your arms to walk in?" They giggled and grabbed my forearms and the three of us marched into the lobby. Sheila and Annette was both dolled up in church dresses, and I wore my best blue jeans and a white shirt, and I was glad the lights was on 'cause I knowed we looked good walking down the aisle toward the front. I sat between the girls. Annette scooted back in her seat so that her legs dangled into mine, but Sheila had to kneel on her chair to be tall enough to see over the heads of the people in front of us. I could hear her breathing so fast, it sounded like she were a panting dog.

When Clark Gable finally showed up on the sofa at the picnic, I felt Annette's eyes on me. I guessed she were comparing me to Rhett Butler, and I cocked my head a little to let her see the resemblance. I swear I think she sighed right then. Sheila sat with her mouth open, her tongue tucked in the side of her mouth. When I walked my fingers across the chair arm and down her thigh, she didn't even feel it. Annette grabbed my arm a couple of times like she were scared of what was about to happen, and I was sure she were just pretending for an excuse to hang onto me, but I let her do it. It was a good show. There might have been more actual battle fighting, but there was plenty to keep me interested. I couldn't understand how Scarlett could love that pretty boy, Ashley, but I seen how it were between her and Rhett. When Bonnie died, Sheila got so upset, she yelled out. "No. No. Don't let her be dead." I shushed her and gave her my handkerchief, which by the end of the movie looked like I had throwed it in a bucket of water.

When the lights come up, I seen Annette were all teary-eyed too. She started talking different, all soft and woo woo like. I could've kissed her if'n I wanted to. Sheila was the most carried off though. She couldn't say nothing, just kept shaking her head, and wadding up my handkerchief in her little palm, but I knowed when we got home, she was gonna come alive. I could near smell her desire for me. I was gonna tease her about Annette having a crush on me, but she didn't give me no time for talk. We was still in the truck when Scarlett let Rhett know how she really felt.

The next night all hell broke loose over to my house. Me and Sheila was just about to turn in when I seen headlights coming up our driveway. We didn't get much company as a rule, and hardly none after dark, so I got my gun and went to stand looking out the front door. Then I seen it were my daddy's truck, and I laid the gun beside the door and stepped out on the porch.

Daddy had brought along Hugh, and I could smell the liquor on them 'fore they come all the way up the steps. Both of 'em was wearing their Sunday hats and long-sleeve shirts, so I figured they'd been in town for something or other and had stopped at Tuck's for a nip 'fore heading home. I crossed my arms. "Evenin', Daddy. Hugh," I said.

Daddy was smiling. He reached in his back pocket and pulled out a bottle. "Hugh and me got a present for you. It's 150 proof. Just wait till you taste it."

Hugh was leaning on the porch rail, grinning. I reckoned Daddy was gonna have to drive him home. "Sheila gone to bed?" Hugh asked me.

I looked back and seen she were coming to the door. She didn't have no robe and her nightdress were thin. She come out anyway and stood with one bare foot resting on the other. "Hey, Sheila," Hugh said. "You want to join us in a small libation here?" He held up another bottle same as what Daddy had.

Sheila shook her head no and just kept standing there with the light behind her showing the shape of her legs. I stepped in front of her and took the bottle. The hooch burned going down and my eyes watered. Daddy set hisself down on the porch chair, and Hugh slid down on the top step. I took the other chair and Sheila leaned back against the door, but didn't go in. We started talking about this and that, swallowing along on the bottles. Daddy told a couple of jokes about niggers and mules, and Hugh told a smutty one about a woman screwing a big dog. Sheila laughed along with us, and I wished she would shut up and go inside, but it were like her feet were welded to the porch boards. Once, she said something about it being late and us having to be at work in just a few hours, but I shushed her up with a warning look.

All of a sudden Hugh stood up and held out his hand to me. "I come to get the twenty dollars you owing me."

I looked at his big hand, his blurry face, and I said, "I ain't got no twenty dollars."

Daddy lurched up from his chair then. "You pay your brother," he said. "You owe me too, and I ain't forgot that." It were like every other time he gets drunk. He started yelling, calling me so many ugly names I don't even remember them all. Worthless, lazy, grifter, shiftless, such as that. I stared hard at him, felt my fist balling up.

I was gonna shut his mouth, but then Hugh seen the way the wind were blowing with Daddy and he started up, calling me worse; liar, cheat, thief. Then he looked over at Sheila and told her she could do better than me, should've married someone with "real" nuts. "Stoney ain't got real ones," he said. I went after him then. Caught his ear before he could move, and blood come shooting out. Hugh knocked me down and jumped on me. I felt a blow upside my rib and I rolled over and come at his pretty boy face, smashing his cheek. Daddy pulled me off him, then put his boot on Hugh's leg and kicked him. "Git up. He ain't worth your fist."

They left then. Sheila went to get a rag to wipe me up and I made it to the bed. The room was a-spinnin' like a kid's top, and my stomach wanted to come up. I told Sheila if'n Daddy hadn't stopped the fight, I'd of won. Hugh used to always win 'cause he outweighs me by ten pounds, but working at the dairy had made me stronger than I used to be. "I could've took him," I said. "I know I could've."

Sheila were bending over wiping my chin where some blood had dribbled down, and she held the rag up and said, "You owe him money?"

"Yeah. Some."

"How much you owe your papa?"

"Another twenty," I said, feeling myself get tense, feeling the red haze coming over me.

"What'd you do with all that money?" Sheila asked. "I ain't seed none of it, and we needin' a coffee grinder. That one your mama gived us don't work."

Then there weren't no way out of that red fog; it were all around me, heavy, pushing in on my head. I remembered her standing in the light in that nightdress, the outline of her legs leading up to her sweet place. Daddy and Hugh had seen it all. I remembered that now. I swung at her, then my belt was in my hand, and I swung again. She covered her face, but I got her arm. I heard her yelling, "I'm sorry. I'm sorry. I shouldn't ask." But it were too late.

I don't remember getting back in the bed or falling asleep, but when I waked up, Sheila were lying beside me, stroking my face. I seen the marks on her, and I kissed them every one. "We're a pretty pair," she said and laughed real soft.

"Don't you know it." I looked into her sweet eyes full of love and pride on being my wife. We were something special together. I knowed that right then. For the first time in my life, I let a woman see me cry. I laid my head between her breasts and cried like a girl. "I love you more'n anything in the world," I told her, and now I knew I did.

The next Saturday I took Sheila into town and bought her a brand new coffee grinder. She held it up like it were some trophy prize she won and she turned to me, smiled and said, "Oh, Stoney. The fightin' is worth the makin' up."

CHAPTER 21

I had big plans for me and Sheila. I wasn't gonna spend my whole life working on a dairy, shoveling grain, and sweeping cow piss. I told Sheila that someday we was gonna be riding in a fine car, a Cadillac with chrome wheels and a wood dashboard. We would leave Mississippians choking on our dust when we drove out to California to the ocean. Sheila hadn't never seen an ocean, and she said she thought it must be like the sky only upside down. I hadn't never seen the ocean neither, but I had a fair idea of what it would be like. Salty, I told her. Like swimming in the water that runs off from the ice around the ice cream churn.

What would we do for work was what Sheila wanted to know, and I said, as to that, I hadn't decided yet, but it would be something that could be done in a big office building where the air was clean and fans blowed on you all day. Sheila said that would be something all right, but she might miss the scent of clover and mowed grass, and wouldn't we be sad to leave our families and friends like the Cottons.

I got mad at her then. We was lying on the porch boards in the sun between milkings. Sheila's face was red and more freckles was already popping up on her arms and legs. I'm dark and the sun don't bother me, but Sheila, she'll blister up if she don't watch out. I shoved her over to where there was a little shade made by a branch of the oak. "Okay, you like it here so much. You stay; I'll go by myself."

Sheila just laughed at that. "You ain't going without me. You wouldn't."

I raised up on my elbows and put my face close up over hers. "I would too leave you. I got a need to see what's all in the world, like in California. That's where the movie stars you so crazy about live, you know."

Sheila flicked her tongue in her mouth and stuck it out to nearly touch my face. "I know that much. Maybe we could go on a trip. A vacation. I ain't never been on a vacation."

I sat up, wiped the sweat off my face with my sleeve. "Mr. Cotton's going on a trip. He's going to Louisiana to take the Ayrshires, but guess who he's taking."

Sheila struggled up to her knees and put her hands on my thighs. "Who? You?"

"No. One of the niggers. Digger most likely. He ought to take me."

"Oh, Stoney. I hope he changes his mind. Louisiana! Ain't that far away? Is it close to California?"

I pushed her hands off me and stood up. "I ain't got time to give no geography lessons. I'm going over to Mama's, see if she's got any sweets to give away." I went in and got my truck keys and when I come back out, Sheila was pulling on her boots. "Don't go messing with them mean Jerseys while I'm gone. You remember what happened that day I went to town with Mr. Cotton."

"I ain't, Stoney. I learnt my lesson on that," she said, rubbing her leg like she was feeling them terrible bruises that cow give her again. I couldn't believe a cow had messed her up so bad, but Sheila can figure out a way to get herself in trouble quicker than any gal I ever knowed.

Mama didn't have no cakes made nor pies neither, but she give me five dollars and said not to tell Daddy, like I was crazy enough to. Hugh come over while I was there, and we went out to the barn to see Daddy's new baler. I couldn't get too worked up over a piece of farm equipment, but Hugh acted like it was a Rolls Royce automobile he was inspecting. I sat down on a hay bale and chewed on a straw while he rattled on about how this baler was gonna make hay bales tighter and better than the old one.

After a while, he sat down on a bale too. "How's that pretty little wife of yours?" he asked.

I didn't know if he was being mean calling her pretty or if he was trying to be nice for once. "She's fine and dandy," I said. "She pesters me all night and all day, can't get enough of me." I had told him this before when he'd bragged about Earlene's big tits.

"She's a little wildcat, huh?" I looked over at Hugh and I didn't like the curl of his mouth when he said that. Maybe he didn't believe his little brother was more of a man than he'd ever be.

I leaned over and stared hard at his sneering puss. "You can't imagine what that hump can do when the lights is out."

Hugh's eyes got big. He didn't say nothing. Couldn't think up anything ole Earlene had to top that. I stood up. "I best be getting back to her right now. Tell Daddy I think that baler is a piece of shit."

"I'll tell him you said that," Hugh yelled after me. "I sure will."

"Do it," I hollered back at him.

When I got home, Sheila was back in the kitchen peeling Irish potatoes for our supper. I reached over her shoulder and grabbed the potato she held next to the knife. I took a bite and dropped it into the pan of water beside her. She jumped as drops splashed up her arms. "Stoney! Wait'll I cook 'em." She turned around with the knife still in her hand. I held her wrist tight and closed my hand over hers. I forced her hand up until the blade was close to her throat. "Stoney! Stop!" she hollered out.

"Take your clothes off right now," I said making my voice tough like a gangster's. "After I rape you, I'm gonna kill you."

Sheila's knees went to jelly and she slid right down to the floor. At first I thought she were pretending with me, but then I seen she was upset like she believed me. I knelt beside her. "It were just a joke," I said in my regular voice. "You know I was teasing."

She dropped her chin on her chest and wouldn't look at me. She were crying, not making no noise, but drops fell and spotted her blue apron. "I'm sorry. You just, you was sounding so real."

When I lifted her face, it was like I could near 'bout see bad memories going on in her head behind her eyes. Maybe her papa had held a knife to her before. Maybe he'd told her he'd kill her if she didn't let him fuck her. I wondered if I was going to have to kill him someday. I knowed I wouldn't be one bit sorry if I did.

Sheila was like that lizard that changes color when it moves from grass to dirt. By the time we went to bed that night, she was singing "Beautiful Dreamer" and pretending her nightdress were a evening gown, and she held it out and danced around the bedroom like she was Cinderella at that ball. I told her I was the prince, and she said no, that I was a king.

I felt like a king two weeks later when Mr. Cotton and me set out on our big trip. I don't know how he come to change his mind and take me, but I was some glad to be going. Sheila was as happy as me. She took an hour ironing my two shirts, and she cooked up a whole ring of sausage for us to eat along the way. Of course, I had duties. It were my job to load the Ayrshires, the grain, water for them. They wasn't much trouble though, and the man who had the bull admired them, said I was taking good care of Mr. Cotton's stock for him.

Mr. Cotton drove straight up there on through the night, and when we got to the farm, he unloaded his gear and spent the night in the big house. I slept out in the barn on a horse blanket, but I didn't mind much. It was warm and the sky seemed bigger overhead so that I got to wondering if there was more stars in this state of Louisiana than there was in Mississippi. On the way home, Mr. Cotton said we was gonna stay at a roadside cabin if we found one handy to us, and I was sure looking forward to that. But it didn't turn out that way at all.

We ran into some trouble on the way home at this roadhouse. I had too much liquor in me and the red haze come back on me when these two fellows insulted a nice woman I think Mr. Cotton liked more'n he should. I don't remember a whole lot about the fight, just the taste of blood and some little pain that didn't amount to nothing much. I slept all the way home, and I remember just before I waked up, I was dreaming about a squalling baby crawling around out in the pasture. I was running after it because Franklin, Mr. Cotton's bull, was headed right for it. I had it in my arms when the sun hit my eyes and waked me up.

I didn't say nothing to Mr. Cotton, but I figured it was his coming baby in the dream. Sheila told me they was gonna have one, and you'd of thought it was her that was expecting it. I said, "Ain't they kind of old to have another one? Annette's gonna be twelve this year."

"Shoot," Sheila said. "My mama's just had one a few months back and she's way older than Miss Rowena." She had this goo goo look in her eyes that warned me what she was gonna say next. "Stoney, maybe we'll have a baby soon too. I used my magic cord on the baby bed they got, and it worked. If you'd let me tie it on you, we could…"

I interrupted her and said, "I told you I ain't wearing no string on my peter. Never. You can go down there and rock the Cottons' young'n or go out to your mama's and get one of hers. She's got more'n she can take care of, probably be glad to get rid of one of 'em."

Sheila shut up then, and I was glad of it.

After we got back from Louisiana, I couldn't quit thinking on Sheila's papa. Wondering if'n he was the first one to have her. If he was, then that could be the reason he hated me so much. Sheila, she tried to pretend her papa would come around to us being a couple, but I seen how her eyes slid away to the floor when she said such.

There was what happened on this one Sunday afternoon. Me and Sheila was sitting on the porch between milking times when she seen her papa's truck going real slow in front of our house. "That's Papa," she said, throwing down her bit of sewing and leaping outta her chair. "Maybe he's coming to visit us, Stoney. Get up and go put your shirt on."

"I ain't wearing no shirt for him, and he ain't coming here noways," I said, watching him come to a dead stop in front of our drive.

"Lookit! He is too. He's coming." And she took off down the drive. I stood on the porch watching her running on the gravel on her bare feet like she were floating on a road of cotton bolls. When she stuck her head in the window where her papa sat, I could hear bits of their talking.

"Git in," he yelled at her. "You needed at home."

I saw Sheila shaking her head, pointing up to me, then I seen him wringing her arm till her knees buckled and she fell up against the truck door. I started running to her then, but Mr. Carruth had the door open and her thrown across him before I got halfway down the drive. He backed out onto Carterdale Road and was gone in less than a minute. I turned around and headed toward my truck, thinking I could overtake him easy, but the piece of shit I got to drive wouldn't turn over. I figured it were the starter or maybe the battery, but it didn't matter which it was since I wasn't going nowhere right then.

I waited all afternoon for her to come back, but it got to be milking time and she still hadn't showed up, and I went on down to the dairy barn in a real bad mood. Them cows got the worst of my feelings, but I took a swing at Shorty too when he said the reason Sheila was late was because she and me had had a fight and she couldn't stand the sight of my ugly face. I told him to mind his own business, there weren't no fight twixt us, and then he smirked like he does with his eyes kinda crossing, and I popped him with my fist in the gut. He doubled over and said, "Stoney, you're crazy. I was pulling your leg, man."

I knowed he were joking, but I needed to hit somebody. 'Course I couldn't tell him that, so I said I were sorry, and we got on with the milking.

When I first started back to the house, I thought Sheila was still gone, but when I got as far as the garden patch, I seen her slumped over at the well. "You alright?" I hollered to her. She didn't answer, and I run on towards her and seen the dark spots on the ground around her weren't water. "Son-of-a-bitch! What's he done to you?" I grabbed her arms and turned her around. Her lip was swelled up some, but I couldn't see where all the blood around her was coming from. "Where you hurt?" I asked her.

Sheila pointed down toward her feet. I lifted her torn skirt and seen a deep cut shaped like a bolt of lightning on the back of her leg. "How'd he do it?"

She started to cry. "Claw hammer. I was running. He throwed it and it caught me."

"I'm gonna kill him," I said. "He ain't getting away with this no more."

Sheila dropped to her knees and wrapped her arms around my legs. "Stoney, he took off again. He ain't home."

I leaned over and kissed the top of her head. "Then I'll wait till he gets back; I'll wait, but I'm gonna kill him soon as I find him."

I carried her into the house and got some rags and salve and helped her bandage herself up. She wanted me to lay down beside her in the bedroom, said she had to tell me what had happened. It was dark by then, and I couldn't see nothing but the outline of her. "I'll light the lamp," I said, but she put her hand on my arm.

"No. Wait. What I got to tell you I want to say without no light on my face."

This kind of rushing, whooshing sound started in my head, and I knowed I didn't want to hear her words, but I was going to have to let her say what she needed to say.

Her voice was low, singsong like she were reading some psalm or poem. I hadn't never heard her read of course, but I thought this would be how she would sound if'n she knew her letters. "Papa took me to the woods. He parked beside a big ole pine, eighty feet or more. He said he missed me."

"I'll just bet my ass he does," I said.

Sheila put her hand over my mouth. "Shush. He said Mama ain't been feeling good. I reckon she's got another one a-coming. But I didn't say nothin' to him. He told me he ain't sleeping good since I been gone." She got quiet then, and when she spoke again, the air in her went out between each word like a wind inside her was pushing them out into the room. "See Stoney, when I lived there, Papa would come to me. Come into us kids' room and shake me awake. We'd go out. Out to the tool shed sometime. The turnip patch. Down to the creek. We'd go to those places.

Once in the rain and it were cold."

I knew what was going to come next. I tried to cover my ears, but Sheila pulled my hands down and held onto them. I could feel her little nails against my skin. "Stoney, you got to hear. It were always when Papa was drinking the corn. When he didn't have none, he never came. He left me be all those nights."

"I reckon he'd had a few today when he took you off."

"Yeah. He got to crying, Stoney. He said he wanted me to come back home. 'Leave that bastard you hitched up to like a mule pulling a plow' is what he said. I told him I love you, how it is with us. I said, 'I'm happier than I ever been in my life.'"

I smiled at that. "I knowed you was. I told Mr. Cotton that on our trip."

Sheila squeezed my hands. "Papa said he loved me too. Like you Stoney. He said he wouldn't hurt me no more if'n I'd come home. I knowed that were a lie. He can't keep hisself from it. We was still sitting in the truck then, and I eased over to the door, thinking to jump out if I had to. Papa grabbed my arm, said, 'Sheila, you're mine. You got to come home.' I said, 'No, Papa. It's Stoney I love now.' Then he hit me on my mouth, and I grabbed the door handle and fell out on the ground. I jumped up and ran, but he come after me with the hammer he keeps in the truck."

I could near 'bout see her flying through the woods, barefoot, her hair a-flying around her, her quiet as a dead person, him in his work boots hollering over her head. "He caught you?"

"No. He seen I was too fast for him. Stoney, I jumped fallen logs like a deer and zigzagged through them trees like a squirrel being chased by a hawk. He didn't have no chance of catching me."

"But he threw the hammer?"

"Uh huh. He throwed it like a tomahawk, but it went low and I thanked the Lord for that. If'n it had caught my head, I reckon I'd be laying dead on them pine needles."

"You think he meant to kill you?"

"I know it. He said so. He said if'n I wouldn't come back to him, then I wasn't gonna come back a'tall." Sheila moved closer and wrapped herself around me like she were a snake and I was a rope. "Stoney, I come back. I'm home now."

I pulled her off. "Sheila, we got to get this settled. Can't be waiting around for him to show up here one day and kill you."

She put her cheek on my back and kissed me between my shoulder blades. "He ain't gonna do nothing of the sort. He'll go off and get hisself sobered up and he'll go home and things will be just like they was. I ain't scared of him, Stoney. Really I ain't." She dug her fingers into my arms. "I want you to promise me you won't go after him. He'd kill you, Stoney. Shoot you with his shotgun like you was a possum frozen in the light of his torch. Promise me you'll stay away from him."

"I can't do that," I said.

She started to crying then. Big old tears like hard raindrops fell on my neck. "Please. Promise me. I won't ask you for nothing else. Not ever."

"I said no." I got up. I wanted to go out on the porch and roll a smoke, think on what she'd told me.

"Stoney," she said. "If'n you don't promise me, I'm gonna put a fairy spell on you and you won't be able to do no loving. I done put one on my papa. That's why I ain't scared of him no more."

I knowed there weren't no such thing as a fairy spell, but I let her think she fooled me. "How'd you do it? You got a voodoo doll hid around here somewhere?" When I said that, I remembered seeing her messing with a little ole rag doll I thought must've come from Annette's toy box, but maybe it weren't Annette's doll, and I reckon I was a little worried then.

"How I done it is a secret," she said. "Don't nobody know it but Mama and me and my grandmama who's under the ground and can't tell nothing now."

So when I heard from Sheila's mama at church the next Sunday that Mr. Carruth was back home, I didn't go over and kill him. Didn't go, but I should have. That's another regret I'm gonna have weighing on me for the rest of my life.

Another thing changed after that Louisiana trip. I couldn't understand it, but Mr. Cotton seemed different to me. I can't say what it was, nor even how he was changed, but I felt uneasy when I went down to milk. It was like he were watching me, expecting me to steal from him or something. Then Mrs. Cotton started acting funny too, just the opposite of him. She smiled at me more, seemed happy when me and Sheila stopped by on our way to town. At first, I thought it was because of her being so het up about the baby, but this was more like it was us that was making her feel good.

I asked Sheila did she notice how Mrs. Cotton was grinning at me like I'd won the bull riding at the rodeo or something. Sheila put her hand over her mouth and pulled her lips out. "Maybe she knows a secret I know, but you don't."

"You and her got a secret?"

Sheila shook her head. "I ain't telling. Not yet."

I got to admit I starting guessing what it was. I sat on my milking stool pulling on teats thinking about that secret. I ran through all the possibilities I could imagine. A new truck, a better guitar, another trip to a better place than Louisiana. Then it come to me that maybe Mr. Cotton was going to give me a big raise with a piece of land to build a better house on. He had plenty; he could afford to show some generosity. That was probably why he was watching me so close like, to see if I was ready to step up to a better life. Well, I was ready. I'd show him that I could out-milk, out-shovel, out-drive, out-do anybody in anything. Sheila had said it. I was her king; all's I needed was some land to rule over, and it looked to me like I just might get it.

CHAPTER 22

The day I found out Sheila's secret marks the end of my life. Not eighteen years old yet and it's all over or it might as well be. Who would have believed that Sheila Carruth Barnes, a plain girl with a hump on her back who couldn't read nor write, would betray her husband. No one would have predicted it. No one could ever understand what I felt when she told me, and even if someone could, I don't have no words to tell it.

On the morning of that day that was to turn out to be my last, Sheila stopped at the Cottons' house to borrow a catalog before she come home from cleaning up down at the barn. She were barefoot, left her boots at the dairy. She had on a yellow dress too pretty and nice for work, and she'd pulled her hair back with some twine and stuck a clover bouquet in the knot she made. I watched her coming back home. and when she saw me, I waved to her. I was hungry, hadn't ate since the night before and she hadn't left nothing on the wood stove.

When she came up the steps, I pointed to the book. "What you got that for? We ain't got no money for ordering nothing outta there."

She grinned. "I know. It's my wish book though. I got things I want to look at and dream on some." She rocked the book against her chest. "It's about the secret."

I sat at the kitchen table flipping through the book while Sheila fried up some ham Miss Cotton had gived her. There sure wasn't no land in the catalog, and my spirits was lowering as I turned through the pages of fancy men doodied up in high-class suits. I turned on back to the home section and seen couches with roses on them, curtains, and dishes, and then hot water bottles, and torches and rubber tires.

When Sheila set the ham down, I grabbed a piece and burned my fingers. "Ow!"

Sheila sat on her chair. "Hot, silly. Use your fork."

I had my elbow on top of the book while I ate and I tapped my finger against the cover. "What you planning on getting me in there?"

Sheila chewed a while on a big bite of ham. "Tonight. I'm telling it all tonight."

She wouldn't say no more, and that left me studying on that catalog all day. If she was just wishing like she said, then it wasn't nothing for me, but then she'd said the secret was in there, hadn't she? I broke my record milking that night, and Mr. Cotton said he guessed I was in a hurry to get home. I said I was. I was planning on heating some water and taking a long bath in the tin tub while Sheila finished up at the barn, and I'd put on some of that sweet-smelling cologne she give me, to be ready for my surprise.

I guess things would have turned out the way they did, no matter what, but I'll never know for sure. I was halfway up the hill when I seen Hugh's truck parked underneath the oak tree. I hoped he and Earlene hadn't brought the boys with them. I was in no mood for their racket tonight. When I opened the door and went in, I saw that it was only Hugh, and I was glad for that until I seen Sheila's face. She was still wearing her yellow dress, but she'd taken her hair down and hadn't combed it so that little bits of blonde stood out in clumps around her ears. She looked real unhappy, and I reckoned Hugh had said something mean to her. "You're late for work," I said. "You better hurry up and get down to the barn."

She didn't say nothing, just ran past me and out the door like a rabbit. I frowned at Hugh. "What'd you say to her?"

Hugh was sitting on the couch and he lifted his hands and shrugged.

"Nothing I know of." Then I saw the jug on the table. He lifted it and held it out to me. "I brought over a little celebration drink."

I took a long pull on the jug, wiped my lips with the back of my hand and set the bottle back. My throat burned like fire. "What we celebrating?"

"I got a big raise today. Bought Earlene a Buick." He took a swallow from the jug and handed it back to me. "That'll make a man outta you. I came by to see if you want to go with me to pick up the car tomorrow. Supposed to be ready around noon."

"I might," I said, knowing I wasn't about to go into town with him to watch him strut around at an automobile dealership. I sat down on the couch feeling all the air going out of me. This was the night I was going to find out the big secret about me. It was my night to celebrate, not Hugh's. I wished he would go on home, but I wasn't wanting him to think I was jealous or nothin'. "Why didn't you get a Dodge?" I asked. "They're better than Buicks."

I didn't get a rise from him, and that made me madder. When we was little, Hugh would pick on me about something or other, and then when I'd get mad, he'd act like I was crazy and tell Mama he didn't know how come I was hitting him. I don't know how long Hugh sat there on my couch, drinking from the jug, passing it over to me, like he was some kind of preacher doling out charity to the poor, but after a while, I knew I'd had enough. I stood up and walked to the door. "Time to go, Hugh. Sheila'll be back soon and we got plans. Say good-bye, brother."

Hugh staggered to his feet and patted the jug. "I'll leave this here for you. I got such a big raise I can buy more."

I opened the door and let it slam behind him. When I turned back to the front room, it wanted to lift up on one side and throw me, but I kept my hand on the wall and made it back to the kitchen table. Sheila had two plates set out and on the center of the table, there was a milk bottle with one of Miss Cotton's roses stuck in. She had covered our dinner with a dishcloth and I thought about going over to the stove and lifting it to see what we were having, but I didn't feel like standing up, so I laid my head down on the plate to wait for Sheila.

When I felt her hand on my head, I raised up and pushed my head against her stomach. She stood for a while, holding my head, not saying nothing. "Hugh's gone," I said.

"I seed that when I come home," she said. "You had some of that jug, didn't you?"

"A little."

Sheila went to the stove. "A little too much. You want your supper?" She lifted the cloth and I smelled fried chicken, and there would be milk gravy.

I sure wanted that chicken, but I said, "I want to know the secret. What's my surprise?"

Her back curled up, and when she turned around, I seen she was finally smiling. "I can't tell you in here. This secret's got to be told in the bed."

I made it onto my feet then. "Okay, let's go."

Sheila puckered her lips out like she does when she's trying to figure out her letters I tried to help her with. "Ain't we got to eat first?"

"We can eat after." I held out my hand. "Come on."

Sheila put on that green nightdress I hadn't never seen before. "Miss Cotton gave me it for tonight, and I got to wear it," she said, when I told her that she didn't need no gown.

I remember her standing there in that gown. The room was a fuzzy blur, but she stood out, a sharp image in my mind. I can still see the way her lashes brushed against her cheek when she looked down at her feet. She had brushed her hair back behind her ears and they sat small and pink against her head. I thought how in the last month her face had taken on more color, was rounder, and she seemed older and softer. I told her she was beautiful. I meant that too. Her eyes held me, and I saw how much she loved me.

Sheila was dancing around then, twirling like a top, her gown floating, rising and falling against her legs. She took my hands and I stumbled around the room, trying to keep step with her, but I was getting dizzy and said for her to stop.

Then we was laying in the bed, but she wouldn't let me inside her. Said I had to wait. Said she was gonna tell me the secret first.

I raised up on my elbow. "What is it?" I asked her.

Her hands went round behind my head and she pulled me to her. I felt her mouth wet and soft against my ear. She whispered the words. "Stoney, you and me is gonna have a baby."

PART TWO

Chapter 23

Leland

The morning after the Barnes girl was found, I made my first trip to the basement of the Lexie County Hospital where Casey Pottle conducted autopsies. I woke up famished, having missed my dinner the evening before, and I asked Alberta to prepare a substantial omelet for me. I was midway through breakfast when Mother came into the dining room in her dressing gown. "You were late getting home last night," she said, sliding into her chair and nodding for Alberta to pour her coffee.

"I was covering a murder case. A girl who worked at the Cottons' Dairy out on Carterdale Road was found strangled and beaten in their cornfield."

Mother rattled her cup as she set it on the saucer. "My goodness! Do you have to be the one to write about it?"

I frowned. "Afraid so. There's no one else to do it."

"I'll have toast and orange marmalade," she told Alberta who was standing at the door pretending she wasn't listening. Even though Mother celebrated her fifty-third birthday, she watches her weight and has the figure of a young girl. "Oh, Leland, I know Rowena Cotton. She must be devastated to have such a thing happen. Have they caught the murderer?"

"No. I interviewed the sheriff yesterday, and he said he doesn't have any suspects, but he seemed confident there'll be an arrest soon." I daubed my lips and folded my napkin beside the plate. "How do you know Mrs. Cotton?"

"Her mother is in the Ladies Auxiliary, and she occasionally accompanies her. They're a fine family. I believe they're related to the Natchez Bancrofts who own the logging company. Eva Bancroft had three daughters. The youngest died of cancer; you may remember the obituary on her,

Doris Vitter was her name. Then there's Leda, who lives with that Sylvia Bartheleme over on Third Street. People talk about that relationship, but I don't know if there's fact in the rumors. Then Rowena is the middle daughter, I believe, and I think she has a child named Annie, or something like that."

"I haven't met Mrs. Cotton yet, but I plan to interview everyone involved. The dead girl was a Carruth from Mars Hill, so I guess I'll have to drive out there too." I looked at my watch. "Eight twenty-five! I've got to rush, Mother. I'll see you tonight." I brushed her cheek with my lips and breathed in her dusting powder, which was a lovely scent to carry with me on this unpleasant day.

Casey Pottle had finished his autopsy and was sitting in his small, cluttered office when I peeked in. "Hey, Leland, you here for the scoop?" He waved me in and I stepped over the piles of books and folders littering the floor. "He reached across the desk and lifted a manila folder. "Sheila Carruth Barnes. That's the one you're interested in, huh?"

I lifted my brows. "Did you do another autopsy today?"

Pottle grinned. "Nope, just making sure. You wanna see the corpse? She's still here, quiet as a mouse."

"No," I said too quickly. "I saw her yesterday before they brought her here. She was so small, looked more like a child than a grown married woman."

"Well, she better be a married woman because she was definitely doing a married one's duties." He tapped a line on the page he withdrew from the folder. "Found a fetus of approximately eleven weeks in her uterus."

I leaned forward to look at the report. "She was expecting?"

"Yep. No doubt about it, but it's a wonder she lived long enough to get that way."

I took out my pad and began to jot my first notes of the day. "Why do you say that?"

"Well, of course, there are the fresh wounds and bruises; she was definitely strangled. I could tell that by just looking at the marks around her neck, but there were a lot of other scars indicating past injuries. Her ribs had calcium deposits indicating they'd been broken some time back. There is evidence of other broken bones, scar tissue where I've never seen it. I'd guess she was used to pain. I'd say she lived with it from her first years on this earth."

"So maybe this time someone went too far?"

Casey closed his file. "I can't say, of course, but in all my years in this job, I haven't seen a young woman's body so damaged. If the person who's been beating on her all this time didn't kill her, he ought to be electrocuted anyway."

I thanked Pottle for his time and hurried over to the jail. I wanted to see what the sheriff thought about the autopsy report, but he had already left for the Cottons' place, so I went on to the office to check in with Mr. Elzey, the owner and publisher of *The Lexie Journal.*

"Nice write-up on the murder, Graves," he said to me. "A little high-toned for a hard news story maybe." He lifted the morning edition and read aloud. "Mrs. Barnes wore a sheer nightdress trimmed in yellow." He leaned forward and retrieved a noxious cigar from the smoke stand beside the desk. He drew on it and for a moment his face was obscured in a gray cloud. "But some folks care about the visual detail, I suppose. Might make for a more interesting story, reels them into the scene, you know."

I'd already read the piece in the paper at home earlier, and I was dissatisfied with it because it was too terse. I thought it was in dire need of more descriptive language.

Mr. Elzey stuck his pencil behind his ear. "So you need to get out to that dairy barn and find out all you can for tonight's print run."

"That's where I'm heading," I said.

"This'll be a nice change for you, boy. You been to too many weddings and soirees lately. Do you good to quit writing about seed pearls and Blue Danube waltzing. Write about the real world, cow shit and bloody bodies. Real life." He laughed.

I formed a pithy retort, but it would have been wasted on Mr. Elzey, who thought the purpose of life was to aim a gun at a beautiful doe and blow its head off so that he could sit beneath it while he dined.

In my blue Pontiac I settled back and cleared my mind of the task before me. I hummed a few bars of the Blue Danube waltz and then couldn't stop hearing it repeat over and over in my head until I reached the Cottons' drive. I saw the sheriff's patrol car parked beneath the oak in the front yard, so I decided to visit the girl's parents out on Mars Hill.

I got lost twice trying to find the Carruths' house. The roads weren't marked, and the directions I had scribbled the day before were vague. I drove past the shack twice before I realized that it was inhabited when several young children appeared in the yard. I called to them. "Hello, is this the Carruths' house?"

The oldest, maybe ten or eleven years old, stepped forward and peered in the passenger's side window. "Huh?"

"Are you the Carruths?"

"Yeah. We them." He backed away while I got out and went around to the front of the car. "Our sister got herself kilt yesterday."

"I know. That's why I'm here. Are your parents at home?"

He pointed to the house, an unpainted box, set beneath a rusted tin roof. "They in there." I walked up to the edge of the porch weighing my chances of falling through the bowed boards that slanted down from the structure. "Hello? Mr. Carruth? Mrs. Carruth?"

I heard more children talking, a baby crying, and then the screen door was flung open by a man smaller than I. His brown hair was threaded with gray stripes, and although his face was lined with deep crevices, I judged him to be around forty. He was wearing overalls and no shirt, and in his hand was a straw hat with a wide brim that for some reason made me think of a picture of Huckleberry Finn in one of my childhood books. There was nothing amusing or charming about this Huck Finn, however. He frowned at me. "Whaddya want?" he said in a near growl.

I backed down the steps. "Good morning, sir. My name is Leland Graves. I'm a reporter for *The Lexie Journal*."

He made no move forward. "What's that? The Lexie what?"

I should have guessed this wasn't a family who had a paid subscription for newspaper delivery. "It's the weekly paper. In Zebulon. The newspaper?"

"Okay, whaddya want?" I noticed his hands then. They were far larger than most, wider than a much bigger man's hands. I shuddered, imagining them around the girl's neck.

"I'd like to ask you a few questions about your daughter. I'm following the investigation into her murder."

Mr. Carruth let go of the door and it banged against the weathered frame. He crossed his arms over his chest, hiding those ape-like hands beneath his armpits. "Ain't no need for no investigating. He done it. I know he kilt her, and I told the sheriff to lock him up."

I scrambled in my shirt pocket for my pen and pad. "Who? Who killed your daughter."

"Stoney Barnes. My no-good-for-nothing son-in-law. He's your murderer. Write that down and print it in your paper."

"Do you have any evidence to support that?"

"Evvv eye dence!" That's the way he said it, accenting the "i". "You goddamned right I got evvv eye dence. He hit her plenty of times. She was scarit of him. He beat her and he kilt her."

I saw the way of it then and put away my pad. I had intended to ask to interview Mrs. Carruth, but I made a hasty retreat to my car. An exceptional writer can fill in any information he's missing in the interest of his safety and well-being.

My interview with the Cotton family stood in stark contrast to the Carruth debacle. Their home was a neat white clapboard, raised in the back, so that from the screened porch there was a lovely vista of rolling meadows and verdant pasture land. Mrs. Cotton was charming, a true beauty with soft waving chestnut hair, delicate bone structure, wide-set brown eyes that filled with tears when she described her relationship to the dead girl. She offered me coffee and tea cakes, which I declined. We settled into the cane-backed rockers and then Mrs. Cotton told me that Sheila

Barnes had worked for them for two years. "Lloyd, my husband, didn't really need her, but we learned that her father was beating her and she needed to get away from him." I thought of those hands of Mr. Carruth's again and nodded my understanding. Mrs. Cotton bit her lip. "I thought she was safe here, but now, oh, dear Lord, she wasn't safe at all." I wanted to offer comfort, but I didn't know what would be appropriate, so I looked down at my pad and waited until she regained her composure. "Sheila was as dear to me as my own child," she said.

This last remark reminded me of the autopsy report, but I kept that bit of information to myself. I was hesitant to ask her about anything too coarse, but I knew that I must if I were to write an accurate account. "Er, Mrs. Cotton, I have to ask you an unpleasant question." She pressed her lips together as if she knew what I was going to say. "Mrs. Barnes, Sheila, did she and her husband quarrel often?"

Mrs. Cotton looked down at her folded hands. "I, I'd rather not comment on private conversations. I'll just say Stoney and Sheila were so very young and inexperienced. All couples have a period of adjustment."

"But they'd been married for quite some time, hadn't they?"

"Mmmm. Nearly two years. That's not long."

Mrs. Cotton's daughter, Annette, came out onto the porch just then. She told me she was "real close to twelve years old." She would most likely grow into a real beauty like her mother some day. For now, she was a gangly child, freckled-faced, with straight brown hair pulled back in a ponytail that hung low on her head. She said that Sheila was her best friend, that she knew her better than anyone in the world, and that whoever killed her better pay for her death in the electric chair. I said her sentiments were those of Sheriff Vairo exactly. When I tried to ask the girl about the husband, Stoney Barnes, Mrs. Cotton frowned and shook her head. "Annette doesn't know anything about their personal lives." So I had reached another impasse and thanked them for their hospitality before heading for the dairy barn to speak to Mr. Cotton and the workers.

CHAPTER 24

LLOYD

I was plenty pissed at Clyde Vairo for locking my niggers up and leaving me short-handed. When he took them yesterday afternoon, I told him there was no way any of them had killed Sheila, but he was just itching to lock somebody up before the night was over. Now they'd missed the morning's run, and I hadn't gotten home until after nine to eat my breakfast. I have to admit though that Annette and Rowena were good help to me. Rowena looks so fragile, I'd have never believed she could grab a teat, give it a strong pull, and shoot foaming milk into a bucket. Annette shoveled grain and helped with Sheila's job. I told her as often as she'd watched us work, she ought to know just what to do, and she tried to smile at that. Poor kid, on top of her grieving over Sheila, Rowena told me she started her menses. She was near comical the way she walked spraddle-legged to the barn, but Rowena gave me a look that warned off my smile. None of us mentioned Stoney; I reckon we were all relieved he didn't show up for work. Hell, what was there to say to him?

I was still cleaning up from the morning run when Leland Graves, the reporter for *The Lexie Journal* showed up at the door to the barn. He's a little fellow, kind of prissy, wears a bow tie up tight against his Adam's apple. He wrinkled his nose against the cow manure, but he stuck out his hand and smiled like he was smelling ladies' perfume in a drawing room.

"Mr. Cotton?" he said. "I'm Leland Graves."

I shook his hand and told him I knew who he was from yesterday up at Stoney's house. I had started to say Sheila's; that's the way I always thought of it. Her house. Graves asked some routine things about dairy life and Sheila working for me, and then he took out his pad and acted like he was reading off it, but I could see there wasn't many words on the paper. "Now, Mr. Cotton, I need to ask you about Stoney Barnes. He works for you also. Correct?"

"He does. Been here over two years."

Graves tilted his hat back a bit and looked around the milking room. I could tell he'd never been in one before just by the way his eyes roamed over the stalls and sacks of grain. "He milks the cows in here, I presume?" I said yeah that we didn't milk them out in the weather, and then he said I must know Stoney very well if I saw him twice daily and must have some knowledge of the relationship between him and his wife.

I knew what he was getting to. I had the feeling Carruth was stirring up trouble for Stoney. Clyde Vairo had told me he was pestering him to death to arrest Stoney for the murder. "They were a nice young couple," I said. "Never caused me a minute's trouble."

"There's been talk," he said, "that perhaps the relationship wasn't always amicable."

I didn't know what the hell he meant by that, so I kept my jaw locked. In the end, I told him that Sheila had come to work banged up some several times, but that as to who done it, I would be guessing.

After he left, I took a pull on the whiskey bottle and sat on the milking stool to sort things out. I'd been so worried about keeping the dairy going I hadn't had much of a chance to think about the murder. I went over the day in my mind, step by step, how it all played out.

I'd overslept, the first time I'd done that in a year. Rowena had kept me up late with her fretting. She was gonna be a trial over this baby. I could see that from a mile off. So I'd pulled on my clothes and gone down to the barn without coffee or a shave. I yelled at Digger when I seen they was just getting started on bringing the cows in. They knew better and I told Shorty, who was sitting on a stool eating a biscuit, to get his butt up and moving. Stoney was milking Bell, but he was pulling on her teats so slow she had her head turned back to him as if to wonder what the hell he was doing. We got loaded up, and I remember seeing Digger and Stoney outside the barn smoking a cigarette as I drove off with Shorty. When I got back, the yard was full of cars and trucks, and a school bus. Rowena came running out and told me Stoney had been there and had said Sheila was missing. I remember my first thought was Rowena had jumped the gun and Sheila would turn up saying she was off on some fairy hunt or some such foolishness. Meanwhile, folks were tramping all over my land, and god knows what damage they'd do to the garden. I had to unload and I left Shorty to clean up and joined up with Clyde Vairo, who was toting his rifle over his shoulder.

Now though, as I took another pull on the whiskey, my thoughts jumped to the how and when of it. What was clear to me was that Sheila had been murdered during the night, maybe while Stoney was milking. He said she was still sleeping when he left the house. He said that, but it might not be true. If he had killed her, would he have come to work, smoked a cigarette before he went back home? That didn't seem likely. But if he hadn't murdered her, who had? I thought of her papa, or maybe it had been a vagabond, a tramp? Why hide her body in the cornfield? I couldn't get my thoughts to come to any conclusion about anything, and I was glad I'd chosen dairying for a livelihood and not the law.

I put away my bottle and rinsed my mouth with some Listerine I kept in the cabinet and started back to the house. Rowena would be in a state, and I dreaded what was before me. I looked over to the tenant house and saw that Stoney's truck was gone. I hadn't seen him since they'd loaded the body, and I wondered where he'd gotten off to. The thought came to me then that maybe he had killed Sheila and he had taken off to hide out somewhere before he was found out. If that were the case, I'd help Clyde hunt him down myself. "Son of a bitch," I said. "Goddamn it to hell and back."

Just as I said that, Annette came out of the house yelling that Digger had called from the jail for me to come and get them. I looked up at the umbrella-shaped cloud over me and said, "Well, thank You for that. At least I can run my dairy right again."

R O W E N A

After Lloyd went into town to fetch the coloreds, I called Mama to tell her that Digger would be coming back soon so that she could pass the word to Angilee, his wife, who works for Mama. I told Mama I couldn't think of anything except poor Sheila and I just didn't see how I could get through a funeral. Mama asked when it would be, and I couldn't answer that. I knew there had to be an autopsy in a situation like this. "Rowena, you know not to look at the body. You don't want your baby marked," she said. I told her not to worry, but I knew she would. Mama tried to sound cheerful then. "We should talk about something else, something pleasant." I told her I was going to give Annette a party for her twelfth birthday, but I couldn't summon any joy over my plans.

When Mama hung up, I sat holding the receiver until Miss Wilda came on the line and asked was I wanting to make another call. I did want to talk to Leda, but I was drained and went in and just collapsed on my bed. I couldn't nap though. I kept thinking about the day before, the horrible horrible day.

Lloyd had overslept, and I turned over and put the pillow over my head, so I wouldn't hear him stumbling around in the dark room trying to get dressed in a hurry. I went back to sleep and didn't wake until nearly five, and I had just gotten my new seersucker bathrobe on that was going to be plenty roomy for the baby and me later on, when I heard Stoney's wild knocking on the back door. I couldn't find my slippers and so I ran barefoot through the kitchen to unlock the door. When I opened it, I smelled cigarette smoke through the screen and I thought my nausea which had eased up some was going to return, but I held my breath for a second and it went away. Stoney looked terrible. I stepped out on the porch and saw that his pants were soaked from the knees down, and his eyes were wet too. I asked him what was the matter, and he said, "Miss Cotton, sorry to bother you, but I was wondering if'n Sheila was down to here." I told her she never visited this time of the morning. Annette wasn't even awake yet. That's when he told me she was missing, and the tears he was holding in his eyes spilled down his face. I felt so sorry for him.

I did ask the question, and I wish I hadn't. "Did y'all have a fight? Maybe she's hiding from you." If I had known she was dead, I'd never have said such a thing, but of course, I didn't know, and I can't take it back.

Stoney just shook his head no though and said, "There weren't no arguing last night. When I left for work she were sleeping on her side like always." His fingers went up to the tobacco tag hanging out of his pocket, but he didn't pull out the pouch. "I think something terrible has happened to her," he said.

I told him I'd get dressed and we'd look for her. I woke Annette, and by the time we got ourselves presentable, Digger had come up to the porch and was talking to Stoney. Stoney said he'd already searched all around their yard, and Annette ran down and checked the smokehouse and the barn again. It had rained the night before and in no time Annette's bare legs were spattered with mud. When we'd been searching for maybe an hour, I'm not sure how long, it was Digger who suggested that Sheila might have gone home to her parents' house. I gave him the keys to the Dodge and told him to drive Stoney out there right away. I remember how Digger's jaw dropped in disbelief that I was allowing him to drive my automobile, but he closed his mouth, took the keys and jumped behind the wheel. I was sorry I'd made that decision when he swung the Dodge around and barely missed the camellia bush beside the drive. I will never forget Stoney's face as he sat staring out of the windshield like he was willing Sheila's face to appear on the glass.

When my automobile disappeared, I suddenly felt so weak I had to lean on Annette to get back to the house. I asked her to pour us some milk and make oatmeal, which she managed in record time. I could tell she was worried about me and the baby, and I tried to comfort her and say I was all right, but she knows me. After the oatmeal, I went in to begin telephoning. I called Clyde Vairo first and then Mama and Leda. They're on different party lines than we are, so they helped with the calling.

It seemed like no time at all before people began to arrive to help with the search. I was desperate for Lloyd to get home. And darn that sheriff of ours; he was nearly the last to arrive, so that I had to be in charge of everything. I wondered if I should serve coffee, but the big urn was stored in a high cabinet, and I knew not to be lifting anything heavy.

When Stoney and Digger returned and said that the Carruths were on their way, my hopes of finding Sheila died and a cold fear came over me. I guess Mama had called Stoney's folks because I hadn't thought to do it and wondered at myself for forgetting about them, but Mr. Barnes drove into the yard and jumped out of his truck with a water jug and a long-barreled shotgun. He had already left for the pasture when the Carruths arrived in the big yellow school bus. I hope the amazement didn't show on my face when I saw them falling out of the bus. Digger had said they couldn't all fit in an automobile and that Mr. Carruth had driven over to the Dunaways to borrow the Mars Hill school bus, but I had no idea there were so many of them. Besides Mr. and Mrs. Carruth and the newborn bald baby in her arms, there were eleven children ranging from around fourteen down to a pair of toddler twins. They were dressed in frayed but clean clothes. The boys' hair, most of them cotton-topped, spiked unevenly in all directions, the obvious result of kitchen shears. The girls wore plaits that hung down to the middle of their backs. All of them were barefoot and wide-eyed. Mr. Carruth's mouth, a deep straight gash across his face, worked itself open as he walked over to me. "Did you call the law?" he asked.

"The sheriff is on his way out," I said and then turned to poor Mrs. Carruth, whose ashen face was literally quivering. "I'm Rowena Cotton."

She said nothing at first. She shifted the baby on her arm, and I thought she was trying to free a hand to hold out to me, but she clutched the baby tighter against her. I patted her back between her protruding shoulder blades that looked like sharp shovels jutting out from her faded, floral-print dress. Her eyes filled and she whispered, "I know she's dead. I know."

"Oh, you mustn't say that. Don't think it. We'll find her." I tried to think of more comforting words to say, but my mind was as empty as our coffee pot by noon. I spread my arms out to the drive where more automobiles and one tractor came toward us. "We have so much help," I finally said.

Sheila's mother raised the baby higher and kissed the pink skin that stretched over its big round head. I was staring at the sleeping baby when I remembered that this was the day we were going to celebrate; I was supposed to make a cake. Sheila would tell Annette about her baby today because she was going to tell Stoney yesterday. Had she told him? I looked for him over the heads of the grim-faced people standing in our yard with guns, hoes, shovels, and rakes. They were shaking hands, talking in fast chatter like they were at a church social. They seemed unsure of how to begin the search, and right then, to the great relief of us all I'm sure, Clyde Vairo finally drove up in his patrol car. He tried to get everyone's attention when he stood up on the bed of Castle Moore's Ford truck and shouted in a deep bass voice for everyone to shut up and listen. The cacophony of voices continued until, after shouting twice more, he shot his rifle into the air and silenced everyone except the Carruth baby, who woke up and began to wail loudly.

Clyde took over the search then, and I brought Effie Carruth into the house to wait for news. Mama came by and Leda and quite a few of the women from both Effie's church and ours, but no one stayed all that long. I couldn't blame them; it was too painful to sit and watch Sheila's mother sitting on my couch gripping that baby as if she thought he might go missing too if she let go of him. Mama had said she'd stay with me until they found Sheila, but she got a sour stomach right after she ate a piece of the peach pie she'd brought over and had to go home. So it was only me and all those children and Effie Carruth in my house that seemed like a crowded tomb. I wondered if Sheila had told her mother about her being p.g., but I doubt if the poor woman could have stood talking about her at all. I went to my room and brought my Bible out and sat beside her reading aloud from the Psalms, which are uplifting if you read them in the right tone of voice. But my breath was wasted on her; I doubt she heard a word I said until hours later when Digger called me out to the porch and told me Sheila had been found in our cornfield.

ANNETTE

I answered the phone when Digger called to say he and Shorty were free to come home. After I told Daddy, Mama called Grandma so she could tell Angilee. Angilee is Digger's wife and she makes the best chicken pie in all of Mississippi. We don't have any help in the house because Mama is just too picky and hard to please. Grandma doesn't care if her sheets aren't folded into a perfect square. Mama went and laid down on her bed and said she was going to take a nap and for me to answer the telephone if it rang.

I got out my Parcheesi game, but it wasn't any fun playing by myself, and I wandered around the house, wishing I could go up to Stoney's. I needed to talk to somebody about Sheila, but Mama didn't want me to talk about her. She hadn't let me say hardly a word to the reporter, and I could have given him a better description of her than anybody else. I wondered if maybe our names would be in *The Lexie Journal*. I thought Mr. Graves was just about the most elegant man I'd ever met. He was wearing spectator shoes, a blue suit with a maroon stripe, and a pink shirt. Daddy wouldn't be caught dead in that shirt or the bow tie that moved up and down when Mr. Graves talked.

I went to the bathroom and stared at myself in the mirror. I was a woman now, not some kid to be shushed up when I had something to contribute to a conversation. That's how it should be, but that wasn't the way things were going so far. I sat on the floor beside the tub and laid my head on my knees. I hadn't gotten to tell Sheila I started my period, and she would never know that my hair didn't curl. And she hadn't told me her secret either.

When Mama had woken me up the day before and told me to get dressed fast, that Sheila was missing, I thought she meant that Sheila was missing some thing, not that it was herself. Of course, I soon realized the truth, and I was sure that I would be the one to find her. After all, I knew all of her hiding places. The first place I looked was the smokehouse, but when I pulled the string cord for the single bulb hanging in the center of the meat hooks, all I saw were a rake, a hoe, a sling blade, and some bags of 13-13-13. Then I got the Ever Ready and pointed it up into the fig tree, expecting to see her legs dangling down, her grinning white face appear in the orb of light. I called her name over and over. "Sheeeeelia, Sheilaaaaa, She Laaa."

After I helped Mama and fixed her some oatmeal, I took off up to Sheila's house. Stoney and Digger had gone out to the Carruths' which I knew was a wasted trip since Sheila would never go out there alone at night. It was around six-thirty now, and the sun should have been rising behind the car house, but later I decided that it knew it shouldn't shine on the sorrow we were all to feel that day.

I saw her house as if I'd never seen it before. I stood in the yard beneath the gloomy sky, and stared at it. The boards holding up the rust-stained tin roof had weathered to a dull gray, having lost their dress of white paint years ago. A pair of narrow rectangle windows matched on either side of the front door, which was shut and unwelcoming. Their bedroom was to the left of the front room, and I imagined Sheila on the patched sheets, curled on her side. I walked around the house and tried to peek in the window, but rising on my toes, I could only see the foot of the bed, a chest of drawers, a small trunk, some clothes on the floor. I staggered back and tripped over an oak tree root and fell, banging my knees. Little red dots formed on my knee cap, and bending over, I licked them and kissed my scratches. Sheila had taught me this routine, saying it was better to soothe your own wounds than run to someone else because you can't count on finding love every time you need it. I got up then and went on around the house, circling the kitchen windows, too high up to see in. When I came back to the front, I walked up the wooden porch steps and then cupped my hands to look through the front room window. I saw the battered couch I always sat on when visiting; there was the big radio Stoney had bought, and some newspapers littering the floor. On the table in front of the couch beside a ceramic jug was an enamel dishpan filled with water and a gray rag was draped over the side of the pan. Did Sheila wash in the front room instead of the kitchen? Suddenly, a terrible thought came up in my head. The well! What if she'd fallen in the well, and I raced across the yard, my heart rat-a-tatting like a drum. But there was the tin bucket hanging on its usual peg and the board that covered the opening was in place.

I stayed away from my own house most of the day. I couldn't look at Mr. Carruth without seeing the poker he'd struck Sheila with in his hand. Mrs. Carruth's eyes scared me too; she looked like a crazy person who might be capable of just about anything. I tried to stay near Stoney, but there were too many people wanting to shake his hand, slap his back, tell him that his wife would be found safe and sound. I could tell he knew different by the way his eyes would slide over people's heads to avoid looking straight at their lies. I caught a glimpse of Daddy a time or two and ducked down behind bushes or whatever was handy to hide in. I knew he'd send me inside to sit with Mama and wait, and I couldn't do that, no, I couldn't have stood it. I had to be looking for my Best Friend. She'd expect that of me.

I stood up and looked in the bathroom mirror again. I was glad I hadn't been the one to find her, and I didn't care a rotten fig if I was never going to have curly hair.

CHAPTER 25

LELAND

After I left the Cottons' Dairy, I drove up to Stoney Barnes' house to inter-view him again, but he wasn't at home, and the house was dark. I nearly sat in one of the pair of ladder-back chairs on the porch to wait for Barnes to return until I saw that the wood was rough and thought better of it, there-by saving my suit pants a snag or two. I did walk around the yard a bit, try-ing to get a sense of the place and its inhabitants. I thought of the girl's body wobbling on that stretcher, of the shack out at Mars Hill, of that father of hers with those unnatural hands. I think I was half-expecting some sort of ghoulish face to appear in one of the windows of the house, which had taken on a gothic ambience in my mind. I decided right then to go back into Zebulon and check in with the sheriff.

Sheriff Vairo was just getting into his patrol car when I steered my Pontiac into the space beside him. He waved me over. "You want some news to write up for your column, boy? Jump in. You can get a scoop if you hurry."

I detest the word "scoop." It conjures a gum-chewing swell with his hat cocked back and a pencil stuck in his ear, and I deeply resent being referred to as "boy," which is what most people in Lexie County call Negro men of all ages. But I didn't hesitate to open the passenger door and slide into the automobile that smelled like a mixture of an outhouse and a cigar factory. I breathed through my mouth, and then said, "What's our desti-nation, Sheriff?"

"Hospital. Got us a fracas going on over there."

"A fight? In the hospital? Who? Why?"

The sheriff pulled out into the street narrowly missing a dog that scuttled out of our way. "The Barnes boy and Thad Carruth. Pottle called and said they were fighting over the release of the body. Said he had her out on the table nicely stitched up, and they both busted in about the same time wanting to take her home to be laid out. Before he knew it they were both pulling on her this way and that. Said Jane Madison, the nurse, walked in and nearly fainted when she saw the stitches ripping out. Pottle didn't see who threw the first punch, but they were into it when he called me."

My mouth was so dry I had to moisten my lips with my tongue before I could speak. "Why, that's, that's, barbaric." I took out my pad and pen, but my hand was shaky, and I looked out the filthy window at the gray stone building that was the Lexie County Hospital. It could have been Frankenstein's laboratory. I half expected a man-made monster with a crooked line of raw stitches to walk stiff-legged across the lawn toward us. But there was only Mrs. Quinn holding up the forearm of her son, Jimmy, who was shrieking like a banshee over, I assumed, the small bandage on his left cheek.

Clyde Vairo and I ran down the cement steps to the basement two at a time and skidded into each other trying to make the turn into the morgue. I had expected shouting, rough language, something of that sort, but all was quiet. Casey Pottle intercepted us before we entered the room and ushered us into his office. "They've gone," he said. "Left just minutes before; I'm surprised you didn't run into them."

Sheriff Vairo's disappointment was visible, and I realized that he'd drawn his gun when I saw his hand return to his hip. "Well, hell, Casey, why didn't you keep them here? You knew I was on my way."

Pottle's shaking hand pulled out a drawer in his desk and lifted a pint bottle. He uncapped it and took a long swallow before he answered. "Keep them here? I'm just lucky they didn't take a swing at me. I don't think either one of them would have cared if they'd killed me."

"Where's the body?" I asked him. "Did they take her?"

Casey shook his head. "No, no. She's still here. Come see." He got up and grabbed his keys from the wooden letter box on his desk, and we followed him out. He unlocked the door to the morgue and Sheriff Vairo stuck his head in and whistled. "Whew, I reckon they did have themselves a ruckus in here." I looked around him and saw that the room was ransacked; tables overturned, steel instruments scattered over the floor, the rollaway table I assumed the girl had been lying on was turned on its side with two wheels pointing up at the ceiling. I realized I had been holding my breath when I began to feel dizzy. I held onto the wall and let the sheriff and Pottle go farther into the room without me.

Pottle stood in the center of the room beside the tipped table. "Now you're catching on, Clyde. There wasn't a thing I could do to stop them."

"So how'd you get them out of here without her?" The sheriff looked down at the sheets that lay on the floor beside his feet. "And where is she?"

Pottle pointed to a door to our left. "In there. When the fight moved out into the hall, I ran to her and dragged her in there. Locked her in the storage closet. When they run back in here, each trying to be the first to get back to her, they saw that she was gone, and got quiet. I told them that I had called you to come and lock them up and that you had the say of who takes her. Mr. Carruth left first and the Barnes boy kept picking up things and dropping them, and then all of a sudden, he wheeled around and ran out too."

I closed my eyes and for a brief moment I saw the two of them pulling her body apart like a wishbone. I thought of Odysseus meeting Agamemnon in the underworld, and I said, "Nor would they close her two eyes as her soul swam to the underworld or shut her lips."

The sheriff stared at me and shook his head, but Pottle nodded agreement. "Never in all my years," he said. Then he turned to Sheriff Vairo. "So where should I send the body?"

"Nowhere. Keep her here. Say she's evidence; say that you got more to do on the autopsy."

"But she's got to go in the ground eventually."

Sheriff Vairo snapped back. "I know that, Casey. I just want some time."

When we got back to the jail, our deputy and the only other full-time law enforcement person, Sam Mueller, told the sheriff Mr. Carruth had been there "all riled up like a setting hen."

I was glad we had missed him.

By the end of the day I knew who the prime suspects were, but the sheriff wouldn't let me write much about his investigation. "I'm giving you the scoop," he said, "but you have to give me your word you won't print anything until you get my okay."

I said that would be acceptable, that I appreciated the opportunity to learn about how a criminal investigation is conducted. I knew the only reason the sheriff was amenable to my presence was that he was anticipating my writing that he was the hero of this story.

My piece was short, but my notes were prolific. Beneath the heading "suspects," I drew lines for three columns. The first subheading was "vagrant," then "Stoney Barnes," and the last column was titled "Thad Carruth." The sheriff was most doubtful that a vagrant had committed the crime. "You go in that house, you'll see they didn't have nothing worth stealing. If I was looking for some cash or valuables, why I'd break in at the Cottons' house, not their tenant house. And the girl wasn't raped, so it wasn't some pervert type."

His deductions seemed logical. "So, Sheriff, what about the father, Thad Carruth?" I was thinking of those plate-sized hands.

"Well, we know he beat her. We know he is a violent man who can't control his temper. You saw that at the morgue. Lloyd Cotton told me he knew for a fact that he had come up to that house when the boy wasn't home. Beat her…maybe violated her." Sheriff Vairo's eyes were on me for my reaction, and I'm sure he was satisfied that I was disbelieving and horrified by his information. After a minute he went on. "So he could have gone up to his own daughter's house, knowing her husband was at work, was going to take her in her own bed. She struggles, tells him to get out, he won't go, she's small and can't fight back none. He chokes her. Then he panics, knows Stoney Barnes will come back home, find her, maybe guess he done it, and then come after him. So he totes her out to the cornfield, hoping that when she's found, people will think she was killed out there."

"Can Mr. Carruth account for his whereabouts when she was murdered?"

"He said he was possum hunting all night on the Whittingtons' land, but nobody was with him to prove it. I asked his wife a few questions, and all she knew was that he was back home when she got up around five that morning, and she said they didn't eat possum for breakfast."

"What about Stoney Barnes? What makes you suspect him?"

The sheriff took a sip of coffee from a stained cup that looked in dire need of a good scrubbing with disinfectant. "Well, he had the best opportunity to kill her. There wasn't anybody there with them after his brother left that night."

"They had company that night?"

"Yeah, the oldest Barnes boy, Hugh. He brought over some hooch and both of them boys was most likely drunk as skunks that night. Every one of them Barnes boys gets wild with liquor in them. The old man too. So could be Stoney gets drunk, him and the girl get into it. Lloyd Cotton knows for sure that he's given her a black eye before, so he's capable. Then he goes too far, chokes her, thinks just like I said with the papa. Panics, totes her to the cornfield, hoping folks will think she was killed out there."

I thought back to my brief interview with Stoney Barnes. His sorrow, his regular features that would be most attractive to the fairer sex, his quiet voice, his youth. He didn't seem like a person who could strangle a young girl he obviously loved very much, carry her body all that way to the cornfield, and once there, raise his boot and stomp her head into the ground.

"So you'll question him too?"

"Yep. I'll go out to the Cottons' place and have a talk with him first thing in the morning."

I rose from my chair to return to *The Journal* offices. I asked one more question. "Who will get the girl's body then?"

Sheriff Vairo smiled. "Whichever one I don't lock up for her murder."

CHAPTER 26

STONEY

I can't stay in this house; I can't. Her ghost is here. At night, I hear her calling me, "Stoney, Stoney, Stoney." Then she starts crying. I listen to her sobbing, and it near breaks my heart. Sometimes it's that baby wailing all night. Its cries are real weak, like it's far away, but I hear it all the same. Mostly, though, it's Sheila I hear, and I cover my head with a pillow, but her voice goes right through the feathers into my head. Last night I got up and I yelled at her. "Hush up now! Leave me be!" But she ain't gonna quit till I get her in the ground. I know that.

I ain't gonna be in this house much longer no how. I know that too. My life is over and I never got to see the ocean or California or any place excepting Louisiana, and that wasn't much.

When the sheriff come out here this morning, I told him that it ain't right that a man can't bury his wife. That's the worst of it. Not burying her. Her lying in that dark basement without nobody who loves her. If I could get her in the ground, she'd stop calling me every night. But that sheriff ain't got no heart; he ain't got no wife, and he don't know how it is. He said he can't release her body yet, and I just got to wait. Sheila's papa ain't getting her. "You ain't touching my Sheila" is what I yelled at that bastard yesterday down at the morgue, and when he grabbed for her, my fist come up against his head. I seen blood dripping off his face, and I knowed I could take him then. I would've too except he run off.

The sheriff wouldn't say no more about Sheila's body, said that wasn't what he'd come to talk about. He kept pulling out his handkerchief and wiping the sweat off'n his face. Me and Sheila ain't got no fan, and I reckon he wasn't used to the heat. I didn't offer him no water though; I wanted him to get the hell outta my house. But he kept on asking questions about Sheila and me. I tried to answer everything he asked, but then he got to tapping his pen on the table and it kept on and on until I got to feeling like thunder was going through my ears and into my head and booming out the other side, and I wanted to put my hands over my ears. He said something else I don't remember, but finally I heard him say he guessed that was all for now, and he drove off in his sheriff car.

Then less than an hour after he left, I looked out the front door and seen Effie Carruth standing on my porch. She was polite, asking if'n she could come in and talk to me about something important. Behind her I seen a Ford automobile I didn't recognize filled up with children and a lady sitting behind the wheel wearing a man's straw hat. Sheila's mama don't know how to drive, and I guessed it were some neighbor lady or church friend of hers giving her a lift over to here.

I let her come on in, and she looked around real interested in what-all she seen. She hadn't never been over before. Sheila's papa forbid it, said he'd never set foot in Stoney Barnes' house. She was clutching a big purse to her bosom like it was her baby, and she eased down on the couch real slow like a person with aches and pains. She crossed her feet that was laced up tight in black men's shoes and swallowed hard a couple of times. Finally, she got to it. "Stoney, Mr. Carruth told me what happened down to the hospital."

That got my jaw tight. I didn't answer her and stayed on my feet in front of the spare chair.

"He said the sheriff's gonna decide on what happens to Sheila." When she said that her voice caught in her throat and she pressed her lips together for a minute before she went on. "I'm headed to town right now to talk to him, and here's what I want to say. There don't have to be no wake at nobody's house. We could just go right to the funeral and burying. The church is the proper place for her now. I can get us a box for her and, if you'll say yes to it, I'll see to it that she gets laid out proper and buried in the Bethel Baptist cemetery out at Mars Hill." Her knuckles was white on her purse, and I seen how hurt her gray eyes was. Maybe Sheila had been calling her mama at night too is what I thought.

I sat down and dropped my head in my hands. I tried to figure what Sheila would want me to say to this, and I seen her little face all lit up talking about them little young'ns she growed up with. Her mama was a good woman too. I knowed that none of her husband's doings was her fault. I raised up. "I'll say yes to it. You tell the sheriff, if he'll let you have her, I said yes to it."

Sheila's mama loosened up on her purse and stood up. "I'll go then. I'll see to it and let you know when to come to the church."

I felt just about as sad as I ever have thinking on walking into the church where Jesus' face would be looking down on her box. I wiped my eyes with my sleeve. "You let me know. I got to be there when she goes in the ground."

ANNETTE

A storm swept across Lexie County on the September night before Sheila's funeral. That Sunday morning we sat at the breakfast table eating our eggs and ham slices and biscuits in slow motion. Daddy had bags as big as small lemons beneath his red eyes, and Mama's face was swollen and sore-looking. "I say let's skip church this morning," Daddy said. "We got the funeral to get through this afternoon." He had just returned from the milk run, and an orange stain ran down his pants in the shape of an exclamation point. I guessed he had broken another bottle of juice.

"Fine with me," I said. I hadn't learned my verse for Sunday school.

"Me too," Mama said. "I guess I should call Mother to let her know; she'll be worried if we don't show up." But she didn't get up; she propped her elbows on either side of her plate and gazed off toward the stove.

"What time is the funeral?" I asked, looking first at Mama and then at Daddy, who was staring at the ceiling.

"Three," he said. "Maybe it'll dry up some by then. Nothing worse than a burial in a water grave."

Mama came back to us and said in a child's voice, "I don't think I've ever been to a funeral when there was no wake before."

Daddy pushed his chair back. "Circumstances are different. Autopsy and hard feelings between the Carruths and Stoney."

That afternoon I sat looking out the window of Mama's Dodge as we drove out toward Bethel Baptist at Mars Hill. While the skies had cleared early in the morning, a dark covering of angry clouds had begun to hover over us. The past month had been dry, and the farmers were glad of the afternoon storms that had visited us in the last week. In a way, I was glad of them too. I imagined a funnel cloud lifting our cows, swirling them in the sky like pinwheels. I saw the corn, torn from the soil, dancing around the cows, and Sheila and I riding a stalk, suddenly finding ourselves on a golden road leading to the castle of Oz. I could wake up from that dream, happy again because these last days were only a nightmare, and like Dorothy I would run into Sheila's house calling her name. She would be there just like Auntie Em, smiling, her arms open to catch me and hold me to her.

The coffin was closed, and I was glad for that. I didn't want to remember my Best Friend in this ugly square room. She belonged out in the pasture, in the fig tree, somewhere where the wind could blow through her hair and she could smell the buttercups that grew wild over our land. As I sat in the pew looking around the church, I couldn't help comparing this funeral to Aunt Doris's. There were only thirty or so people scattered around the room. Sheila's mother and all of the Carruth children sat on the first two pews on the right. Sheila's papa stayed away, and Grandma said Mrs. Carruth told her he'd gone off somewhere, but she didn't know where. We all saw the swelling on her bottom lip and knew that he must have done that before he left. Across from the Carruths Stoney sat with his head down, beside his mother. Stoney's father laid his arm on the back of the pew, patting his wife on her shoulder pads which stuck up like little bobbed-off wings. None of Stoney's brothers came. Hugh's wife, Earlene, sat on the other end of the pew, sniffing into her lace-edged handkerchief. She told Grandma that Hugh had gone to Jackson with the two other brothers, Pete and Daniel.

Although I had attended only one other funeral, I knew that this one was most unusual. There was no cloying scent of flowers, no sad music, no appropriate verses from the Bible the minister held up like a torch. The blanket of flowers on the closed pine box looked cheap and scraggly. A few of the white carnations were brown-edged, giving me the thought that perhaps they had been taken from a corpse already laid to rest.

Except for the toddlers and baby, all the Carruth children carried the box. It looked light and unsteady in their hands as they crept down the aisle after the blistering sermon about sin and damnation was over. By the time we all walked to the cemetery, where a red clay mound awaited Sheila's body, it had begun to rain and black umbrellas popped open in all directions. Mama looked up at the sky as Daddy ran to the car to get our own umbrella and said, "Oh no. The grave is going to fill up with water."

She was right. By the end of the last prayer, dust to dust really meant mud to mud. Poor Mrs. Carruth slipped on the red slick clay and skidded several feet before someone caught her by the arm and lifted her up. I heard her sobbing, and then I looked back at the grave and saw Stoney kneeling there in the mud with his hands held up like he was catching the rain for a keepsake of the day.

There was no post-funeral feast, but Mama had brought a cake for the Carruths, which Mrs. Carruth, wearing a black dress that was so old it had a purple sheen to it, nodded for one of the older boys to take from her. We had a pie, too, for Stoney, but before we could give it to him, Earlene Barnes walked over to where he stood beneath the lone oak tree in the cemetery. I couldn't hear what they said, but Stoney's head was bowed, and when her hand reached out to touch his shoulder, he threw it off, ran to his truck and drove away. I hollered to Daddy to flag him down, but Mama shushed me. "But he didn't get his pie," I said, and immediately burst into tears. Mama knew it wasn't the pie that made me cry, but she pulled me close and promised we would drop it by his house on the way home.

CHAPTER 27

LELAND

I had what I hoped was a brilliant idea for a slant to the Barnes' murder story that would keep my byline on the front page of *The Journal.* Actually, I have to give Mother credit for it. On the Sunday night after the Barnes girl was finally buried, we were having our nightly tea in the sitting room adjacent to her bedroom. Mother was reading Willa Cather, frowning over her spectacles, and I had taken out a volume of the collected poems of Byron, Keats, and Shelly. Although I knew it by heart, I was just finishing "To Sleep," and I closed the book and said the last lines, "Turn the key deftly in the oiled wards, And seal the hushed casket of my soul."

Mother looked up and said, "I suppose they laid the Barnes girl in a pine box today, poor as they all are."

"Yes, Mother. It was pitiful, really. The family didn't have the money for a decent coffin. And there wasn't the usual feasting and visiting after the burial. Everyone left before I had an opportunity to offer my condolences. I found it interesting, too, that Mr. Carruth, the father, didn't come to the funeral. I heard his wife tell an older lady, a friend of hers, I guess, that she didn't know where he'd gone off to. And I noticed that she spoke with a swollen lip."

Mother pulled the lapels of her rose dressing gown tight around her neck. "How terrible! Oh, Leland, I wish I could stop thinking about those two women."

"What women?"

"The two mothers. Mrs. Carruth and Mrs. Barnes, especially Mrs. Barnes."

"Why is that, Mother?"

"My dear, you might well imagine that, if you should marry some day, someone much different from the Barnes girl, of course, and your wife should be killed, well, think how I would feel."

"Tragic no doubt," I said, but I couldn't truly visualize such an occurrence in our lives. I had yet to meet someone I felt strongly enough about to want to marry, let alone someone Mother would approve of. Once, when I was ten, just weeks before my father died of a virulent flu, I had brought home a little girl, Charlene was her name, for tea, and Mother had found her mannerisms deplorable, her nails ragged, her hem uneven, her tangle of dark wild hair heathenish. I had taken a second look then, and I saw what Mother did. Charlene was not invited back. Then when I was attending university up in Oxford, I had met a young lady whose sensibilities seemed more in keeping with ours, but she had an annoying habit of saying "I do declare" over and over, which Mother said would surely drive us into the madhouse in no time. Since then, I have settled into a routine that is most comfortable and pleasurable, and I have decided that, when the right woman comes along, Mother will probably know it before I do. Until then, I couldn't imagine her empathy with Stoney Barnes' mother.

Mother closed her book and removed her glasses. "Leland, of course you can't understand, you'll never bear a child, but if you could, you would sympathize with the boy's mother."

This conversation was the genesis of my idea to do a piece on the two mothers, and the next morning, I drove out to the Barnes' farm to interview Mrs. Jane Barnes. Mrs. Barnes welcomed me into her front parlor and served coffee with plain milk and sugar cookies, which were a bit dry, but I complimented her on them anyway. I think she imagined I was bringing a photographer because she was wearing a two-piece dress with lace collar and cuffs, which I'm sure was reserved for special occasions. Her hair was tightly curled around her lightly powdered face, and although she wore no lip color, her lips were shiny with a Vaseline coating. She was of a nervous disposition, fluttering hands, tapping foot, fussing with strands of her hair that escaped a fake jewel hair clasp.

After twenty minutes or so of a nasal recitation of the history of her family, I was ruing my decision to do the piece, and then Mrs. Barnes led me toward a startling discovery. She had risen from her rocker and brought two photographs from the mantel above the fireplace to show me. "These are Hugh and Earlene's two boys," she said.

I took the wooden frames and said in what I hoped was a sincere voice, "They're handsome lads." One of them was. He resembled Stoney Barnes quite a bit. Dark hair, square face, heavy brows that arched over beautiful eyes. The other boy, the youngest, had a jutting jaw, bucked teeth, and oddly shaped ears which I finally determined were upside down, the fleshy lobe sitting high on the boy's head.

Mrs. Barnes took the photographs back and looked at them again with a maternal smile. She sighed. "It's such a shame Stoney and Sheila couldn't have any children."

I sucked in some air. I certainly had no intention of telling her that her grandchild had been murdered along with her daughter-in-law. I didn't envy whoever would have to give the autopsy report to the family, and I wondered if Stoney Barnes knew that he would have been a father had his wife not been killed. "It is a shame," I said. "I'm sure your son wishes he had a child, too. That would help ease the pain of his great loss."

Mrs. Barnes lined the photographs side by side on the coffee table between us. "Well, he knew that wasn't a possibility, of course."

It took a moment for me to recognize the significance of her words. She, the wife, certainly was able to have one, so it was her son Mrs. Barnes meant. I spoke too quickly and loudly. "He couldn't have children?"

She looked away and clasped her hands in her lap, and I saw that I had offended her. "No. The mumps. No, I don't think I should…it's not something…"

"I apologize for my rudeness," I said. "I'm afraid my question has upset you." I did feel badly for causing her distress, but I wanted to end this interview quickly and rush over to the sheriff's office to share this information. I forced myself to ask a few more questions that Mrs. Barnes was eager to answer, and after complimenting her on her refreshments and lovely home, I finally backed out of her drive and drove as fast as I dared on the winding country roads toward Zebulon.

L L O Y D

When Clyde Vairo drove up in his patrol car, Annette was washing the supper dishes. Rowena had gone in to lie down, saying her pork chops didn't agree with her at all, and I was reading *The Lexie Journal* sitting at the kitchen table Annette had cleared. She had been pouting over the extra chores Rowena had given her, and I had to agree that her mama wasn't in the best of spirits these days. Truth be told, Rowena had become downright ornery and stubborn as a mule. I tried to joke with Annette a little, told her the miracle baby was causing all our troubles, keeping Rowena up all night, kicking her because he was mad as hell that he wasn't gonna get out in time for Santa Claus. Annette didn't laugh though and she snatched the plates off the table and said she wished she could go live with her grandma until the baby was born.

I opened the paper then and ignored her banging the dishes. If she broke something, maybe she'd feel better. I felt like throwing a milk bottle ever' now and then myself. "Daddy," she said. "The sheriff's coming round to the back door."

I laid the paper down and stood up. "Wonder what he's wanting this late?" I walked out on the porch and stuck out my hand to him. "Clyde, what brings you out this time of night?"

"Got some questions I need answered," he said. "How's the wife?"

"She's all right, I guess. Sit down. This one's going hard with her. You want some iced tea, coffee?"

He sat in the far rocker, and I took out my pouch as I sat down beside him. I was pouring the tobacco along the paper when he said what he'd come for. "Lloyd, did you know that the girl, Sheila, was pregnant?"

"Yeah. Well, I knew she told Rowena she thought she was. She hadn't been to the doctor yet." I finished rolling my smoke and lit it.

Clyde rocked back and breathed in deep. "Smell of tobacco always makes me want one, but then when I take a toke, it don't taste like it smells." He laid his head back on the chair. "Well, the girl was right. Autopsy showed a fetus. So Rowena knew and you knew. Did Stoney know? That's my big puzzle."

"I'm not certain on that. Sheila told Rowena she was gonna tell him, but we don't, neither one of us, know if she got the chance before she died. She was planning on telling him the night she was killed. Rowena was supposed to make a cake the next day, and Sheila was gonna tell Annette and they'd have a little celebration. Of course, it never got to that."

"Hmmm. So she must've told her husband. She was planning on it."

"I guess."

Clyde stopped rocking and sat up. "Stoney says he didn't know."

"And you think he's lying?"

"I do."

"Why would he?"

Clyde stood up. "Oh, he had a good reason for lying. A real good one. I'll see you, Lloyd. Gotta get going. It's late, and you dairy farmers get up before the rooster crows."

I went over Clyde's words again in my mind. Stoney had a good reason for lying. He'd done it! Sheila had told him about the baby, and he'd gotten mad over it, and killed her. Hadn't he told me he didn't want any children? But, if he was the murderer, why would he stick around to get caught? It didn't make any sense at all. I knew though that Clyde wouldn't have said what he did without good cause, and I decided that I'd send Stoney out to the field when he came back to work. I didn't want him close to the house until we knew more.

CHAPTER 28

ROWENA

Oh, dear Lord, what will you bring down on this family next? It's only been one week since we buried Sheila, and now this. What have we done to deserve such trouble as you have bestowed on us? Why didn't you give us some kind of warning that Stoney was the one we should fear? I sit here in this small church, looking at your portrait above Brother Yarbrough's head, and your eyes have compassion in them; your raised hands with open palms seem to be saying, "Come to me and I will give you ease." But you haven't offered any comfort. You won't even still this baby inside me that keeps flipping around and pulling on my insides so that I can't get one decent night's sleep. No, you're not seeing to your flock. You aren't listening to my prayers. I may as well be asking one of the cows to help our family overcome these trials you have given us.

And here's Lloyd sitting here beside me with his chin dropped down on his chest. I'm the one who should be nodding off; he is getting plenty of rest. Annette's eyes are fixed on Brother Yarbrough, strutting back and forth in front of the pulpit like he was in a marching band. Mama said we weren't going to be pleased with any preacher under thirty-five, and she was right. I miss Brother Westler. Why'd he have to retire? I guess he's praying on some white sand beach down in Florida this morning. Well, Annette does like our new preacher, and I need to keep my feelings about him inside. Poor Annette. I think Stoney's arrest upset her more than Sheila's death.

A N N E T T E

Dear Sheila, are you up there in heaven? Can you hear me? Are you an angel now, flying above us, seeing what-all has happened? Can you send me a sign to let me know if Stoney killed you or not? I don't believe it. The sheriff is wrong. He didn't do it, did he? Brother Yarbrough keeps talking about forgiveness and turning the other cheek. Did you forgive who murdered you? Was it your papa? Mama told me you were going to have a baby, and when she said that, I cried till my eyes swelled up. To think of a little dead baby. It's too awful. Stoney wouldn't hurt you and he wouldn't hurt his own baby either. If you have any supernatural powers as an angel, could you send us some help? There's too many shadows to walk through now. And I've forgotten how to anyway.

I can feel Mama's eyes on me, boring right through Daddy's suit into my head. They both believe Stoney did it. My own parents were the first ones to call him a murderer. They don't know him like I do. They never saw him kissing you and hugging you, looking at you like you were a special gem that God had sent just for him. But I was with y'all plenty of times to see how it was between you. You wouldn't have loved him so much if you'd thought for one minute that he was capable of choking another person to death. I wouldn't love him if I thought that.

L L O Y D

Love your neighbor, forgive them that do evil. Ha. What horseshit! I say an eye for an eye, and damn them to hell. If Rowena thinks dragging us to church after yesterday's mess is gonna change my feelings, she better think another thought. Who knows what's in her mind these days. She says don't tell Annette about Sheila's baby, and then she goes and tells her herself. She says we ought to think like Christians at a time like this, and she says she hopes Stoney gets the electric chair. I know Annette doesn't believe he did it. She's hanging on to her innocence, not wanting to see the facts as they are. Well, let her. Stoney can't hurt her in jail, but it's gonna go down hard with her when he gets convicted. And he will. I'll have to hire another hand to replace Stoney for the dairy soon. There's a lot of work to be done on the place, too. I should have told Digger to make sure that back fence was gonna hold until we get it fixed proper. That's all I need, half my herd wandering out onto Carterdale Road to get killed by an automobile. I'd say with my luck lately, if Brother Yarbrough ever gets to the benediction, I'll go home to find my Ayrshires dead in the road.

The Lexie Journal
September 16, 1941

STONEY BARNES ARRESTED FOR MURDER!

Stonewall Buford Barnes, age 18, was arrested for alleged-
ly murdering his wife, Sheila Carruth Barnes, on August
31. According to Lexie County's sheriff, Clyde Vairo,
Barnes beat and then strangled his wife, and carried her
body to the cornfield owned by Lloyd Cotton, who was his
employer at Cottons' Dairy. Barnes, a resident of Lexie
County, denies the allegations, but is being held in the
Lexie County jail without bail. His lawyer, William
Calloway, a native of Zebulon, who is senior partner in the
Jackson law firm of Calloway and Green, told this reporter
that evidence he will offer at trial will prove his client's
innocence. — *Leland Graves*

L E L A N D

I had expected my interview with Bill Calloway to be a waste of time. I
would listen to him proclaim his client's innocence in bombastic tones,
and I would be back at Mother's in time for dinner, but my day didn't go
as planned. I assumed that Mrs. Barnes had hired him because the local
lawyer, Randy White, the court-appointed attorney, had not managed to
get bail for her son. I learned from a secretary down at Mechanics State
Bank that Mrs. Barnes had been forced to mortgage their house to pay
Calloway's fee.

The Mechanics State Bank, an impressive two-story building on the corner of Second Street and Locust, is where we met. Calloway was using the offices of his friend, Jeremy Foxx, and Foxx's secretary ushered me in to the conference room, which was furnished with a mahogany table and forest-green leather chairs. On the credenza there was a magnificent brass lamp. Calloway looked exactly right in the surroundings. When I entered the room, he was seated at the end of the table in front of a stack of legal pads, blue-backed vellum documents, and a silver cylinder filled with pens and pencils. As I came toward him, he rose and offered his hand. He was an imposing man. Fifty-plus years old, solid, a bit too thick in the middle, with a mane of hair, not silver, but white. His three-piece suit, of a dark blue hue, covered most of a lighter blue shirt with long collar points. The red and black striped tie was, in my mind, a fashion misstep.

His heavy gold ring cut into my hand. "Leland Graves from the newspaper, correct?"

"Yes. Pleased to meet you, Mr. Calloway," I said taking the seat he indicated. His big teeth shone in the dimly lit room, and suddenly I felt small and insignificant in his presence. I gave myself a quick pep talk by reminding myself that Napoleon was several inches shorter than I. "I've been assigned to follow the trial, as I told you on the telephone, and I'd like to ask you a few questions about your client."

Bill Calloway was relaxation in the flesh. He leaned back in the big leather chair and crossed his legs. "Fine. Will this be your first murder trial?"

How did he know this wasn't a routine assignment for me? "Yes. I was on the society page, but the hard news reporter moved away. I expect my position is temporary." I hoped so.

"But aren't you the fellow who found out that Stoney Barnes is sterile and reported it to the sheriff? That's not cub reporter work. You're obviously an astute young man."

I swelled a little with the compliment, but then wondered if he were saying that — if not for me — the sheriff wouldn't have arrested his client. I had told Sheriff Vairo that here was Stoney's motive. I had said, "Here's our Othello snuffing out the life of his Desdemona." Then, when the sheriff had looked at me with blank eyes, I said, "Jealousy! Murderous jealousy."

"Mrs. Barnes is the one who told me about Stoney's condition," I said.

Calloway leaned forward and clasped his hands over the legal pad in front of him. "Yes, and I'm grateful for her assistance in helping our case along."

I didn't understand his cheerful tone nor how her blunder could be construed as something to be grateful for. "Helping your case?" My pen was poised on my pad, but I hadn't stroked the first curve of one letter until now. I wrote, "Mrs. Barnes helping how?"

"Yes, since the child wasn't conceived by the husband, painful as it is for Stoney Barnes, he now knows that a love triangle existed. His wife, Sheila, such a pretty name, had taken a lover." He smiled at me like he was about to hand me the keys to a new automobile or give me some other extravagant gift. "She had unwisely taken a lover, who went up to her house for a forbidden tryst after her husband left for work. When she rebuffed him and threatened to expose him, he murdered her."

I was writing as fast as my pen would allow. My voice came out loud and adolescent. "Who? Who was the lover?"

Calloway's smile stretched wider. "Oh, we'll find out eventually. I've got an investigator working on it. For now, you just print what you have there. That's the true story of what really happened to that poor girl."

After I left the bank offices, I drove straight to the jail and told Clyde Vairo what Calloway had said to me. "Who do you think it is? Who's the lover?"

Clyde looked annoyed. He needed a shave and he rubbed his cheeks like the stubble was worrying him. "Hell, I don't know. I don't have any evidence of who was sleeping with her, except maybe the papa, and I haven't any hard proof of that."

"Can I see Stoney? Interview him in his cell?"

"Yeah, you can go back there, but he ain't talked much since I locked him up. Just sits on his cot kinda staring at the floor like he don't know where he's at. His lawyer was here a long time this morning. I reckon he talked to him, but he hasn't spoke more'n a few words to me or Sam."

I'd never gone through the locked door that led to the cells behind the sheriff's office, and I wasn't prepared for the stench of urine and stale whiskey and unwashed armpits that assaulted us when the sheriff opened the door. Sheriff Vairo motioned me to follow him down the dark hall that divided the two cells. I looked first to my left where I saw two Negroes sitting on the floor throwing dice. A third black man lay on the stained mattress with his forearm resting across his eyes. They were all barefoot. The man holding the dice wore overalls with no shirt; his hair was shot with gray patches around his temples and ears, and he cocked his head and nodded to me as we passed. The man sitting across from him was much younger and his unbuttoned shirt revealed a huge raised scar that crossed his chest like a hyphen. He greeted us with a lift of his hand and the word "Boss." The third prisoner ignored us, and I decided most of the liquor smell was rising from his damp khaki pants.

Turning to my right I saw Stoney Barnes leaning against the back wall of his cell. Like the sheriff, he needed a shave, but his beard was much darker and heavier. When he saw me, he pushed himself off the wall and walked on his sock feet across to the bars between us. Behind him I could see a mattress partially covered with a rumpled tan blanket, a pillow with no case, a tin slop bucket, a roll of tissue paper beside it, and beyond that a small cardboard box with the words "Astor Golden Delicious" written on its side. Barnes wore loose-fitting jeans with no belt, a blue and green checked shirt with gray buttons, and white socks. He stepped back when Sheriff Vairo opened the door to the cell. "Call me when you're done," he said to me, closing the door behind me.

I stood, uncertain as to jailhouse etiquette. After a moment, I stretched out my hand. "You may not remember me. I'm Leland Graves, reporter for *The Lexie Journal.* I spoke with you at your house, the day of... the day your wife was found."

The boy smiled at me and took my hand. "I remember now. Yeah, you was asking me about how was I gonna feel that night." He leaned against the bars and crossed his ankles. "I reckon you want to know how I feel now being locked up in here."

I pointed to the cot. "May I?" He nodded, and I straightened the blanket a bit and sat on the very edge of the cot and took out my pen and pad. "Yes, I am interested in how you're feeling, what you're thinking."

He began to pace, completing a square. He walked past the bars to the back wall, in front of the bucket and box, back toward the bars inches from my feet. I followed him with my eyes up, across, down, across. I tried not to breathe too deeply each time he passed. Looking around the cell, I saw that there was nowhere to wash. "So you were taken by surprise when you were arrested?"

"Yeah. I reckon I was. Didn't know anybody thought I done it, except old man Carruth." He stopped pacing and looked at me. "I didn't do it. Write that down." Then he continued on his route around his cell. "I was in the peanut patch, pulling peanuts for Mr. Cotton. He said it was best for me not to come down to milk yet what with Sheila's memory still there. So I was out pulling peanuts, the sun weren't high yet, it weren't hot, and I was kinda enjoying being out there alone, and then I looked up and seen the sheriff and Mr. Cotton coming. The sheriff had his hand on his hip like he was ready to draw on me. I ain't sure 'bout what he said for exact, but he said something like, 'Stoney, I got to take you in.' And I says, 'What for, Sheriff?' and he says, 'Murder.'" He shook his head and his dark hair fell across his forehead. "I couldn't get my mind around what he was saying, but I held out my wrists for them cuffs and said, 'All right then. Let's go.'"

The sun, which had been obscured by cloud cover all day, suddenly broke out and an elongated rectangle of light shone through the window, and now Stoney walked in and out of the light as he traversed his course. Dark, light, his face clear and vivid and then shadowed and dim. His monologue followed the same pattern. He smiled speaking of his mother, telling me that she brought his supper to him every night. Then his voice slowed and his tone was mournful. "But I didn't get no bail. I ain't never going home again unless a jury says I'm innocent."

"You think you'll be found not guilty?"

He hesitated. His mouth moved and he nodded as if a disembodied voice was telling him what to say. I suspected the person who was speaking was Calloway. "Can't nobody prove I done it."

Stoney's voice held no conviction and brought to my mind a child's voice denying his naughtiness. "I spoke with your lawyer, Mr. Calloway, and he says that you weren't aware of your wife's infidelity. You didn't suspect that she was having an affair with someone, some other man?"

Stoney walked to where I sat and stood looking down on me. His eyes frightened me, and I'm sure I shrunk back from him just a bit. "*No!* She never let on nothing. She and me, we, we was happy." He looked up at the ceiling as though his wife was there nodding agreement. "She were happy, said so all the time. I satisfied her in ever' way." He looked back down on me. "Ever' way. She didn't need no other man for that."

His reaction was, I knew, typical of a man cuckolded by another. Although I had only experienced a physical relationship with a woman twice, I understood how painful it must be for him to realize that his wife had lain in another's arms.

The stench was getting to me, and my stomach wasn't going to stay settled in place much longer. I needed to ask the question I'd come here for. "Do you know who your wife was seeing? Who the father of the baby is?"

Stoney held onto the bars and turned his back on me. His voice was low and angry and frightening. "Yeah, I know all right. I know him. It's his fault Sheila's dead. He killed her, not me."

I stood up, but stayed safely away from him. "And what is his name?"

Stoney turned and stared at me with such intense hatred spread over his face that I thought for a moment he was going to say my name. But he lifted his hands to his head and ran his fingers through his thick mane of blue-black hair. It was as if he'd just awakened from sleep and realized where he was. His eyes opened wider, revealing his fear. "I ain't supposed to be talking to nobody about my case. You better go."

CHAPTER 30

ROWENA

I might have known Kevin Landry, the prosecutor for Stoney's case, would pick today of all days to come out here to talk about the murder trial. Lloyd thinks the world of him, but I know his type. He's too ambitious for my taste. The good Lord knows I believe in doing your best in this world, getting ahead to give your children a bright future, but his hungering after success is all for himself. Those two children of his look like ragamuffins running around the churchyard, and Eloise, his poor wife, wears run-down heels and doesn't have a decent hat. Last Sunday she had on a cloche that I could see had been patched with thread that didn't match. Lloyd says that a district attorney doesn't have to be a family man to be qualified for the job, and we ought to be glad he's more interested in putting criminals in jail than he is in fashion.

I'll admit he's plenty smart. And with me he was quite the gentleman. You would think he was a knight come to do my bidding as his fair lady. The first thing he said after I brought him a cup of coffee was that I would not be receiving a subpoena due to my "delicate condition." He admired nearly every piece of furniture in the house and he did recognize the copy of Gainsborough's *Mrs. Siddons* hanging over the piano. After two bites of my pound cake, he said he'd greatly appreciate it if I would pass my recipe to Eloise. Even so, I just don't like him. Here lately, lots of folks are getting on my nerves, especially Lloyd. He can't remember two items on a grocery list, and when I asked him to move the couch from beneath the window because the morning sun is fading the fabric, he acted like I'd asked him to move the moon from the sky.

Kevin Landry finally got around to asking me what-all I knew about the murder. I told him we were never as shocked in our whole lives as we were when we found out Stoney was the one who killed Sheila. He asked me if I would be willing to come down to his office and give a deposition about Sheila telling me she was p.g. and how she was going to give Stoney the news on the night she was murdered. He also asked about the morning Stoney reported her missing and what he'd looked like, exactly what he said. I told him so many weeks had passed now that I couldn't be sure my memory would be all that good, but that I'd try my best.

Lloyd came in and Kevin changed like a chameleon. Really, he could be an actor on stage. He went from soft and refined to a man right at home walking over pastures, stomping on cow piles. I looked at his immaculate wing tips and knew his lie. "How's the dairy business?" he asked Lloyd in this booming voice. Lloyd said fine, and then Kevin asked him about our Ayrshires and said he'd heard they were the finest breed of milk cow in the world. I got up to refill his coffee, and by the time I came back into the front room, Kevin had taken out the pad he had written my words on and was writing down what Lloyd said he knew about Stoney and Sheila.

"So that morning, you were an hour late getting down to the barn?"

Lloyd frowned. He didn't like having to admit to that. "Yeah. That one time."

The two of them talked on a while about what would be Lloyd's testimony when he was called to the witness chair, and then Kevin took out another smaller pad and said, "I've got Bill Calloway's witness list here, and I'd like to talk about it with you, Lloyd," he glanced over at me, "in private."

I never felt so insulted in my life. I looked to Lloyd to say that he was a man with no secrets from his wife, but he ducked his head and mumbled, "All right." I stood up. Without a word, I lifted Kevin Landry's cup from the table, opened the front door, and walked out onto the porch. I broke the cup. I don't think I meant to, but somehow it fell from my hand and crashed on the brick walk. I had gotten out the good Haviland china with the patterned rose chain that I only used for special occasions, and when I saw the broken flowers, I burst into tears. I hated Stoney then more than

I believe I've ever hated anyone. This was all his fault. Everything bad that had come into my life was his doing. I wished I could go into that courtroom and testify against him. I wanted to see his face when the jury found him guilty.

Lloyd looked upset when he came out with Kevin Landry. His face was crimson and he took out his handkerchief and wiped his palms. I was cool to both of them. I stood with my chin in the air, holding the broken shards of china, and nodded only slightly as they came down the steps to me. Before he got back into his automobile, Kevin thanked me for my hospitality, but he didn't mention the recipe again. I turned and went up the steps and back into the house to wait for Lloyd to come inside. He would tell me what had just transpired in my own home, and had been kept from me.

But Lloyd didn't tell me a thing. He tried to pretend that Kevin Landry had just wanted the privacy to avoid talking about the ugly details of Sheila's death in front of a "lady so delicate." That was the way Lloyd put it. I wasn't fooled one bit. His face wasn't that color because of me. He made hurried excuses and scuttled down to the barn like a rat running for grain.

By the time Lloyd returned for his dinner, I was loading my suitcase into Mama's Buick. I told him that I was going to live with Mama whom I could trust and who didn't keep secrets from me. I didn't risk looking at his or Annette's faces as Mama backed over the camellia bush and turned out onto Carterdale Road.

ANNETTE

Daddy really goofed up this time. I didn't know what the fuss was about, but whatever it was must have been a doozy. We both knew Mama's mind was teetering, and I judged that Stoney's upcoming trial had sent her over the cliff. Or it could have been the baby that made her plummet over the edge.

It seemed like overnight, her stomach had ripened like a prize pumpkin that couldn't sit still on the vine. One minute all of her baby-filled womb would be riding below her breastbone and the next it would lurch over to her left side, nearly throwing her off balance. Other times Mama's belly would quiver and then roll across the front of her like a lava flow. The baby wouldn't stop its acrobatic feats long enough for poor Mama to sleep anywhere. She tried the couch, the guest bed, the porch daybed, and then she moved into my own sanctuary. One morning I had found her there crying all over my pillowcase.

I tiptoed in. "Mama?"

She wiped her wet cheeks and sat up on my bed. "I'm a freak. Just a sideshow freak."

She was really, so I studied the yellow-ruffled curtains and wondered what was an appropriate response to an ugly truth. Finally, I decided to blame it on the baby. "You're not the freak, Mama." I pointed to her lurching stomach. "It is." Mama's face crumbled and she began to cry loud enough for Daddy to hear her down at the barn. I tried to help with good advice. "Maybe you could try listening to some waltzes or lullabies. Sing it to sleep like we did for Lil' Bit when he got overtired."

Mama laid back down. I wanted her out of my bed and back in hers, but I didn't know how to evict her. She mumbled something. "What?"

"Lil' Bit. I want him, not, not," she gasped, just saying the treacherous words, "not this crazy baby." Then she covered her face with her hands. "I didn't mean that, Annette. You know I don't mean it."

I thought she certainly did mean it, but I said, "I know you don't. Grandma said this baby is unsettled because of all the goings-on since it started sprouting up inside you. It may have heard all the talk about Sheila's murder, the funeral, Stoney getting arrested." My selfish motives rose up then. "And you've been mad at me a lot lately. The baby might be agitated by all your fussing. You need to start paying more attention to what you're doing and saying."

As I said these words, something momentous happened. A new element turned up inside me, a purple mist that coated all of my organs with a radiant glow. This powerful aura, floating out of my body, soared out into the room and wafted around me. It smelled like magnolia blossoms, so sweet that my best perfume seemed as putrid as stinkweed. I turned away from Mama, scared she would ruin the moment. I walked to my dresser and searched my face in the mirror looking for evidence of my transformation. Although I looked the same physically, there was a hint of something new and different about this girl with more womanly eyes than any near twelve-year-old I knew. Maturation was coming on me like a blizzard in July. I could nearly feel my breasts growing, hair sprouting between my legs and under my arms. The color of womanhood is purple, I thought, and now as a full-grown woman, I could give advice, point out Mama's errors and mistaken ideas. I pivoted toward her and saw submission on her face.

She nodded. "Maybe you're right. I have been upset throughout most of this baby's time on earth. With you, I was calm, had no more to worry about than what day I would prune the roses." She sat up and tried to hug her knees. Her face took on the glow of soft memories. "Your daddy was different back then too. He would lie with his head on my stomach and talk to you like he could see you laughing when he told a corny joke." Mama was smiling big now, and I felt a wonderful relief inside my purple body. "And you know, we did listen to Brahms and Handel and Strauss. Doris and Leda and Mama and I would sit on the sofa and drink sassafras tea while the music drifted out from the console radio. My papa would come in and take turns dancing with us girls. And then your daddy would come to take me home, and he would cock his hat, offer me his arm like a swell, and we'd dance down the hall out to the buggy we had back then." She was crying again, but the tears were the nice surprising kind that people aren't so quick to wipe away.

I was thinking she was about to get her fanny off my bed and back to Daddy's and hers where she belonged when her crying signaled a back-slide to her earlier misery. "Oh, Annette," she wailed. "What's the world come to? Why can't everything be like it used to?"

I sat down on the bed then, my purple feeling fading, and I felt a terrible rage building up inside me. What right did she have to ask me questions like that? She was the mother, the one who was supposed to have all the answers. Suddenly, I felt cold and scared. If your own mother doesn't know what-all is happening on this green earth, who does? What if Stoney did kill Sheila? Or what if he didn't do it, but was found guilty anyway? Sheriff Vairo would send for the traveling electric chair, and Stoney would fry like a slab of bacon. I saw his eyes bulging out of their sockets, his hands turning black, his beautiful hair in flames. I fell over on Mama's big stomach and held on to the bucking baby who was practicing his punches for all the fighting he somehow knew life would require.

If Mama wasn't an A student on the answers to life's questions, Daddy was about to flunk out. When I finally got Mama out of my room and back into hers, Daddy was less thrilled than I had thought he would be. Mama's fussing fits were mere warm-ups for her attacks on Daddy, who had no intelligent defense. Grandma told him the hormones made her throw the iron against the wall when he forgot to buy grapefruit in town. And it must have been hormones that made her cry for over an hour when Daddy told her he was too tired to take her to the picture show. I knew their married bliss didn't include the words "rapture" and "ravished," but I was sure that they loved each other. Until now. Now their loud voices traveled down the hall and into my bedroom and angrily bumped me out of peaceful sleep.

I covered my ears with a pillow, but I could still hear the unexpected roar of my good-natured father and the shrill cry of my gentle mother. I longed then for my Best Friend Sheila. She knew how to handle discord better than anyone in the world.

But Sheila was dead and Mama had never been more alive as she loaded up her suitcase filled with maternity clothes, Pears soap, and the good linen tablecloth that needed ironing. She turned to me and said, "Annette, you're in charge now. Feed your Daddy and keep the bathroom picked up. Wet towels will mildew." Then she marched out of the house with her jumping-jack baby and stood in the drive waiting for Grandma to come and rescue her.

Before Mama and Grandma drove off, Daddy came up from the barn. He stood silently beside Grandma's Buick with the look I saw on his face when one of his Holsteins came down with hoof and mouth. "Aren't you going to stop her?" I asked him as we both gaped at her through the passenger window. She was sitting ramrod straight staring out the front windshield as though she didn't know two pairs of astonished eyes were boring into the side of her head.

"Nope," Daddy said. "Her mind's made up. No use in trying to make sense of her now." He waved to his runaway wife and then stepped back from the car. As we watched the Buick bump over the camellia bush and buck out of the drive toward Carterdale Road, Daddy lifted his arm, "Good-bye, Rowena," he called after them. Then he turned back to me and said, "Well, what's for supper, Annette?"

CHAPTER 31

LLOYD

I couldn't tell Rowena yet. She'd have to know eventually, and maybe if I'd come out with it, she wouldn't have left us and gone over to her mama's. The way I saw it though was that a change of scene might be just what the doctor ordered. She wasn't getting enough sleep, the baby was twisting her guts up like a knotted rope, and she couldn't quit thinking about how she had been entertaining a murderer in her parlor. Over at her mama's she'd most likely sleep better and she'd get the pampering from her mother she was craving for. Meantime, I had to figure the best way to tell her what I would have to hit her with when she came home.

Hell, there wasn't nothing in this world I could do or say to make Rowena feel better when it came time to tell her that Virgie Nell Jackson was the name on Bill Calloway's list that Kevin Landry asked me about. What me and Virgie Nell's little fling twelve years ago had to do with Stoney's murder trial had been a mystery to me, and I said as much to him that day he came out to the dairy. "You're sure Calloway is calling her to testify for Stoney?"

Kevin had tapped his pencil on the line where her name was printed in block letters. "Yes. She's on the list."

"But why do you think she's going to tell about our affair? Maybe it's something else."

Kevin frowned. "I don't think so. The word from the rumor mill is that Bill Calloway snooped around town until he heard the old gossip your sister-in-law, Leda, spread about your and Virgie Nell's affair, and that's the reason he's calling her to testify."

"But how would that help Stoney's defense?"

Kevin took a deep breath and looked me square in the face. "Sheila was having an affair with someone. The baby wasn't Stoney's. He's sterile."

It was like hearing Rowena wasn't born on earth, was from some planet far away in the sky. I couldn't get my mind around what he was saying. It was just crazy. Sheila wasn't laying with another man, not in my tenant house. Then I thought of the time in the barn when I'd guessed that her papa had been at her. Stoney had thought so too, hadn't he? "Well," I said, "my God, it could be her papa's baby. I thought he might be coming round there, suspected him of it."

Kevin was staring at the piano like it was going to start playing a song on its own accord. "I don't think Calloway believes it was him."

"Well, then who? Who else could it be?" When I asked him that question, I felt a rushing in my head that sounded like a gale wind blowing through the tops of our pines. I could nearly feel Sheila's hump in my hands, her forehead against my lips. Kevin didn't say anything, just kept his eyes on the piano. I said my next words in a near whisper. "They're gonna say it was me. That I'm the father of the baby."

Kevin Landry's next words were like fists striking my gut. "I think that's right. Virgie Nell Jackson will testify that you had an affair with her, and then Calloway will say you had another one with Sheila Barnes."

My first thought was that this was going to kill Rowena; or more practically, she could lose our baby. So later that day, when I saw her getting in her mama's car, I was so relieved that I wouldn't have to look at her accusing face, I felt plumb numb with an odd kind of happiness. I imagine it's the way a man feels when a doctor tells him his chest pains are just gas. He knows he's gonna have that heart attack one day, but for now, he can just belch away his pain. I knew I was a coward and that I was gonna have to face what was coming, but not yet, I said to myself. Not yet.

The following night I went over to Howard's house; we sat at his kitchen table, where we usually played poker, and talked it over. My big brother has always been known around town as the ladies' man, not me. I thought he might know better how to handle this situation, but he kept shuffling the worn deck of cards like he didn't know how to deal them. He said, "Lloyd, you got any proof that you didn't fuck her?"

I held my head in my hands and raked my fingers through my hair. "No, but there isn't any proof that I did either. I think it's her old man's kid. I think he went up to her house and beat her up and raped her. Maybe more than once."

"But he'll say he didn't. And that lawyer will say you are the one that's already screwed around on your wife. Hell, Mrs. Carruth must have twenty kids, when would he have time to fuck somebody else?" He was grinning, trying to make me feel better, but nothing short of Landry calling and saying it was all a mistake was gonna make me smile ever again.

Howard began laying the cards out face up. Five-card stud. He dealt four hands. He held an ace high and across from him a pair of queens stared at him. He raked the cards back in. "Shit," he said. "Lloyd, I know you got worries enough, but I think you're not looking at the whole sky here. You're just seeing a little piece of it hanging over your head."

I watched him shuffle the cards. Listened to the rhythm of them falling against each other, then the tapping as he began again. I said, "Okay, what do I need to know about the sky over China or wherever you think I ought to be looking at it?"

He stopped shuffling and held the deck in his right hand. I could smell the eggs and bacon he'd cooked for supper still lingering over the table. "It's this. We know Stoney is gonna accuse you of screwing his wife, being the daddy of that baby." I nodded yes to that. "But he's not on trial for not being the parent; he's up for murder."

"Howard, what do you take me for, a mule in the field? I know all that."

"Shut your trap a minute. Just listen to me. The only reason he could have for making you out to be his wife's lover is that he's gonna say that you killed her."

I don't remember getting up, but I saw the chair on the floor lying on its side. My fists hit the table. "No," I said. "He can't say that. He can't accuse me."

Howard stayed calm. That's the way he is when he's about to lose a big poker pot, calm, his breath coming out smooth and even, like he's about to fall asleep. "Lloyd, you better get yourself a lawyer."

I didn't hire a lawyer, but I went down to Kevin Landry's office and asked him did he think I was gonna be accused. "You're not on trial, Lloyd. Clyde Vairo hasn't arrested you. All Calloway will be trying to do is cast doubt in the minds of the jury so that they can't convict Stoney. There isn't a shred of evidence to support his theory that you killed the girl."

I leaned over his scarred desk covered with books and papers and pushed my face up close to his. "You better be right about this, because everybody in this town is going to know about me and Virgie Nell, and if you don't get a conviction, some of them are going to think I did kill Sheila."

On my way back from town, I pulled into Rowena's mama's yard and sat in the truck for five minutes or so. I couldn't open the truck door. I sat frozen there, just staring out the windshield at Mama Bancroft's gray house. I looked over at my face in the rearview mirror and saw the fear my eyes were holding. "Not yet," I said. Then I backed out of the drive and drove on home.

ROWENA

I knew it was time to go home. Annette and Lloyd needed me, and I wasn't doing right staying over at Mama's eating chicken pie, reading magazines, and taking a nap whenever I felt like it. Mama was so thrilled to have my company, she fussed over me like I was royalty. I could nearly forget all my troubles, and it was hard to think about returning home to what-all I knew I'd have to face. Every time I telephoned Annette, she was on the verge of tears; I knew she worried I wasn't coming back, but still, I sat in Mama's parlor, rocking my little baby who had finally calmed himself in my womb.

Then Lloyd telephoned and said he was coming to get me, that he couldn't take my being gone any longer. He said that he was ready to tell me what Kevin Landry had told him and it was best that I hear about it in my own home where I belonged. Then he said the words that I was waiting to hear. "Rowena, I love you more than life itself. I need you, honey. Please come home."

It was worse than I could possibly imagine. I sat on the side of our bed watching Lloyd pace around the room as he told me all that had happened in the six days I'd been away. I couldn't believe it. How anyone in this world could think that Lloyd and Sheila had...I couldn't even say that out loud. And Stoney! I wanted to go straight down to that jail and strangle him myself. How could he do this to us? To the people who had been so good to him, giving him a job, a home, helping them out time and again. "You go talk to him," I said to Lloyd. "Tell him it's not true, tell him to make his lawyer stop this insanity."

Lloyd said it wouldn't do any good to talk to Stoney or that Mr. Calloway, his lawyer, who was probably the one who came up with the idea to accuse Lloyd. I agreed with that; I couldn't credit Stoney with sense enough to think of it.

"Annette will have to be told," I said. "We should tell her before she hears about it at school or somewhere else."

Poor Lloyd literally groaned out loud. "God, I'd give anything not to have to tell her. It's bad enough causing you so much pain. If only I hadn't..."

I went to him then and put my arms around him. "Lloyd, this isn't your fault. I forgave you a long time ago for the other. Annette will forgive you too." I felt his muscles beneath my hands, and I dug my fingers into his shirt, hanging on to him, wondering if she would forgive him, realizing with a cold fear coming on me that I didn't know what thoughts might be in my own daughter's head.

ANNETTE

My happiness over Mama's coming home evaporated like rain on a hot tin roof when Daddy called me into the kitchen for a family meeting. I slid into my usual chair, back to the stove, and looked over at Mama, who was hugging her arms close to her body. Daddy didn't look too good either. His normally sunburnt face had turned to the color of a bar of Ivory soap, and his deep voice rose to soprano a couple of times as he told me the unbelievable news. My own daddy had had an affair with another woman, and she was going to tell the whole world about it. No, that wasn't possible. My daddy was a churchgoer, a good husband and provider, a father who played Chinese checkers with his daughter and never got mad when he lost. It was all lies.

"No! It's not true!" I yelled at him.

Daddy reached across the table and took my hand in his. "It was a long time ago. A terrible mistake. Your mother forgave me."

I snatched my hand back. I hated him. I hated men and their stupid things that hung between their hairy legs, and I hated God for making us all have desires we couldn't control. I stood up. "You committed adultery. You sinned."

Daddy's face fell about a mile, and I was afraid he was going to cry. I didn't dare look at Mama who was so quiet I had nearly forgotten she was sitting beside him. Daddy's voice was firm. "Sit down." He grabbed my arm and pushed me back onto my chair. "Listen to me, Annette. As much as I'd like to be, I'm not perfect. No one is. There isn't a single person walking on this earth who won't make a mistake at some time in his life. You'll make your own mistakes, and I hope you'll remember this day when you do and find forgiveness from the people who you hurt."

I knew I wasn't going to commit adultery. I wasn't going to grow up to be like him. But then I remembered Aunt Doris. I had prayed for her to die. I had lusted after Stoney, and he was a married man, just like Daddy. Maybe Grandma was right; the fruit doesn't fall too far from the tree. I bowed my head. I didn't know if I could forgive him, but I hated hurting him too.

Daddy stood up and held out his arms. "I love you, and I'm sorry you're suffering."

I let him hug me, but I didn't hug him back.

Mama made a little sound, like she was going to start bawling out loud, but she held herself back. "Annette, there's more you'll have to know."

Daddy let go of me and walked to the back door. "You should be the one to tell her, Rowena. A daughter needs her mama at times like this." Then he was gone and I stared over at Mama. Her face color deepened to near plum, but she patted Daddy's chair for me to sit in, and said, "Annette, there's a reason Virgie Nell Jackson is going to tell about her and Daddy."

She told all of it. Stoney couldn't have children. Mama said she didn't want to get into the why of it, but that it was so. Sheila's baby had to have been fathered by some other man, and Stoney's lawyer was going to try and make people believe that that man was my daddy. That my father could be perceived as a seducer of a young girl was monstrous. I saw him daily in his white shirt, with the embroidered red letters over the pocket that said "Cottons' Dairy." He smelled of milk and cow manure and Vitalis hair lotion on Sundays when he wore his blue suit with the gray and white swirl tie. I saw him with his brown hair matted with sweat beneath a straw hat, then wet-combed into a straight part on the left side under his gray fedora. Like most country men, he was stingy with words and money, but he had always been generous and kind to his family and hired help. I could no more picture him lying with Sheila in some narrow bed than I could imagine myself astride one of the camels standing in front of the pyramids of Egypt in the drawings I had seen in my history book. The notion seemed that exotic. And yet, yet there was the idea of it. Who knew what images were in people's heads when they smiled and nodded at you on the street in town. And if they saw you as a camel-rider, did that make you more likely to sit atop one someday?

No, I knew that no matter what anyone thought, no matter what mistakes Daddy had made in his life, he would never never lie in a bed with my Best Friend. I said this to Mama, and she looked like I had told her the best news she'd ever heard. She pulled me out of my chair and hugged me so tightly, I thought for a moment or so that the baby was kicking in my stomach instead of hers.

I headed out to the fig tree to sort things out in my mind. I climbed to the highest branch and sat staring up into the charcoal sky. If Daddy hadn't lain with Sheila, and Stoney couldn't be the baby's father, who had Sheila loved besides him? She had lied all those times she told me how much she loved Stoney. I closed my eyes and saw her wispy hair falling over blue eyes, the ugly hump that now took on greater proportions. I heard her stupid giggles, her moronic jokes. I had thought she was so wise, telling me on this very limb how to walk through shadows, but she was dumb. Her shadow was big and dark, and she was a sinner. Sheila wasn't my Best Friend; she wasn't a friend at all. She had told her big secret to Mama, not me, and she had lied about my hair curling too. Angry tears came, fast and hard and warm on my cheeks. I wiped my nose with the back of my hand. "You're no angel, Sheila. You're burning in hell, and I'm glad because I hate you. I hate you."

CHAPTER 32

LELAND

Bill Calloway gave me a scoop for my story for the Thursday edition of *The Lexie Journal.* Since my discovery about Stoney Barnes' sterility, I had begun to like the word "scoop," deciding that one didn't have to affect the mannerisms of a callow young reporter to be an ace in the field of journalism. My writing style precluded anyone from putting me in the same category as a hack, and I was beginning to feel comfortable with my role as hard news reporter. Truth be told, I suspect most of us human beings have a fondness for detective work; solving riddles and puzzles does satisfy one's innate curiosity. And while I certainly don't plan on journalism as a lifetime profession, it suits me until I complete my novel. So I wasn't offended when Bill Calloway telephoned me at the office and asked me to come over.

And what a scoop he gave me! After I left Calloway's office at the bank, my first thought was to rush back to my desk and let my fingers fly over the keys of my old Underwood. My copy was sure to be read and talked about by the citizens of Zebulon, but by the time I got to my Pontiac and had driven no more than a quarter-mile, I chided myself on my overeagerness. Something about Calloway's readiness to feed me information about his upcoming case didn't ring true, and I decided I needed to investigate things further before I wrote my next piece on the Stoney Barnes murder case.

I thought about driving out to Cottons' Dairy to interview Mr. Cotton again. Did he know that Bill Calloway was accusing him of being the father of Sheila Barnes' baby? And if he did know, had he figured out that Calloway was trying to throw suspicion on him as the murderer? But I turned my automobile around before I reached the dairy. He would say it was all a lie, of course. What else could he say but that? On the drive back into town, I thought about Lloyd Cotton and his comely wife and sweet little girl. They were a family right out of a children's storybook. Oh, Mr. Cotton was a bit rough around the edges, but clean his boots of cow manure and put him in a proper suit, and he could pass for a gentleman. I couldn't believe him capable of murder.

But he was an adulterer; Calloway said there was plenty of proof of that in Virgie Nell Jackson's deposition. I had bumped into Miss Jackson several times over the course of the last few years, and I now recalled a brief conversation we had maybe two months prior in the post office while waiting for Mr. Gravier to open his window. I had been embarrassed by her flirtations. She is most definitely not someone Mother would welcome into our parlor, and I remember thinking that Mother would swoon at the sight of her large breasts spilling over the top of her dress. I admit it took considerable effort to force my eyes up to her crimson lips, rouged cheeks, blonde curls that spilled down over her forehead. If Miss Jackson had not been so heavy-handed with the makeup, I saw that she might be quite lovely, even though she was on the downslide of her thirties. Still I couldn't visualize Lloyd Cotton and her together.

When I returned to town, I stopped by the Lexie County courthouse intending to run up to the second floor where Kevin Landry occupies a corner office. The Lexie County courthouse is, in my opinion, the ugliest building in our town. Our county board voted to tear down the beautiful old neoclassical gem that had served our citizens since the early eighteen hundreds and hired a German architect, named Grunewald, to design a "modern utilitarian courthouse." The result of Grunewald's efforts is a three-story red-brick edifice that resembles a department store. Nature provides the courthouse's only beauty. Lacy light green ivy grows up the left side of the building and a magnificent two-hundred-year-old magnolia shades the brick walk leading up to the center door, which opens into a foyer where a line of stern-faced judges frown down from the walls upon those who pass beneath them. The center stairs lead to the offices of the circuit clerk, the archives library, and the district attorney's offices. Behind them lies the courtroom itself, where what was now dubbed "The Dairy Murder Trial" would begin the following week.

I peeked into the courtroom, and seeing that it wasn't occupied, I stepped inside. I imagined a film director panning the scene with his camera. Directing the lens from right to left, he would first show the windows that looked out onto the parking lot where Cab Nelson, Zebulon's oldest citizen, sat on a bench already dozing in the early morning sun. Inside beneath the window, sat the court stenographer's small desk, and five feet beyond was the raised witness box beside the judge's bench. Flanking the judge were the U.S. flag and the Mississippi state flag and between them hung a framed replica of our state's seal. Panning on across the judge's high bench, there was the closed door which would open to admit the judge, the prisoner, the guard and bailiff. Beside the door two steps led up to the jury box, where two rows of folding chairs were unevenly aligned, awaiting the citizens who would decide Stoney Barnes' fate.

The upcoming murder trial would be the first to occur in over a decade in Lexie County. There had been several other murders, but none of them had gone to trial. One, which had been covered by my predecessor, was the murder of a Mr. Otis Fancher, who had been shot by his neighbor, Sidney Odom, for severely beating Odom's five-year-old son after the boy had dropped the oak bucket into the well the two families shared. Fancher was shot in the back after he jumped off his porch and ran across his yard trying to escape Odom's double-barrel. When the sheriff and another neighbor had gone to Odom's field to arrest him, he had handed the hoe he was using to scrape cotton to his son, reached into his coveralls, handed his wife a crumpled one-dollar bill. He then turned to the men, saying in a soft mournful voice, "I kilt the son-of-a-bitch, all right. Let's go." Before they took him away, he looked at his wife and said, "That dollar's all we got. Spend it wisely." Sidney Odom served two years for the murder and was released on parole to go home to help his family before they starved to death. No one, not even Mrs. Fancher, was sorry Otis Fancher was dead.

She told the sheriff that Sidney Odom spoke true when he called him a son-of-a-bitch and gave testimony on Odom's behalf to the parole board.

I walked over to the defense table and sat in the chair from which Stoney Barnes would view the proceedings. I heard a noise in the back of the courtroom and quickly turned around, feeling I had been caught in some unlawful or immoral act, but I had no idea what. The woman standing just inside the door hadn't seen me, and I sat quietly observing her. I had seen her once before, at Sheila Barnes' funeral, but I hadn't had the opportunity to meet her. I guessed her to be around twenty-five years old, and although big-boned and sun-browned, she was quite beautiful with rich red hair piled high on her head. She wore a lemon-yellow suit and beige high heels, and as she began to come toward me, she seemed to glide across the room on her long legs. I stood and cleared my throat.

Startled, the woman stopped and her hand reached for the back of the courtroom bench beside her. "Are you Mr. Calloway?" she asked.

"No." I started up the center aisle toward her. "I'm Leland Graves, reporter for *The Lexie Journal*." I stretched out my hand to her.

She hesitated, but then proffered her gloved fingers. "I'm Earlene Barnes," she said. "I was looking for Mr. Calloway. I thought, I thought, he said to meet him here." She looked around the room. "But maybe I got it wrong."

"His office is in the Mechanics State Bank building," I told her. "Maybe he's waiting for you there."

"Oh, god! I think he did say the boardroom, not courtroom." I could see the yellow flecks in her brown eyes as she lifted them, and I found myself searching for a reason to delay her just a bit longer.

"Barnes, you said. Are you related to Stoney, then?"

She frowned. Almost a pout, impossible for her full mouth to lose its loveliness. "Sister-in-law."

My spirits fell. "You're married to the oldest son, then. Hugh, I believe?"

"Yes." She seemed nervous now, upset. Her eyes went to her feet.

"And then you must be the mother of the two fine boys Mrs. Barnes showed me photographs of when I had the pleasure of visiting her home."

She smiled, and I admired her straight white teeth, the dimple on her left cheek. "Yes, guilty of the crime of mothering two hooligans." But then her smile was gone as if she remembered why she had come here. "I shouldn't say guilty in this room."

"Oh, if these walls could talk, they would repeat guilty and not guilty verdicts for days. Months. Years." Why, I chided myself, are you trying to be facetious; she will think you only ridiculous. I searched for something more impressive to say to her. She would be gone in seconds. "May I escort you to the bank building?"

I nearly ruined our parting with that question. She looked offended, lifted her shoulders, and pivoted on her toes toward the door. "No thank you. I'm sure I can find Mr. Calloway without assistance." Her hand was on the door. She turned. "I'm glad I met you though. And, well, I don't know what's come over me, but I want you to know, I'm pleased it was you I saw today."

"Me too," I said. I think I may have blushed. "Thank you." I stood in the courtroom doorway watching her walk down the hall until she left the building. "Thank you for what?" What was wrong with me? Earlene Barnes was a married woman with two children. She was also the sister-in-law to a man who may well have murdered his wife. No, I wouldn't think of her anymore. I needed to keep my mind on the upcoming trial.

CHAPTER 33

STONEY

Tomorrow I got to go to court. Ma brought me some nice clothes to wear. Brand new shirt and trousers good enough for church. Mr. Calloway said I need to look like a stand-up citizen. I figure it don't matter much, but I says okay to him. And Ma, she wants to believe her buying them clothes will save me. But there ain't nothing on this earth that will save me. No, they're gonna execute me. I know they will. I sit on my cot here in this cell and see the wall across the room, and I see the word "guilty" carved into the stone. At night Sheila comes in here and lays beside me, and whispers, "Guilty, guilty, guilty." Over and over she says the word, and then she cries for me. She still loves me. She knows it's Hugh's fault, not mine. It's Hugh they ought to strap in the electric chair, not me. He done it as sure as if he'd put his hands around her neck and choked out her life.

I told him so. I told him it were his fault the night I went over there after the funeral. I had to wait a long time for my chance 'cause he run off to Jackson on the day Sheila were found. But he came back after we put Sheila in the ground. I had left her grave and gone straight home, and Miss Cotton come by with some pie for me, and I ate that. I seen the bottle of hooch Hugh had left that last night he come up to my place, and I drunk up the rest of it. Then Daddy come by and told me that Hugh and the boys was back from Jackson. He was mad they had missed the funeral, and I was surprised at that. I reckon he liked Sheila a lot, but he hadn't never showed it. After Daddy left, I knew I had to drive over to Hugh's and kill him for what he had done to Sheila. Ma would have to survive it. I couldn't do nothing else.

I remember I had my gun sitting on the truck seat where Sheila always sat. I run off the road once into a ditch and I had a helluva time getting the truck out 'cause it were muddy and the tires kept spinning. But I got there all right. The house was dark, so I shined my truck beam on the porch so's I could see to shoot Hugh when he come out. I stood in the yard and hollered for him, but it were Earlene who come out first. I reckon she seen the gun 'cause she started screaming "no" or "don't" or something like that, and went running back into the house. Before I knowed it, Hugh was diving off the porch, coming at me fast. He wrestled the gun away from me and it went skidding across the yard. I don't remember what-all I called him, but ever' time I hit him, I said what he done. "Sheila told me. You forced her," is what I said. And he wasn't hitting me hard; it was like I were fighting a girl.

Then all of a sudden, he pins me on the ground and says that she wanted it, that she liked him better than me. "You're lying," I said. "She cried when she told me how you hurt her so bad when you done it." Then I told him everything about that night that Sheila died. I told all of it, and I was glad of it. I heaved him off, but before I could get up, he lit out across the yard. I chased him, but I don't know where he went to 'cause I never found him. I was gonna go after him in the truck, but it were the next morning when I waked up behind the wheel and seen I'd hit a tree. Hugh's truck was gone and Earlene wouldn't answer the door, so I went back home.

If'n Hugh comes back, I'll find a way to get outta this jail and I'll do what I should've done that night. I'll kill him. But he ain't coming back till they strap me in the chair and I take my last breath. When Mr. Calloway asked me how come my brother run off like that, I said what Earlene was telling Ma and anybody who asked — that he had business in Memphis to attend to. I ain't saying no more about it, and when Earlene went to her meeting with Mr. Calloway, she probably didn't tell him nothing. But she knows that when he comes back, I'm gonna kill him. She knows, but I'll bet he ain't coming back until I'm gone from this earth.

Mr. Calloway is smart though. I don't know if he believed Earlene's story, but he's hunting with another dog now. Virgie Nell Jackson gave him that dog when she told about her and Mr. Cotton. Mr. Cotton could've been the one who forced her. I seen the way he looked at her, and there was that time she showed him her titties on the night I asked her to marry me. I said to my lawyer, "He could be the one." But I'm the one they're gonna electrocute. I know it. No matter what Virgie Nell Jackson says from the witness box, ain't nobody in this town gonna believe that Mr. Cotton done it. Mr. Calloway keeps telling Ma that I'll get to go home, that all we need is doubt in the minds of the jurors. "They won't convict unless they're positive he did it," he said to her. "I'll get your boy off." And Ma, she kept grabbing his hands, saying, "Thank you," like he were Jesus about to perform a miracle.

Jesus does forgive us for our sins, and I reckon that's a kind of miracle 'cause I ain't never gonna forgive Hugh. If he hadn't done what he done, Sheila wouldn't be in the ground. If'n I get to kill him, I hope Jesus don't forgive him. I hope he sends him to hell where he burns for eternity. I won't go to hell. I'll be up in heaven because Jesus knows how much I loved her. Love her still, even through death.

CHAPTER 34

ROWENA

I am trying to take care of myself for the baby's sake. I truly am, but Lloyd keeps fussing over me like a mother hen and doesn't believe I'm eating enough, or resting enough, or, my lord, taking care of my skin. Just last night he came in with the lotion to rub on my stomach, said I was scratching in my sleep. I took the bottle, but something came over me, and it flew out of my hands and went right past his head. Lloyd says I'm furious with him and won't admit it. I guess maybe he's right. Yesterday Virgie Nell Jackson testified at Stoney's trial, and now the whole town of Zebulon and half the people living in the State of Mississippi know that Lloyd left my bed for hers. I have forgiven him. At least I thought I had, but it's like twelve and a half years of my life have been stripped away, and I feel just like I did when I first found out about the two of them. Lloyd said he could've lied to me, made up some excuse for his truck being parked in front of Virgie Nell's house, and wasn't I grateful he told me the truth. Well, no, no I was not grateful. He only admitted it because he wanted forgiveness. I remember him saying how much this had tortured him. Him!

Mama wouldn't come over this morning when I telephoned her and asked her if she'd like to have coffee with me. She won't talk about the trial. All she said when I told her about Virgie Nell's testimony was "Rowena, you'd best stay home for a while. You're getting too big to show yourself in town anyway." Mama, and, well, a lot of people think a lady who's p.g. shouldn't go out in public much. She says a ripe womb is proof of a man's knowledge of the woman, but the old ways are changing now. I read in *Liberty* magazine that, if we get into the war, women might have to take some of the jobs men have been doing all these years. And women could too. Leda says that she and Sylvia are already planning to form a female brigade should war come. I believe, if she could, Leda would strap on a pair of aviator goggles and fly to Europe to drop bombs on the Germans. But Leda doesn't have a husband to worry about like I do. She can do as she pleases, but me, a married woman, I have to sit here in my house, humiliated and branded by the town as "the woman scorned by her husband for another." I can just imagine what-all folks are saying. "Poor Rowena Cotton." And the men! Oh, they'll wink at Lloyd behind my back. They'll all be thinking of Virgie Nell's big breasts when they look at me. I might as well be wearing the big scarlet "A" like in Mr. Hawthorne's novel. And I'm not the one who committed adultery.

Lloyd has been called to testify tomorrow, and I can tell he's nervous by the way he keeps whistling. He's driving me mad with it. It's a soft little "wheet wheet wheet" that sounds like a little bird, and every time there's a lull in the conversation, he starts up with it. Annette noticed it too and asked me what was wrong with her daddy. I told her to just quit being so hard on her parents, judging us by every little thing we say and do. Then I felt bad when her eyes got watery, and I told her we would get through this. And we will. Somehow. But I don't know how yet.

L L O Y D

Leland Graves tried to get a statement from me after I left the courtroom, but I told him nothing doing. That little fellow is getting pushy, sticking his nose in everybody's face, scribbling on that pad like he's Moses writing on the tablets. Hell, what was there to say anyhow? I'm being falsely accused and there's not a damn thing I can do about it. Kevin Landry did get me the chance to say I hadn't had any affair with Sheila Barnes and that I didn't know who was the father of her baby. I hated to hurt Mrs. Carruth, God knows she's been through enough, but I said how I thought maybe it was Sheila's own father. I knew though that my words were spilled milk. Worthless. Stoney's lawyer, that Mr. Calloway, twisted my words around to where I got so confused up there on the witness stand that it sounded like I had something to hide. Calloway suggested that Rowena had left me and gone to her mama's because she found out I was the father of Sheila's baby. I tried to tell him that wasn't the reason, but he shut me up and said I could only answer the questions he asked. The law ought to be changed on that. There ought to be a way for a man to defend himself from lying lawyers. And goddamn Kevin Landry, he didn't do his job, just sat there in his chair with his head down, looking at the mess of papers on his table. He should've done something. My being late getting down to the dairy that morning went against me hard. Where was I? Calloway asked me and then he told everybody in the courtroom I was lying. Said I wasn't home in my bed oversleeping; I was up at Sheila's, killing her, and after that dragged her like a sack of potatoes down to my own cornfield where I thought she wouldn't be found for a long time. I couldn't even look at Stoney Barnes' face when I got down from that witness chair. If I had, I probably would've taken a swing at it. After Calloway got done with me, I don't think anybody in that courtroom didn't suspect that I could be the man who fucked her, and then killed her to keep from being found out.

Before I got in my truck, hoping to cool down enough to drive home without killing myself, a woman came up to me and introduced herself as Earlene Barnes. She's a pretty lady and I'd seen her a couple of times before somewhere or other, but I wouldn't have remembered her name. But her face was all pinched up like she had a burr up her butt, and at first I thought she was gonna lay into me, maybe accuse me of killing her sister-in-law like Calloway was saying. But she held out her gloved hand for me to shake. "I'm so sorry for what happened in there," she said, nodding back to the courthouse.

"Not your fault," I said.

She swallowed hard. "Well, maybe you…there are things…" She stared off to where Leland Graves was standing on the walk watching us. "I've got to come out to your dairy later today. There's something I have to tell your wife."

The last thing I needed was some woman coming out to fuss over Rowena, tell her she ought to divorce me, or pray on it maybe like her mama was doing on an hourly basis. "Rowena's pretty upset. She don't need any company right now."

Her hand went up to my forearm. "Please, Mr. Cotton. It's important."

There wasn't any meanness in her eyes. She didn't look like a woman who was about to help get me thrown outta my house. "Okay," I said. "I'll tell Rowena to expect you."

"Thank you."

She turned to walk away, but I grabbed her arm. "You better not upset her. She's expecting a child you know. When she hears about my testimony, it's gonna go down hard with her. I wouldn't want you making matters worse for her."

I thought the woman was about to cry for a minute, but she looked hard into my face. "Believe me. That's the last thing I want to do," she said.

ANNETTE

Well, just nobody in the whole entire universe is acting like they're supposed to. As soon as I got home from school, Mama said Grandma was on her way over to pick me up and bring me to her house to spend the night. "It's a school night," I said.

Mama didn't even blink at that. "Right. Well, she'll take you to school tomorrow. Now go get packed. She'll be here any minute."

Grandma could see I wasn't in the best of moods, and she believes that there is nothing better than work to take your mind off your troubles, so as soon as I put my suitcase in Mama's old bedroom, she sent me out to pick up pecans. Grandma's pecan orchard stretches for nearly two acres on the side of her house, and the crop of nuts this year was abundant. As I tossed the brown shells and green hulls into my bucket, I thought about Sheila and Stoney. I didn't know how to feel about either one of them anymore. I didn't even know how I felt about my own parents. Daddy and Sheila had both committed adultery. Stoney could be a murderer, although I still believed deep in my heart that this wasn't true, and then there was Mama who had left us and now that she was back, she was snapping at me every time I walked into the house.

Beneath the towering pecan trees, I sat on the cold ground and considered the coming months. I had expected life to go on just as it was. Sheila and I would make pecan pies and divinity candy for Christmas; we would go into Zebulon and stroll down Main Street to admire the holiday decorations. If she were still alive, we would be buying baby clothes for two instead of one. I closed my eyes and imagined Sheila's stomach swelling like Mama's. She would have looked comical with a big belly jutting out between her stick arms, but I was certain that she would have been a good mother. I cried then, for her and the little baby who would never know any of us, for myself and for missing Lil' Bit, and for Stoney locked away from the little sad house and the winter pasture and the crisp fall air.

Grandma said there is a reason for everything, and until now I had believed her. "God has a plan," she would say. But what sense was there in His taking Lil' Bit away, in Sheila's death, in Stoney's arrest? If there was a plan, it was surely the devil's. Grandma also warned me that sometimes bad things happen to us when we need to be taught a lesson. To avoid painful instruction, I should try hard to be a good girl every day of my life. But I didn't feel like being good; I felt like sinning my head off. I was plain mad, and I didn't think what I did made one whit of difference to the Lord. Hadn't I obeyed nearly all ten of the commandments? And how did He reward me? He had taken away half of all that I loved, that's how.

I lifted my bucket and started back to Grandma's house. Right then I couldn't think of any sin I could accomplish given my limited opportunity, but I was sure one would come along.

Grandma frowned at my half-filled bucket, but something about me must have warned her off her fussing because she said she had tea cakes baking in the oven for me. I sat at the old scarred wooden table watching Grandma in her blue apron wiping up spilled flour and sugar with a faded rag. Her wavy gray hair was held back with black bobby pins and flour streaks ran down her fat cheeks. She was smiling and humming like there was a lot to be happy about. It was all an act; I knew that. Then Grandma looked over her shoulder at me. "Why the long puss?"

I shrugged. "I hate everybody and everything. That's all." I kicked the pecan bucket beside the table.

Grandma is a big woman, weighing close to two hundred pounds, and she came at me like a bulldozer about to plow down a tree. When she reached the table, she shook her rag in my face. "What are you saying? You don't care about your mama, your daddy, the baby that's coming?"

I leaned as far back away from her as the ladder-back chair would allow. "Yes ma'am, of course I do. It's just all the other things. Sheila and Lil' Bit and Stoney, and stuff at school." Already kids were looking at me whispering about my daddy and Virgie Nell Jackson.

Grandma sat down at the head of the table. She pulled my hands into hers and squeezed them into a tent for praying. "Annette, I know. The good Lord knows I understand. Haven't I lost my husband, one of my daughters, my sister, and two brothers to Him?"

I nodded. I was surprised to think about Grandma being mad at God too. I had forgotten He had taken so much from her. "But how can you still be happy?"

Grandma smiled. "How? I don't know as I ever thought about how I can, I only know that life is too long not to be happy."

"I don't get it."

"Oh, when your Grandpa died, I was still a young woman then even though my children were grown. After he departed this life, I thought about dying too. At night I would lie in my bed in the dark feeling the cold sheet where he used to lie. And I would pray for God to take me. I knew I was too cowardly to take my own life, but I hoped I would get gored by a bull or run down by a train or just die quietly in my sleep. But every morning the sun came up and so did I. My stomach still rumbled when I was hungry, the jasmine growing by the porch still smelled sweet, your mama's arms around me were as soft as ever." She glanced at the clock over the table and, grabbing a dishcloth, she slid the pan of tea cakes out of the oven. "And tea cakes still tasted like heaven," she said, lifting them one by one with a spatula and placing them on a plate. When the dish was piled high with the cookies, she brought it to the table. "So there's no how to it. There's just the going on with the living. We're not made to be sad; we're put here to rejoice in all the things the good Lord leaves to us. He didn't have to give us anything, you know." Her arms swept out and waved around the kitchen. "But look at all we have to be thankful for."

I looked at the old coal stove, the peeling paint on the cabinets, the wallpaper steamed half off the wall. "Well," I tried to think what to say. It wasn't a time for honesty. "Well, I guess you're right, Grandma." I watched her lips spread into the smile she wore whenever she thought she had helped somebody out. She pushed the plate of tea cakes toward me, and I took one from the stack. It was burned on the bottom, but I ate it anyway.

CHAPTER 35

ROWENA

It's funny how you can know something, and not realize you know it, but then after you find out what it is, you say to yourself, "Yes, yes. I knew it all along." That's the way I felt after Earlene Barnes left my house.

I was nervous about her coming after Lloyd told me. He wouldn't talk about what had happened in the courtroom that day, said he'd tell me after supper. He needed to get down to the dairy because he'd been gone most of the day. When Annette came in from school, I sent her packing to Mama's so that she wouldn't be at home when Earlene came. I changed my dress, smoothed down my hair, and applied a bit of scent to my wrist. I knew she'd be looking at me with an eye as to why Lloyd would cheat on me, and I wanted to show her that it wasn't my looks.

I felt confident, even though I was wearing a maternity smock. It was my prettiest one; the print is little purple flowers with green curved stems on a white background, and my skirt, a lighter shade of lavender, matched nicely. When I opened the front door, Earlene barely looked at me. "Come in. I'm Rowena Cotton," I said. "I saw you at the funeral, but I didn't have a chance to introduce myself."

She went straight to the piano bench and sat there even though my hand was extended to the couch. "I won't stay long, Mrs. Cotton," she said. "I, just, I need, I have to talk to you."

I could see then how upset she was. She kneaded her hands against her stomach like two loaves of bread dough, and I saw that there wasn't any point in offering coffee. I sat down in the armchair across from her. "Well, I hope I can help," I said, wondering what in the world she was going to say.

She closed her eyes, took a big breath and let it out before she sat up straight and looked up at me. "Mrs. Cotton, you know, of course, that your husband is being accused of having an affair with my sister-in-law."

So it was about that! I decided right then and there that if she insulted me in the slightest, I would order her out of my house. "That's not true," I said. I stood up. "I am absolutely positive of it, and if you came here to make more accusations against my husband, I'll have to ask you to leave." Now my hands were shaking harder than hers.

Earlene Barnes jumped up and stretched out her hand to me. "Oh no! That's not what I've come for. I didn't think he had. No, I didn't think that."

The clock started bonging just then. Four o'clock. They'd begin milking soon. I backed up to my chair and eased down. I held onto the chair arms. "Then that is why you came here? To hear me say my husband didn't have an affair with Sheila? I'm sure he said that under oath today on the witness stand. He told me that you were there in the courtroom."

She sat back on the piano bench. "Yes. And I believed him, Mrs. Cotton." Her voice was so soft I could barely hear her, "It was Hugh, my husband, not yours. He is the father of that poor dead baby."

I couldn't speak. I can't imagine how I must have looked at that moment because all sorts of thoughts and words were crowding into my mind all at once. The pieces of that minute I remember are these: Earlene was crying; I saw the image of Hugh coming up my back-porch steps that day we were making Christmas decorations; I saw Sheila barefoot, her saying, "I'll get my shoes." Hugh was the father, and hadn't I known that all along? Hadn't I suspected that day? Sheila hadn't come back like she said she would. And lastly, in a rush, I remembered the truck being up there when Lloyd and Stoney went on that trip, Annette's being so upset, Sheila not letting me in.

I went to the poor woman and knelt on the floor in front of her. "I think maybe I knew. I mean I saw the way he looked at her, but I never thought she…she would. She loved Stoney so much."

"She didn't, Mrs. Cotton. He raped her."

I think I said, "Oh dear Lord" or maybe "Oh no," but I may have said nothing at all. I was so stunned I doubt there were any words in my head.

She crossed her arms and held herself tightly, rocking back and forth on the bench. "Hugh has cheated on me from the second year of our marriage. He's weak about women, and I just put up with it, for the boys. I guess it was always easier to turn a blind eye. That's what I did, but..." She lifted her eyes back to mine. "I never suspected Sheila. I could see how crazy she was about Stoney, and, of course, there was the hump and she was so skinny. Not Hugh's type at all."

I remembered his dark good looks, his thumb in his belt, my cheeks firing red and looking away from his privates. He could have easily coaxed a lot of women into his bed. "No, she wasn't," I said. "Are you sure he did this?"

"Oh, God, yes, yes I'm sure," she said. After a moment, she got up and walked to the couch and stood looking over it out of the window. I followed her there and saw a small brown wren standing crookedly on a broken branch of the camellia bush. I took her hand and pulled her down to sit beside me on the couch.

She took a deep breath and said, "This is what I know. After Sheila's funeral, Hugh came back from Jackson, and I guess Stoney found that out somehow. He came over late. Drunk. He had a gun, was yelling he was going to kill Hugh. I ran back into the house, begged Hugh not to go out, but he went anyway. I stood just inside the front door, watching them. I heard it all. Everything that was said that night. When Stoney accused Hugh of raping Sheila, he tried to say she was willing, but I knew better. They fought. I thought one of them would be killed, but then somehow Hugh got away and took off toward the woods. Stoney went after him, and I ran back to the kitchen to call the sheriff." She bowed her head and twisted her wedding ring on her finger. "I thought better of it. I didn't want Hugh arrested, not until I could decide what to do. So I waited, sat there at my kitchen table thinking and worrying myself sick." Earlene's voice changed then. Her emotions were more in check. "Mrs. Cotton, I loved my husband, but I never liked him. Really, the only one of the Barnes family I liked at all was, is, Hugh's mother, and she has the blindest eye of them all where her sons are concerned. She spoiled them, especially Stoney. I guess she was trying to make up for some of their daddy's meanness. But all of those boys have a mean streak, Hugh more than any of them.

"Hugh finally came home that night, tiptoed up the back steps and just appeared like a ghost in my kitchen, scared me to death. The first thing he said to me was, 'Stoney's passed out in the truck, hit the oak tree. I got to get gone from here before he wakes up. Help me get packed.' I told him he wasn't going anywhere until he told me the truth about him and Sheila. He said it was none of my business and to fix him a sandwich or biscuit to take."

While she talked, I sat with my hands folded in my lap. I was conscious of trying to look calm for her sake, but my insides were twisting and turning with emotion. I tried to relax my facial muscles and soften my voice. "This must have been the worst night of your life, Mrs. Barnes."

She smiled then. "Earlene. I think we should be on a first-name basis." Her smile vanished then. "Yes, until now it was the worst. Having to tell it to strangers will be more painful. I doubt Hugh would have told me anything, except I threatened to call the sheriff. I was afraid he'd call my bluff; there were two boys sleeping in our house who would see their daddy get arrested, so I wouldn't have called, but Hugh didn't think of them. He started with a lie, saying he hadn't done it, but I stood up to go to the telephone, and he said, 'Okay, I'll tell you, but it was Stoney's fault. He couldn't shut up about her, bragged about their lovemaking, how she was like a bitch in heat.'" Earlene paused, looked down at her hands. "I'm sorry to say these ugly things, but Hugh said, 'Stoney told me that hump of hers made it more exciting.'"

I clenched my fists to keep from crying out my disgust. I wanted to cover my ears to block out her words, but her voice grew louder as she went on with her story.

"I asked him if he had beaten her, and that was the only time Hugh looked the least bit sorry. He said, 'She fought me the first time, and the second a little until I told her I'd tell Stoney what she and me were doing and that he wouldn't want her no more then. I said he'd throw her out.' I don't remember what I said to Hugh. I know I was too shocked to even cry though. He left then, and I stayed up, walking the floors of my house, all the rest of that night. Around dawn, Stoney knocked on the door, but I didn't answer. I was scared he was going to use the gun on me, and when he went back to his truck and drove away, I cried with relief. I waited all the rest of the day for Hugh to telephone me, but he never did. I don't know where he is, or if he'll ever come back. I told his mother he was in Memphis on business, but I guess she'll have to be told the truth now."

She started to say more, but she was sick. I saw it coming on her and I jumped up and helped her down the hall to the bathroom. When she came out, I guided her to the couch and got a cold cloth for her forehead. She was so pale, I told her to rest a while, but she shook her head and said, "No. You've got to hear it all."

I sat on the floor beside her and held her hand. "Go on then. I'm listening."

"At first I wasn't going to tell. There's my boys, and Hugh's mother; she'll hate me, but I made my decision this morning." She closed her eyes and said, "Rowena, there's more. There was another time before this." Then she opened her eyes and stared at the door as if she expected it to open, and I realized there was fear behind her words, which came faster now. "I had hired a colored girl for cleaning and cooking. She was good help, dependable, a treasure really, and then one day she just didn't show up for work. I had this feeling something was wrong, and so I drove over to her house. When she answered the door, I saw that she had been badly beaten. She wouldn't tell me what had happened; she just said she wasn't ever coming back to our house and slammed the door in my face."

Earlene struggled to sit up, and I moved over to the couch beside her. "Can I get you something?"

"No, I'm okay. I can go on. I have to." She took a breath and began again. "I think I knew right away. You see, the boys and I hadn't been home the day before, but Hugh had been home, and I'd asked him to drive the girl to her house when she finished her work. That night I noticed some scratches on his arms, one on his face, and he told me the cat had made those marks. But after I saw the girl, I knew what had really happened. I knew, but I never said a word about it. I didn't have the courage to accuse him. I guess I didn't want to know." She covered her face with her hands and sobbed. "If only I had. If I'd said something, then maybe Sheila would be alive today."

Now, understanding what torment she had been living with, my own eyes filled with tears. I searched for some words of comfort, but I knew that no matter what I said, Earlene's guilt wasn't going to leave her for the rest of her life.

She wiped her tears and stood up. "I talked to the girl last night, told her that I knew what Hugh had done and that I'd see to it that he paid for it. She cried and asked me not to give her name." She fell silent then and took a few wobbly steps toward the door. "I've got to get home to my boys now."

I asked her could she drive, and she nearly smiled when she said she'd been driving around in a trance ever since the night her husband had left. I helped her into her Buick, and before she turned the key she gripped the steering wheel and stared out the windshield. "I thought about her and poor Sheila all morning as I sat in the courtroom, listening to your husband's testimony. I knew the pain that was going to come from it. For you, your husband, your daughter, too. If I had told what I knew, your family wouldn't have had to suffer. And that's why I came here. To ask for your forgiveness."

I reached in the car and laid my hand on hers. "You have that. I'm so sorry for your own suffering."

She lifted her hand and squeezed mine. "Pray for me to find the strength to do what I have to do." She turned the key and the motor roared to life. She spoke louder over the noise of the engine. "My boys' lives will be ruined, but I have no choice now. I'm going to call the prosecutor and tell him everything I've told you."

I leaned my head in the window. I had to know, had to ask. "Earlene, did he, is Hugh the one who killed her?" I held my breath then, waiting for her answer.

Slowly, her head turned toward me. "No, he didn't. It was Stoney. I heard him say it in our yard on the night he fought with Hugh. He said, "'I kilt your seed, and I'm glad of it.'"

CHAPTER 36

LELAND

My next story ran a 10pt. double column down the front page of *The Lexie Journal* and began with the headline, "Stoney Barnes Found Guilty of Murder." I was there in the courtroom three seats back from Kevin Landry's table when the verdict was read. Each day I had taken copious notes on the parade of witnesses and their testimony. My best two pieces were about Lloyd Cotton's testimony and Virgie Nell Jackson's. Miss Jackson made her appearance in court dressed in an ill-fitting skirt that was stretched so tightly across her buttocks that one could clearly see the outline of her underwear. I suspected that she enjoyed telling about her affair with Cotton because when she was excused and told to step down from the witness box, she said, "Already? That's all?" Of course, the other star in the case was Stoney, who aroused great sympathy in all of the women spectators. There was nearly a collective sigh from them when Stoney cried and said he couldn't believe his "little sweetheart" was dead, and there were nods all around the room when he said that the man who had taken advantage of her and then killed her should be the one on trial for murder. I think most of us thought he'd get off at that point. But then came the bombshell, the headline every reporter dreams of.

Kevin Landry stood and asked to call a witness who had just come forward with new evidence. No one was more surprised than I to see Earlene Barnes walk into the courtroom. I had been unsuccessful in erasing her from my memory, and now I felt heat rising to my face as I watched her glide past my seat. I sat mesmerized by her testimony, so engrossed in her soft voice, her lace-edged handkerchief, with which she daubed her eyes many times, her long legs crossed at the knee, her red hair I now decided was the color of a roan stallion's I had once seen, I nearly forgot to take notes. Earlene Barnes maintained her dignity through all of the distasteful facts she was forced to tell the court. She held her shoulders erect, her chin lifted to the lawyers as they asked her question after question. She was on the stand longer than any other witness, nearly two hours, but time passed too quickly for me. When Earlene Barnes repeated the words Stoney had said in her yard that night, that he had killed Hugh's seed, Bill Calloway objected, but the words had been spoken, and I knew then that Stoney's fate was sealed. It was with regret that I watched Earlene, with head bowed, slowly make her way down the aisle toward the exit. The sobbing of Stoney's mother was so loud at that point that I nearly didn't hear Earlene's soft, "I'm sorry," as she passed by her mother-in-law.

It took the jury the rest of that Tuesday afternoon to come back in with the verdict, but by five o'clock, it was unanimous. It had to be in a capital murder case, but Mr. Calloway asked that the jury be polled anyway. One by one they stood and said the words, "Guilty, guilty, guilty." Twelve times, and I couldn't see Stoney Barnes' face, but I saw his body jump with each pronouncement as if the words were lances sticking into his back. Earlene Barnes wasn't there for the verdict, nor were any members of the Cotton family, but the Carruths were there, him with his large hands stretching out to Kevin Landry in a triumphant shake, her with tears streaming down her pale face. She looked like she might be carrying another child in her womb.

The next day the sentence was handed down, and I rushed back to *The Journal* offices to write the final copy on the murder of Sheila Carruth Barnes. My fingers trembled above the keys on my Underwood, but I took a breath and typed out the sentence. "Death in the electric chair." It was done. The tragedy was complete. Our flawed hero would die. The gods sitting in the ugly Lexie County courtroom had decreed it. I had played my part in the tragedy, not as protagonist, nor antagonist. Only the minor role of commentator had been mine.

I sat at my desk for a few minutes staring at the black lines I had made on the cheap paper Mr. Elzey provided. Although my sense of relief was overwhelming, I experienced a sense of discomfiture that I could not explain. I typed "-30-," left my desk and handed my copy to Mr. Elzey. Before I went home, I stopped at the Hamilton Hotel for a whiskey.

Mother was waiting for me at home in the foyer. She was beside herself with worry, said I was too pale, hadn't I lost weight, shouldn't I make an appointment with Doc Reynolds. After dinner she fretted that I hadn't eaten my lamb chop, and that was my favorite since I was eight years old. In the sitting room she grew quiet when I poured a large brandy for myself and ample sherry for her. We didn't read that evening, sat in our chairs in the dark, pretending to listen to our radio programs. I vowed to put all thoughts of the boy and his dead wife behind me and so suggested to Mother that we might take a trip over to Natchez or perhaps take the Illinois Central down to New Orleans. She liked my idea, and by the time I left her to retire to my room, she was smiling again.

The next morning I learned that Mr. Elzey had another journey in mind for me.

When he told me I wasn't going on any vacation because I had to stay in Zebulon to cover the execution, we had our first major altercation, which ended with my saying I would resign. He then offered me a substantial raise. Against the protests of my inner voice that said nothing could possibly be worth having to view a man die, I took it. Fate played a hand in the decision; three nights before, I had received a long distance telephone call from Van Potter, my former roommate at university. Shortly after graduation, Van had taken a position with an antiques dealer in South Carolina, brokering paintings, furnishings, even an occasional automobile of exceptional quality. Van knew my passion for books, and he said that the war in Europe had been a boon for business; Americans were flooding out of every country on the continent, their arms laden with treasures the natives were eager to sell. He had come upon a first edition of Thomas Hardy's *Jude the Obscure*, which he knew I'd covet. The price, $85, was exorbitant, and I told him I couldn't afford it. Then I asked him to hold onto it for a week or so while I tried to raise the funds. Now, here I was offered the means to buy that book. How ironic that my love of words would make me witness to a man's execution.

I decided that the best way to handle my distasteful assignment was to lose myself in research. I hoped that learning abstract facts about executions would shield me from the reality of the one I was going to attend. So I immersed myself in fact-finding as though I were a scientist seeking a cure for a dreaded disease. My first discovery was a story I found in a Florida daily about the sheriff in the 1926 Williams execution in that state. Like Stoney, Williams was sentenced to die for killing his wife, but when he sat in "Old Sparky," Florida's electric chair, the sheriff had asked one of his deputies to pull the switch. Not one was willing to do so, nor the sheriff himself, and finally, after the terrified man had been sitting in the chair for over ten minutes listening to them argue, the sheriff unstrapped him and ordered him back to his cell. Years later Williams jumped from a prison truck and saved a woman and her baby from a mad bull, and for that heroic act, he was granted his freedom. I didn't for a minute think Clyde Vairo incapable of pulling the switch, and a pardon was a pure pipe dream for Stoney Barnes.

Our Zebulon library was woefully inadequate, so I was forced to drive up to Jackson for further research. There I found a wealth of information. I sat at one of the long wooden tables in the reading room of the Jackson Public Library, engrossed. I learned that it was the competition between Westinghouse and Thomas Edison that led to the development of the electric chair. Edison hired people to kill scores of cats, dogs, calves, and even a horse to prove that death by electrocution was quick, efficient, and painless. But then I found an account in a New York newspaper of the 1890 execution of William Kemmler, the first convicted killer to be put to death in that state. Witnesses said he smoked and bled, and that the smell of his charred flesh filled the room. When high voltage enters the body, the temperature rises to 138 degrees, and the eyeballs may pop out, the sweat turn to blood, and the skin and hair may burst into flames. After I had taken all of the notes I'd need for my column, I went to the men's room, where I doused my chalk-colored face with water, carelessly soaking the collar of my shirt.

On the drive back to Zebulon, I knew what I had to do. I couldn't save Stoney Barnes from the monstrous chair that would be his last seat in this world, but I intended to write a piece that I hoped would prove to the citizens of our town that they had made a terrible mistake. I had heard many of them quote the Bible, "An eye for an eye," but I would remind them that Jesus said, "Forgive them that persecute you." I would write up these horrific accounts of botched executions, and I would show them that taking an eye for an eye could only lead to blindness.

By the time I returned to Zebulon, I was charged with my own kind of electricity, and I was determined to visit the Barnes boy in his cell. I needed to see his unharmed flesh, touch him, feel his blood flowing at a normal temperature through his body. I wanted a clear vision of him in my mind when I wrote my piece. But Clyde Vairo said I would have to sign up for an appointment.

"What? An appointment to see a prisoner?" I was standing in front of the sheriff's desk, and he handed me a clipboard. I looked down at the paper attached and saw dates, times, and names scribbled in various shades of black and blue ink.

Sheriff Vairo grinned. "We got us a celebrity back there now. You wouldn't believe how far some people have come to say good-bye to our condemned man. I reckon it's you that's responsible for a lot of them."

"Me? What do you mean?"

The sheriff held up *The Jackson Clarion-Ledger.* "They're covering the execution too. Your stories are getting picked up all over the state."

"But who are these people visiting him?"

"Some are reporters from other towns, but a lot of them is just good-looking women who saw his picture." He nodded to Sam, the deputy, who was coming through the door leading to the cells. "Sam, here, says he wants to get arrested hisself so he can share some of them cakes, pies, and cobblers all the ladies have been toting back there."

I backed away from the desk and sat on the chair beside the door. I needed to collect my thoughts on all this new information. "How does Stoney feel about all of this? Has he said anything to you?"

The sheriff tilted back in his chair, crossed his arms behind his head. "He ain't said much, but he sure is enjoying hisself back there. I hear him telling the ladies he ain't never ate so good, that he appreciates their visits. He's been pestering me to let him have his guitar so he can serenade his visitors."

I stood up to leave. The charred flesh, the eyeballs, the flames rising from his head, all receded from my mind. "Sounds like he should be asking for an organ and a monkey instead," I said. I don't know why I felt shame, but my ears grew hot, and I wanted to cry like a child. As I got back into my Pontiac, lines from Thoreau came to me: "Even the death of friends will inspire us as much as their lives." Maybe there was some sense in it all, but I had yet to understand it.

I understood even less the convicted man himself. When Clyde Vairo got word that Calvin Nunnery would be bringing the chair two days before Thanksgiving, he telephoned me and told me that when he informed Stoney of the date, he said, "Well, I reckon Ma will have to cook her turkey early this year."

"What else did he say?" I asked. Surely, there was more to his reaction that he had only three days left to walk on this earth.

Sheriff Vairo chuckled. "Asked if he could have his guitar and be allowed out of his cell to play for all the folks that have been so nice to him."

I was glad the sheriff couldn't see my face. My jaw had gone slack. "You're not going to allow it, are you?"

"I'm thinking on it. Seems like a small thing to want before you die."

The small request turned into a colossal event. The word about the concert spread so rapidly that, by seven o'clock on the evening before Stoney was to be executed at six the next morning, I couldn't find a parking place within a quarter-mile of the jail.

November had been mild, but now the weather had changed, and as I was putting on my topcoat in the front hall, Mother caught me by my sleeve and begged me not to go; she said it would be barbaric to look upon the face of a man who was about to die, but I told her there was no escaping my responsibilities as a reporter. Then she had pressed her lips together the way she does when Alberta overcooks the standing rib roasts. When she left for her room, she said I needed to think about changing careers.

Now I meandered through the crowd toward the jailhouse steps where Stoney was to perform. I didn't recognize many of the people that stood in small groups on the moonlit lawn and sidewalk, but I came upon the Barnes family, the mother, father, and the two youngest brothers. I took out my pad, thought better of it, and moved on toward Gavin MacNamara, who had been the jury foreman. "Evening," I said. He frowned, nodded to me, but turned aside to speak to another man. Incredibly, a few people had brought their children, and they ran zigzagging in between the adults.

At 7:06 Stoney Barnes, Clyde Vairo, and his deputy, Sam, appeared on the narrow stoop in front of the jailhouse. Sam cradled his rifle while the sheriff handed Stoney's guitar to him after he took his seat on the top step. In the dim light I jotted fast notes as best I could. "Light oak-colored guitar, dark blue jeans, checked green shirt." All that was absent was a handkerchief around his neck, and he could be Roy Rogers singing to Dale. He bowed his head over his instrument, tuning it, turning the keys with slow, but deft fingers. Then, he lifted his head to survey his fans who fell so silent I could hear the rustle of leaves blowing across the street. Stoney strummed a few bars and then sang, "Lil Liza Jane," which seemed an odd choice, but I later learned from the Cotton girl that this had been one of Sheila Barnes' favorites. When the last note died, there was a scattering of applause, and a slow smile spread across Stoney's face. "Thank you," he said. "I'm kinda rusty, but I'll try a few more." He chose "Amazing Grace" and "Just a Closer Walk With Thee," changing the lyrics of the chorus to "Jesus, grant my humble plea. Daily walking close to Thee. Set me free,

Dear Lord, set me free."

A woman behind me sobbed, and I imagined that it must be the boy's poor mother. I swallowed and gripped my pen. Stoney shifted his guitar on his knee and said, "Sheriff says I got time for one more, and then I got to go back to my cell. This last one you all know, 'Down in the Valley.'" I wondered if he knew the genesis of the song. *The Birmingham Star* had run a story about it. The lyrics were written by a prisoner in the Raleigh State Prison in the form of a letter to his girl in Birmingham. After the *Star* published the lines, it had become popular with criminals and citizens alike. I guessed though that Stoney chose it because of the romantic line, "Roses love sunshine and violets love dew, Angels in heaven know I love you."

When the last chord died in the crisp night air, Stoney stood and bowed from the waist. Before anyone clapped, he raised his hands above his head reminding me of a preacher giving a benediction. "Folks, tomorrow morning, y'all are executing an innocent man. I loved my wife, and I didn't mean her no harm." Someone switched on a torch, illuminating his face. "Turn that thing off," the sheriff yelled. Stoney moved a step sideways. "Good-bye, everybody. I'll see you all in heaven someday." And then he was gone. I stood looking at the guitar lying on the top step, and I fought the urge to lift it, to feel the warmth of his hands on the wood. If not for the children calling out to each other, I might well have thought this night had been a bizarre dream.

CHAPTER 37

STONEY

I done all right playing for them folks, I guess. I wish I had had more time to practice, but I reckon it went okay. Ma said she'd always think of me when she heared them songs, and Daddy said he would too. I asked them to go on home. I knowed they was wanting to, even though they said, no, they'd sit with me the rest of the night. I told that preacher to go home too. He stood in between Ma and me and said that I needed to get right with God, ask for His forgiveness before I died. And I told him, I ain't needing no forgiveness 'cause I ain't sinned none. That preacher, I don't even remember his name, left his Bible on my cot, said he'd be back in the morning. Ma was the last to leave, but Daddy had to come back to help her down the hall. Her knees gived out on her. When she first come into the cell after I got back from playing on the steps, she said to me she knowed I was innocent and someday people was gonna know that Earlene had lied about Hugh and Sheila, and about me saying I done it. She hung onto my sleeve and said how was people gonna live with it when they found out they'd executed the wrong man. Then she got to talking about what a pretty baby I was, and remembering how the very first time I picked up a guitar, I started making music out of it. She kept on talking, going over things that had happened in my life, crying, then talking some more. Daddy just stood staring down at his Sunday shoes. Before he left, he shook my hand, said "I love you." He ain't never said that before this night.

I ain't gonna think on them no more. I got to live through this time I got left the way I planned out. It's gonna be just me and Sheila, nobody else. I know she'll come. I got to make sure she understands how it was with me that night, tell her how I tried to get her back, that there weren't nothing else I could've done excepting what I did. She knows that, I reckon. Sheila always knowed things that was in my head, sometimes before I knowed them myself. But she didn't know I couldn't have no babies. I wish I had told her that. If'n I had, I don't reckon things would have turned out no different though, but maybe they would've.

It's so cold in here I can't hardly stand it. I ask the sheriff for another blanket, and he brung me an old holey yellowed one, said that was all he had. He's staying down here at the jail all night, even though he don't usually. When Sheila comes, I'll tell her how much I loved her, how she were the only one who knowed me, who could get her mind around the why of things I said and done.

I can near 'bout see her that night, her standing in the bedroom in that green nightdress. I told her she looked pretty in it. Beautiful, I said. Then she was lying there beside me, smiling, as big a smile as I'd ever seen on her face. I remember her words, "Stoney, you and me is gonna have a baby." Baby, baby, baby, that word kept on going around the room. I said, "It ain't mine." I know I said that out loud. "It can't be mine."

And that's when the red fog come on me and it gets harder to remember just how it was. I know I dragged her off'n the bed, twisted her arm up behind her, felt the bone between my fingers. "Whose is it? Who? who? who?" She said my name first. I heard it over and over, "Stoney. You. Stoney. You. Stoney. Please." Her throat was so white in the red fog. I could see it stretched up, her mouth open above it. Her hair slid through my fingers like oil. Her eyes, they was too big. When she screamed his name, "Hugh," I felt her tears wetting my hands. "Forced me. Hurt me. Don't kill him." All them words she said that didn't mean nothing to me right then. I couldn't hear some of them through the red air. And then her tongue bowing up, blocking up her words. And she were laying there on the floor, so quiet. I dragged her in the front room, told her she was gonna be okay. I had to leave her and I was running in the rain then. Drawing water, hurry hurry. It ain't too late. The dishpan, the rag. Hurry, Stoney! Mopping her face. Hurry. More water. I seen it go in her mouth, but she don't swallow.

Her eyes won't quit staring at me. "Sheila, Sheila, oh god, Baby, come back. Oh god, I didn't mean to."

She'll come back. Tonight she'll come. She ain't gonna let me die alone. She knows I didn't mean to. She knows I loved her, love her still.

If I could just get warm, maybe I could eat some of the turkey and dressing Ma left for me. But I can't eat nothing.

I got this Bible here beside me, but I can't open it. I don't need to read it noways. I know what it says in there. Jesus loves me.

"Now I lay me down to sleep. I pray the Lord my soul to keep. If I should die... Oh, sweet Jesus, have mercy on my soul."

LELAND

I didn't sleep at all, didn't even get out of my clothes. I sat in the green armchair by the window looking out on the starless night. The crescent moon shone pale yellow through the clouds intermittently through the night, until the sun began its ascent, tinting the sky pink and purple and tangerine. I changed my clothes in silence. Usually, I listened to Mozart, Beethoven, or some other classical music in the morning, but not today.

I left the house before Mother rose. I needed no conversation, no worried looks, no free advice. I wished I could avoid everyone. When I arrived at the jail at 6:00 sharp, Calvin Nunnery was backing his truck into the narrow alley behind the jail. I followed him into the storeroom that would serve as a death chamber today. The sheriff was pale, unshaven. His hand shook as he held it out to me in greeting. Without words, I entered the room and sat on the first folding chair of the second row of four. Behind me, stacks of boxes rose nearly to the ceiling, and beyond the empty chairs to my right, more boxes, and a table with a broken leg. The brick wall on my left was bare and cold against my hand when I reached out to touch it.

Sheriff Vairo, Calvin Nunnery, and Sam carried in the heavy chair. It was wooden, slatted, and made of red oak lumber, and they grunted as they laid it on the square mat of thick black rubber in front of me. I didn't think of its use as I wrote the description. "Leather straps on the chair arms, a larger waist strap, foot braces, leg shackles, two wires for the electrodes which will be connected to the portable generator on the truck bed behind the jail." While I wrote the other witnesses had entered through the door leading to the front office. I knew some of them. I recognized the reporter from Jackson and nodded to him, but I crossed my legs and turned my back to the men who were nervously talking in loud tones. Someone told about the last Texas execution, another man called out to the sheriff, still standing in front of the chair helping Calvin adjust the straps, "Hey, Clyde, you need to take a rest. Have a seat there in that chair."

The sheriff ignored him, but when the Jackson reporter said, "The boy will probably shit in his pants before he dies," he turned around and said, "That's enough. No more talking." The room fell silent, and just at that moment, Mr. Carruth walked in, his hat dangling between his large hands. Sam followed Carruth and handed out paper bags to each of us. "What's this for?" someone asked. Sam smiled. "In case you puke, Dave. Sheriff don't want vomit on his floor."

It seemed like we sat for hours in the cold room, listening to each other's coughs, shoes scraping on the cement floor, pocket watches clicking shut, throats clearing, and in absence of those sounds, we could hear each other breathing, assurance that we were all alive on this gray morning.

When Sam and Sheriff Vairo brought Stoney in, his eyes went to the chair and his legs gave way, but he regained them and walked calmly across the room. As he turned and sat in the chair, I noticed that both legs of his gray pants were slit to the knee. The sheriff held out a glass half-filled with amber liquid to him. "You want a shot or two before you get strapped in?" Stoney's hand shook as he took the glass, and Clyde Vairo moved his hand over Stoney's and held the glass to his lips. He took two swallows, nodded up at the sheriff, and then lifted his arms to the straps. After he was strapped in, the electrodes checked, the sheriff asked him if he had any last words to say to the world. He hesitated for a moment, then said in a loud voice, "I'm off to heaven now. Good-bye, everybody."

He was crying when the mask was pulled down over his face, and so was I.

I didn't write that it took two charges of 2,400 volts to enter his twitching body before it stilled. I wrote only these facts. "Stonewall Buford Barnes was pronounced dead at 7:18 a.m.; he was eighteen years old."

L l o y d

I don't know if things are ever going to return to normal around here. Today is Thanksgiving, and we always go over to Mama Bancroft's for turkey, but we're having the big feast in our dining room this year. Rowena is in a snit because Annette's run off somewhere and she was supposed to be helping out in the kitchen. That daughter of ours is a big worry to her mama right now. I know she's been through a lot, finding out about me and Virgie Nell, losing Sheila, hearing about her getting raped, and then the kick in the teeth, Stoney dying in the electric chair. But she needs to snap out of it, get on with her life. We can't just sit around crying over what can't be changed. Hell, if I did that, I'd still be living with my daddy eking out a living selling farm equipment. I can't afford to sit around and mope over life not going the way I want it to; we got another child coming. And the Ayrshires will be coming to term before long too. I'll have to get Henry Blankenship out to look 'em over soon, make sure there won't be no big surprises when they're ready to drop calves. Rowena now, I reckon she's stronger than I thought. I reckon both of us are feeling such relief that the truth has come to light. My god, for a while there, I was wondering if Clyde Vairo was gonna drive out here one day and arrest me. I never told Rowena I thought that, but the words didn't have to be said out loud for both of us to see the fear in each other's faces. I kept thinking, if Rowena hadn't made me hire Sheila in the first place, none of this would have happened, but it isn't her fault. Who could have ever known? And I will say Sheila was a good worker, a fine friend to Annette and Rowena, and I had a heart for the girl. The boy too, I reckon. Stoney had his good points; he was crazy though. Had to be to do what he done. But I'm putting all that behind me.

Won't spend any more time thinking on Sheila or Stoney or what might have been. I just hope we don't get into war; that's all I need. The draft is already beefed up, and if things continue on the way they look, I'll be losing all my help to Uncle Sam. But I'm not gonna borrow trouble; I leave that to Rowena and her mama. Women, they always come up with something or other to worry over before long.

ROWENA

I am going to skin Annette's hide when she gets back here. In one hour Mama and Leda and Sylvia will be here, expecting the table to be set. And Lloyd hasn't been a bit of help to me either. He might still be mad at me about my going out to Earlene Barnes' house for a visit. He doesn't like me driving anymore, but if he won't take me, then I'll just have to drive myself. Poor Earlene needs a friend right now. Mama wasn't too happy either when I told her I'd gone out there yesterday, but she'll just have to get over it, too. I told her that all the rumors the Barnes are spreading just aren't true. They're saying she is crazy, that she made up that story, that Hugh hadn't done any such thing as rape his sister-in-law, that he's off on a business trip. But if that's so, I said to Mama, then why don't any of them know where he is? That reporter, Leland Graves, believes Earlene. He came by while I was visiting her and asked if he could be of help to her. The good Lord knows she needs help. Earlene is putting her house out on Dawber Road up for sale; she said she can't live in this town any longer, not with all the nasty gossip about her. And she's worried sick over her boys; Mr. Barnes has threatened to steal them from her, he's saying she's not a fit mother. Oh, I know different. I've seen her with them; she keeps them spic and span. Last time I went there I smelled hair tonic on them both, and they were dressed in nice trousers and polos, cute as they come. That's what I told her, "These boys are cute as they come." I hope I have a boy. Not that Lil' Bit could ever be replaced in my heart, but I long for a son more than I'd ever admit to Lloyd. I tell him, just so it's healthy, that's all I care. And truly that is all that matters, but still a son is what I'm asking God for. Along with help handling Annette. I swear to goodness, I don't know what to do about her. Ever since she found out Stoney was guilty, she's been staying in her room, mooning over old pictures of her and Sheila and Stoney, writing in her five-year diary which she locks every morning with a key she wears around her neck. She puts on her sadness like a heavy cloak everywhere she goes. Annette was hanging onto hope that Stoney would be saved, and for a while, I let her hang onto that wish, but finally, I told her the truth, that there wasn't going to be any appeal. Mr. Bill Calloway returned to Jackson to his fancy law offices, and Stoney's family didn't have any funds for a new lawyer. He had to pay for his sins. That's all there is to it. And although I'd never say it to Annette, I say good riddance to bad rubbish. I'll never forgive him for hurting our family the way he has. I told Annette that she's got to learn that bad things do happen, and there's no escaping pain in this world. We've got to accept that. I think about how Sheila never seemed to feel much pain. All those beatings beginning with her papa, then Stoney, Hugh. She never complained, always saw the good in others, in life itself. I remember her standing there in our bathroom grinning down on me sitting there in my birthday suit in the midst of all those flowers. That first morning when she came to us, I would never have believed that I was going to learn one thing from her, but wisdom can come from unexpected sources. And in a way I guess she did possess magical powers. I think God gave them to her because He knew she was going to need them for the short time she lived on this earth. Well, none of us know how long we've got and that's why Mama says you've got to live each day as if it were your last. But I know Mama is planning on living long enough to eat a lot more Thanksgiving dinners. I'm not going to cry. I will not grieve for those I have loved and lost; there's Sheila, Doris, Lil' Bit. I still miss my daddy. No, I can't keep on with this sorrow, this heaviness in my heart. Today is the day set aside to count our blessings and give thanks to the Lord for all He has bestowed on our family. "Thank you, Jesus, and make Annette get herself back here in time for dinner."

ANNETTE

I couldn't take being in the house any longer. Before I came down here to the creek, I told Mama that I couldn't think of a thing to be grateful for, and real quick she said, "What about our baby?" I'm sick of hearing about her miracle child. Mama thinks I'm fooled by her smiling like she's got a lot to be happy about, but I saw how she hung her head down while she was whipping the red velvet cake batter around in the bowl. She was hiding tears. I think I'm all cried out. I don't feel like I've got anything inside me at all. It's like I'm a paper doll, flimsy, one-sided, unable to stand without help. But I walk, talk, act like a real person with eyes that see everything around me. I sit here on the bank of this creek and I see that it is low, the water sluggish and dark.

The creek was low on that day when Sheila and I came down here to catch frogs. I remember that, like today, it was sunny with thin, wispy clouds sauntering across the sky. We sat on the bank watching the dragon-flies swooping over the brackish water. The switchgrass and alligator weed that lined the far side of the small stream have died, but I'll bet that pickerel frog we saw that day is still around here somewhere. Sheila heard him first. With his snore-like cry, he hopped out of the grass, and I saw the flash of dark brown spots, white stripe, and yellow underbelly as it leapt into the water. Sheila jumped up and dove for him. She had heard that folks in Louisiana ate frog parts and she wanted to fry one up for Stoney. She didn't catch the frog though and disappointment showed on her face as she stood looking down into the grass for another. "It doesn't matter if you don't get one. Stoney wouldn't eat it anyway," I said.

Sheila grinned. "I wouldn't tell him it was frog meat; I'd say it were rabbit or squirrel or chicken gizzard. I trick him all the time."

I was surprised. Sheila was so honest. "You fool him?" I had asked her.

She squatted down, her bare toes digging in the mud. "Sure do. Once I told him I was a fairy just pretending to be a human girl. I was going on from a story my mama had told about this fairy that sprinkled magic dust on things that turned them into gold. I pretended cornmeal was fairy dust and sifted it through my fingers onto Stoney's boots. Then I put them under our bed and told him that in the morning they'd be solid gold."

I giggled. "Oh, Sheila, he didn't believe you."

She wagged her finger in my face. "Don't be so sure of that. Next morning I opened one eye and seen Stoney hanging upside down looking under our bed. He said he knowed I was teasing and he was just making sure I hadn't hid them boots somewhere else in the night." She poked the grass with a stick. "Huh. I fooled him. He wouldn't own up to it, but I know he was expecting to see two big lumps of gold winking out of the dark."

But Sheila's cornmeal held no magic and she hadn't fooled Stoney into believing Hugh's baby was his. I wonder what would have happened if Stoney had been able to bear children? Would he have killed her someday anyway, over something else? Or would she be sitting here beside me cradling a baby in her arms? But Stoney did kill them both. He did it. I have loved a murderer, and I know now that for the rest of my life, I can't trust my heart.

I have to go home, back to the house to pretend I care about getting the turkey leg on my plate. I think of all those times Sheila and I ran across this ground, laughing, singing, feeling the joy of just being alive and having a friend. I have betrayed my Best Friend, believed she was a sinner. I was happy that she was burning in hell for cheating on Stoney. She would never have doubted me the way I have her. I'm the stupid one, not Sheila.

If she were here, I would beg her to forgive me, and I know she would, too. She would put her arms around me and smile and tell me to just walk through that old shadow.

And I did one time, on the day that Lil' Bit left us. The sun sat up in the sapphire blue sky exactly where it is now. I can nearly see Sheila pulling me out into the field of crimson clover, hear her saying, "Look, Annette, ain't it pretty?" This shadow walking along beside me now doesn't show the changes I feel inside. It looks exactly the same as it did that day, big head, long legs and long arms, but Sheila isn't here to tell me when to turn and take a step. I didn't learn half the things she tried to teach me. And now she's in the ground and I guess Stoney is too. There was no funeral for him, no visitation, no after-burial feast. Grandma said she was sure the Barnes had a graveside service for him, and although I can't forgive him for what he's done, I hope that Grandma is right about that. If they did pray for his soul, Sheila would have been glad. I don't know how I know, but I'm sure that she has forgiven Stoney. He took her life, but he couldn't take her love. I remember her saying that it's a lot easier to hang on to love than it is to cling to hate.

I know what I have to do. I'll stand here and watch the sun exactly like Sheila did that day, and I'll remember what my Best Friend taught me. I'll know the true moment to take my step and then I will walk through this shadow of me. If I can get it right, do it perfectly, then I will forgive myself and Stoney too, and maybe someday I will believe in magic again.

A C K N O W L E D G M E N T S

First, with great pleasure, I thank Emily Heckman, my Best Friend Editor, whose magic pencil guided me, whose optimism uplifted me, and whose immense talent amazed me. Thanks to Lisa Bankoff, who, simply put, is the agent every writer dreams of; no one could be more grateful to her than I. To the gifted people at MacAdam/Cage, I offer my gratitude for their assistance and congratulate them for their creative vision.

Thank you to the writing teachers I have been so fortunate to meet: Jay Paul, so long ago at Christopher Newport College; Douglas Glover at Skidmore, who told me to quit my day job; Tim Gautreaux at Southeastern Louisiana University, my mentor and valued friend; and Nicholas Delbanco at the New York State Summer Writers Institute, whose friendship and talent are true blessings.

I thank those who gave my first stories an audience: Chester Hedgepeth at *Maryland Review,* Thomas Bonner at *Xavier Review,* and Polly Swafford at *Potpourri*; in England at Mildenhall Air Force base, the wonderful women of the wives' clubs, the "gang at PA," who served under the leadership of General Dwight Keahola, and to all of you military members, who are ever present in my writing and in my heart.

At Southeastern Louisiana University I received support and encouragement from Dr. Sue Parrill, Dr. William Parrill, Dr. William Dowie, Dr. Richard Louth, Dr. John Miller, and too many colleagues and students to name. Thanks to all of you.

Thank you to Picket Randall for sharing his boyhood story, while sitting beside me at Maggie's graduation, and Dr. Bruce Belt for sharing his professional knowledge.

For phone calls for research, for passages read, for dreams shared, I thank Mandy and Joey Marshall, ever there, ever in my heart.

Thanks to the loveliest of readers, Amy Acosta, Wanda Trahan, and the members of the St. Tammany Writers Group: Katie Wainwright, Melanie Plesh, Karen Maceira, Dan Butcher, and Phillip Routh. With your various pencils and pens of red, blue, and black ink you give insightful comments and suggestions for which I continue to be greatly appreciative. I offer my heartfelt thanks to three other members: Andreé Cosby, Jan Chabreck, and Tana Bradley. You are the trio who sustain me through the darkest shadows and dance with me on the brightest days. Your friendship means more to me than I could ever say.

For the support, enthusiasm, and love that only family members can give, I thank James Forrest, Shirley Tate, Zora Marshall, and the rest of my many relatives, who love me for no good reason.

From birth to this moment, I am indebted to my dad, Ernest Forrest, the storyteller, and the most extraordinary man I will ever know.

Finally, thanks to wonder boy, Chess, for patiently watching the blinds opening and closing through so many months, and for his loving hugs and infectious laughter. Thanks to Angela for being the daughter every mother dreams of giving to the world, and to my amazing husband, lover, and friend, Butch, I say thank you for choosing to fly with me through this life.